NEMESIS IN THE NIGHT

THE NEMESIS FILES - BOOK 1

ANNA J. STEWART

Copyright © 2018 by Anna J Stewart

Previously published in 2015 as Asking for Trouble.

All rights reserved. No part of this book may be reproduced in any form or by any means without the prior written consent of the Publisher/author, excepting brief quotes and excerpts used in reviews.

This is a work of fiction. Characters, names, places, and incidents either are the product of the author's imagination or are used factiously, and any resemblance to actual persons, living or dead, business establishments, events, or locales is entirely coincidental.

For my mother,

Marjorie McLetchie Stewart

For always believing, always encouraging, and always saying yes when I wanted to buy a book.

This, and all the rest, are for you.

CHAPTER 1

"I THOUGHT I might catch you here, Inspector."

Gage Juliano's hand froze on the slender metal handle of the glass door to Lorenzo's café. The sound of the District Attorney's voice kicked the jackhammer headache pounding behind Gage's eyes into sync with his caffeine-neglected blood. His spine stiffened as his boss approached. "Sir?"

"I thought we agreed to ditch the 'sir.'" Evan Marshall pushed off from where he'd been leaning against the real estate office next door and stopped beside Gage. He lifted his chin, took a deep breath, and smiled, no doubt catching the addictive roasted aroma that brought Gage to this door every afternoon at this time. "You didn't think you could keep this place to yourself forever, did you?"

The corners of Gage's mouth quirked. As a matter of fact, he had. "Can I swear you to silence?"

"Depends. How good is the coffee?"

"Good enough I'm regretting not bringing my gun. Sir."

Evan laughed and slapped a hand on Gage's shoulder. "My lips are sealed and the coffee's on me."

Gage may have only worked for the D.A. for a month, but he'd learned early on that Evan never went anywhere or met anyone without proper motivation.

"What's so important you had to stake out my afternoon escape instead of knocking on my office door?" Gage asked once they had coffee in hand and were headed back to the historic brick warehouse that housed the D.A.'s office. The instant Gage took a long, throat-scalding swallow, his system calmed and zinged at the same time. The day righted itself once more.

Evan pulled out his cell phone and accessed his pictures, then turned the screen toward Gage. "Do you know this guy?"

The picture was blurry, as Evan had obviously snapped it through a glass window, but Gage couldn't place the middle-aged, paunch-heavy, over-tanned man. The shit-brown suit he wore told Gage the man wasn't a conformist. He had his own way of doing things. "No. I've never met him before. Cop?"

"Close. He's a Fed."

Despite the steaming coffee, Gage's blood turned to ice cubes that clattered one by one into his stomach.

"An Agent Kolfax," Evan said. "He called me into the FBI's temporary office this morning for a meeting, and while I was waiting, I saw this on his desk." Evan flipped to the previous photo, handed the phone over so Gage could see the document.

A fluorescent pink sticky note with mostly illegible scribbles topped a solitary page of official FBI letterhead listing a string of contact. Gage's gut clenched as he made out a smattering of phrases and names, but one word stood out enough to raise the hair on his neck. "Why would the FBI be interested in the Nemesis case? And what does Nemesis have to do with the Tremayne family?"

"I'm thinking that's what he wants us to find out. Whoever this Kolfax is," Evan said, "he knows you. I got the impression he didn't think you'd been up-front with me about your time working with them on that joint task force. Or about how it ended."

"Shocking to think the FBI might be wrong about something." Gage's left shoulder throbbed—a quick burn shooting through him like a match had been struck against his skin. As fast as the sensation appeared, it was gone, but the flash ignited embers of resentment he'd worked hard to bank.

"Look, Gage, I know your history with the Feds isn't the greatest, but if they're looking into the Nemesis case—"

"They can look all they want." Gage squinted into the late afternoon sun and tried not to sound edgy as they rounded the corner. His so-called "history" with the FBI had nearly gotten him killed. Having the Feds pop up now, just when his life was getting on track again, felt like another knife in the back. "It's my case. I agreed to head up your new investigative unit provided you get me the Nemesis case. That was our deal."

"And I have no plans to change that deal, Inspector," Evan said. "Which is why I agreed to your plan to use the press to our advantage. But if this Agent Kolfax has gone to the trouble of coming out here from Washington, D.C., to hover over *your* case, not to mention one of our most prominent families, I'm damned well going to take notice."

"Good to know. In my experience, the FBI uses whomever and whatever they need to produce the results they want." Bitterness cut like a razor through Gage's words. "Even if it means innocent people get caught in interdepartmental cross fire." And it sounded to him as if the Tremaynes had been moved directly into their cross hairs.

"That I'm used to." For the first time, Gage caught a hint of strain on Evan's face. "I kept my word, Gage, but I do not need to add the Feds to the mix, which is why I'm going to do a little digging. I'm counting on your experience to stay one step ahead and keep them in check. Beginning with that note Agent Kolfax just happened to leave out in the open for me to see."

Gage eased the throttle back on the anger. "You think he wanted you to see it?"

"Considering everything we talked about could have been handled with a phone call?" Evan shrugged. "I have no doubt he wanted this note in our hands. The question is why?"

"Did you make out anything else that might be important?" Gage couldn't begin to fathom what this Kolfax's agenda was.

"A couple of Nemesis' victims, I think. But then I saw he'd made a special note of the Tremayne family along with the Tremayne Foundation, and while I'm not convinced I was meant to see that, today's meeting can't be a coincidence. There's a fundraiser for the foundation tonight, and Kolfax didn't strike me as the party crasher type."

"He's trying to distract us." Or maybe Kolfax was one of those agents who hoped to make a name for himself by closing a case with the potential for national media exposure. "I didn't walk away from fifteen years on the force to let the Feds come in and take over."

"I know it hasn't been easy for you," Evan said, "taking this job. Especially given how your former bosses at the police department feel about me."

"I try not to let politics interfere with any job that needs doing." But Evan was right. It hadn't been easy to walk away from the job, not to mention the cops at his hometown precinct who had welcomed him home after the time he'd spent away.

Gage cleared his throat and swallowed the bitterness. Dwelling on a past he couldn't change didn't do anything other than raise his blood pressure. He was moving on, finding where he fit. For now, he was content with the skeleton staff and refinished office two floors below Evan's. Just in case this Kolfax was on to something, "This fundraiser tonight. Were you invited?"

"I was."

"Too bad you won't be able to go." Gage popped the lid off his cup and tossed it into a trash can as they passed.

"I won't?" Evan frowned.

"Nope. Something came up, but luckily I'll be able to fill in for you." Gage gestured to Evan's coffee. "That's the price you pay for horning in on my coffee house."

∼

Three hours before the annual Cancer Treatment Center fundraiser, Morgan Tremayne wasn't wearing the hand-beaded designer dress and kill-me-now Manolo Blahnik sandals. She wasn't walking into the Winstead Salon and Spa with the other socialites. She wasn't applying the makeup she hadn't worn in months. Instead, she was jammed under the kitchen sink of her late grandmother's Victorian, grey sludge squishing between her fingers as she tightened the lugs on the garbage disposal.

She swiped at the sweat dripping down the side of her face. Ugh. The glamorous life of a landlord made even more challenging by the overly curious, determined-to-help nine-year-old sprawled across Morgan's chest. Morgan wasn't sure what was more difficult—repairing the disposal or trying to do so without knocking Brandon Monroe in the head.

"Okay." Morgan grunted as her arms and fingers went numb. Given the positions she found herself in these days, she could hire out as a contortionist with Cirque du Soleil. "Turn the faucet on. Slowly this time," she added as a touch of panic kicked in her belly at the thought of having to start over for the third time. She was already behind schedule.

Brandon scooted out, the buckle of his plastic tool belt clacking against the cabinet. Morgan took a deep breath as cool air swooped in under the sink. She lifted her head as Brandon rose up on tiptoe. Seconds later, water rushed through the pipes. "Now flip the switch on the disposal." *Fingers crossed.*

The grinding of the blades above her head may as well have been a performance by a philharmonic given the surge of joy it produced. Morgan twisted her way out of the cabinet.

"It works." Brandon dropped down to Morgan's level, a huge smile on his pale, round face.

"It works." Morgan got to her feet and turned off the disposal before washing up. "Just be careful next time, okay? We can't afford to lose any more spoons."

Brandon plucked the mangled teaspoon, this week's weapon of mass destruction, off the floor and examined it with a narrowed gaze. Morgan wanted to ask what the poor spoon had done to deserve such a horrible end. Not that the utensil was the first sacrifice made in the name of mechanical investigations. As much as Morgan appreciated Brandon's quest for knowledge, it was only a matter of time before professionals would have to be called in for repairs.

No wonder Morgan's bedside reading consisted of *Dare to Repair* and *Home Maintenance for Dummies*.

"We don't have to tell Nico and Angela, do we?" Brandon's voice lowered to a whisper as he asked about his foster parents.

"*We* don't have to. But you know the rules. Secrets are as bad as lying, and we don't lie in this house." Morgan glanced out the window, searching for the lightning strike headed her way. No lies? Guilt and anxiety made her heart spin like an out-of-control slot machine that never paid off. She hadn't lied exactly. She just hadn't confided in anyone how dire her financial woes were or how far she'd gone to solve them.

"O-kay." Brandon rolled his eyes as Morgan's cell phone buzzed. As she read the text from Angela and Nico that they were on their way home, Morgan's schedule shifted back on track and the tension in her chest eased.

All she had to do once she reached her apartment over the garage in the backyard was shower off the remnants of the day's repairs, wash and dry her hair, unearth some makeup—if she could find it—and cram herself into the stunning and outrageously expensive dress her mother had bought her.

Grief surged in her chest. Her mom wouldn't see her in the dress she'd painstakingly chosen. Her mom wouldn't be there as Morgan attended her first charity event as chairwoman of the Tremayne Foundation. Her mom wouldn't be there for anything. It had been almost a year, but Morgan wondered when the feeling of loss would lessen. Or if she'd ever stop missing her mother so much she ached.

"Got your repair journal, Brandon?" She couldn't dwell. No time. Morgan picked up her grandfather's old toolbox before someone tripped on it and set it on the table. "Make note of how we fixed the disposal before you forget." A renewed gleam brightened Brandon's face as he skipped out of the room, tool belt slipping down his narrow hips, the deformed spoon still clutched in his hand.

So far Nico Fiorelli's suggestion that Brandon keep a repair journal had prevented any repeat experiments. How one little boy could cause such innocent destruction in such a short amount of time was a question that as yet remained unanswered. Not so long ago, Brandon hadn't been able to get out of bed. The chemotherapy to treat his stage two kidney cancer had been so intense he'd ended up in the emergency room three different times and been bedridden for weeks. All the more reason to consider Brandon's current hands-on curiosity a blessing.

Morgan scrubbed tired hands down her face. What she wouldn't give for a six-pack of Red Bull about now. Instead, she settled for making a cup of coffee.

NEMESIS IN THE NIGHT

Time to gear up and raise more money in one night than the Tremayne Foundation ever had before. Her mother would expect nothing less, and Morgan needed nothing less. It was the only way out of the mess she'd made. Besides, every second she spent worrying about money was energy stolen from the kids and the work she still needed to do.

Morgan had just grabbed her travel cup of coffee when footsteps sounded behind her and eight-year-old Kelley Black ran to her, her poofy ice blue princess dress billowing around her thin frame.

"Can't I come to the party with you?" Kelley plucked at the hem of Morgan's shirt. "I have a pretty dress, too. I'll be good. I promise. I won't get sick or anything."

"I'm sorry, Kelley." Morgan bent down to meet Kelley eye to eye and took her hand in hers. She never liked talking down to kids. "This is a grown-ups-only party. It has nothing to do with you being sick. I love you no matter what."

"But I'm not sick," Kelley insisted, swinging their linked hands as she shuffled her feet.

"No, you're not." But the leukemia, or rather the chemo-radiation treatment, had hit Kelley hard. Losing her waist-length blond curls had been the least of their concerns. But three months later, save for her slight stature and the peach fuzz dusting of hair, all outward signs of Kelley's fight had faded. "And we'll see about the next party, okay? Maybe you can come then."

Kelley brightened, her baby blue eyes sparking. "Really? And I can have a party dress like yours? Lydia, too?"

Morgan laughed, grateful for the reminder that there

was life beyond financial issues and the desperate measures she'd taken to solve them. She pulled Kelley into her arms, amazed that such a small child could endure so much. "I said we'll see."

"Yeah, but that means maybe, and maybe isn't no," Kelley squealed, jumping away. "Wait 'til I tell Lydia she's getting a princess dress, too. Make sure you watch out for him tonight, Morgan."

Morgan blinked. "Who?"

"Prince Charming. He'll be there, I just know it. Lydia!" Kelley called, racing out of the kitchen again. "Guess what?"

Morgan rubbed her eyes. Prince Charming. Because what was missing in her life was a high-maintenance prince. She heard the familiar muffler rattle of the Fiorellis' minivan pulling into the driveway. Now, if Prince Charming came with a huge bank account that wasn't filled with fenced goods, a set of power tools, and an overgenerous heart— Morgan grinned, secure in the knowledge that a man like that didn't exist. But if one did—yeah. She'd find a way to make that work.

CHAPTER 2

The boy band jingle blaring from his phone would repeat for hours in Gage's head, just like the undercooked Chinese food in his stomach. He really had to learn how to un-program the torture his teenage sister kept inflicting on him.

He tapped the Bluetooth in his ear as he swung his Dodge Charger into a parking space across from the Tremayne estate, avoiding the packed driveway as guests waited for the valet service. "Were you able to forward me those additional files on the Tremaynes, Janice?"

"Just sent them to you." Janice's schoolmarm voice reminded Gage a little too much of his mother.

A drill sergeant when it came to organizing and scheduling his time, a bit obsessive about keeping his office and desk tidy, Janice's attention to detail was the reason he'd hired her after her previous boss retired. Unfortunately for him, she'd since become best phone friends with his mother. Now the two of them were tag-teaming him on everything from his social life to his eating habits, both of which, according to the two of them, needed vast and fast improvement.

Gage snatched up his phone, accessed his email, downloaded, then tapped the icon where he'd saved it. He frowned. Well, he thought that was where he'd saved it. Any idiot could operate an iPhone. But as his mother was fond of telling him, he wasn't *any* idiot. "Any chance you can leave a printout—"

"On your desk? Already did."

A classic cherry red 1966 Mustang pulled effortlessly into the space in front of his car.

Gage's drooling was pure macho reflex. Glistening paint job, polished black top, nary a scratch on the body. There was just enough daylight left to shine an appreciative gleam over the surface. Not so long ago he'd have sold his soul for a car like that. No doubt that's what the owner had done. Lucky bastard.

He caught a flash of long bright blond hair in the Mustang's driver's seat. Huh. So, *not* a bastard.

"Evan just confirmed the story should leak sometime midweek. He asked if you wanted to do the follow-up interview, but I told him I didn't think you'd be interested." Was that a cackle on the other end of the phone? Janice knew how fond Gage was of anything relating to the press. In his experience they used law enforcement to promote their agenda any chance they got. It felt good to return the favor.

Speaking of favors, Gage wasn't convinced Evan appreciated Gage circumventing his plans for the evening, but Gage needed the perfect escort during the Tremayne Fundraiser. Someone who could get him into the middle of action. Someone to make his foray into Nemesis' hunting ground all that much smoother.

He only hoped the youngest Tremayne offspring would be more forthcoming than the picture he'd seen on the foundation's website indicated.

Had the twenty-five-year-old been born with that string of pearls around her throat? Despite the stoic expression on her round face, and given the level of irritation in her eyes, he got the feeling she shared his opinion of the media. Or maybe he was reading too much into a picture.

The family had a sterling reputation, Jackson Tremayne in particular. It didn't make any sense to him why this Agent Kolfax would be interested in either the patriarch of one of Lantano Valley's most admired families or their charitable foundation. But Gage's curiosity had been piqued.

The Mustang's door opened.

Toned, tanned female legs emerged from the car, gossamer blue fabric sliding over her skin like a lover's fingertips. Gage's hand twitched, eager to feel the smoothness of her legs. From his vantage point he could see she had curves. Lots and lots of curves. A shoe dropped to the ground. He felt like a voyeur, but couldn't pull his eyes away from the tempting vision unfolding from the Mustang as he bid good night to Janice.

He got out of the car, tugged the hem of his jacket straight, and rolled his shoulders as he headed her way. He stopped to hook a single finger through the strap of the sandal. Dangling the shoe from his fingertip, Gage squatted down and looked into a pair of surprised emerald eyes.

Jackpot.

"Ms. Tremayne. I believe you dropped this."

∽

Evening gowns and battle armor weren't sold in the same department, but as far as Morgan was concerned, they provided the same protection.

The confidence that descended the second she'd draped the formfitting, strapless peacock blue fabric over her ample figure could only be described as exhilarating. This time last year, she might have resented her mother's extravagant purchase. Morgan could have paid three months' worth of electricity bills with what the gown had cost.

A shadow cut across the late spring sun and she jumped, pulling her feet in as the shadow transformed into a man who leaned down and scooped up her shoe.

Her lungs emptied as if her dress had transformed into an overeager python. The way this man wore a tux made George Clooney look like a grunge rocker. Oh, and that hair. Jet black strands so dark it seemed almost blue. Morgan swallowed as summer sky blue eyes pinned her in place. Her sandal sparkled in his grasp as if each stone had been imbued with the sunset-emblazoned sea.

Hot embarrassment flooded her cheeks as she tried to reclaim her confidence along with her shoes. Morgan slid her foot into what she considered modern-day torture devices. How did her sister walk in these things every day? Morgan placed her hand in his outstretched one, allowed him to pull her from the car. "Thank you, Mr. . . .?" She arched a brow in invitation for an introduction, glancing down to straighten the cameo pendant her mother had given her for Christmas over a decade ago.

"Juliano. But please, it's Gage. Morgan, isn't it? You've recently taken over as CEO of the Tremayne Foundation."

Morgan forced a smile. "Yes." The job was both a badge of honor and a source of grief. She shouldn't have inherited the position for years, and wouldn't have except for the accident that took her mother's life. Which made potential failure all the more petrifying.

"Congratulations on the progress of the Pediatric Treatment Center. A little over six months until opening?"

"If all goes according to plan." Morgan's sadness was swallowed by the queasiness that descended whenever she thought about the balloon payment due on the center's property in a little over a month. All the more reason to get her butt inside and start raising cash.

The subtle strings and flutes of Bach drifted from across the street, drawing her into the cool embrace of the house where she'd grown up yet never felt comfortable. The wealth, the opulence—none of it had ever sat well with her. She'd take a broken garbage disposal any day.

Gage reached again for her hand. "May I?"

"Oh, well, I guess." He tucked her hand into the crook of his arm. "I'm supposed to meet someone inside."

"My loss," he said with what appeared to be a genuine flash of regret.

Morgan didn't often find herself at a loss for words. After all, she spent hours every day conversing with people in all kinds of environments about an array of topics. But when it came to upscale events like tonight's fundraiser, or more personal interactions, her brain and tongue took great pleasure in fighting each other. Add a man like Gage—handsome, charming, confident—and the Morgan Tremayne who'd spent the morning fixing garbage disposals and replacing porch rails may as well have been drowning in the middle of the dating pool without a life jacket.

There wasn't room for her insecurities to loom tonight though. Instead, she focused on donning the mask of her professional self: the woman who didn't care that men skimmed their uninterested eyes over her size fourteen figure before moving on to whatever svelte, posh, polished socialite stood nearby. She was Morgan Tremayne and she needed to raise a truckload of cash or risk a financial scandal that could destroy her family.

When she noticed Gage had shortened his stride to match her unsteady one, Morgan wished she could have pulled off tennis shoes under the gown. If she had, she'd be able to zip around the party like the Road Runner on speed. Instead she'd spend the night hoping she didn't topple into the salmon mousse.

"Would you mind joining me for a drink while you wait for your date?" Gage asked.

"Oh, it's not a date." Morgan tried to remember the last time she'd even had a date. "Just a favor for my father." Of course her father had no way of knowing how dangerous his request that she escort the District Attorney this evening was. Putting Morgan in the vicinity of law enforcement was akin to planting a time bomb at the base of the family tree.

"Then it's his loss." Gage smiled, displaying a set of straight, white teeth behind full, quirked lips. It was then that she noticed the crooked slope to his nose, as if it had been broken more than once. She'd bet there was a story or two there. "If you'll excuse me for a moment, I need to check in with my donation. Don't go too far, okay?"

Morgan watched Gage walk away before she blinked herself back to reality. A few moments around Gage had locked her in some sort of trance, one that broke as she caught sight of her father heading her way.

To anyone else, Jackson Tremayne was the picture-perfect host. Only those closest to him noticed the specter of grief hovering around him like a fog that might never lift.

For over a decade, Catherine Tremayne's Annual Foundation Fundraiser was the season's biggest social event. Morgan couldn't help but feel that tonight's, the first since Catherine's death, was decidedly somber despite the celebratory casino atmosphere.

"Hi, Dad." Morgan heard the telltale twitter of her phone's appointment alert chime from her purse. Her father smiled, shaking his head as Morgan plastered on her "everything is perfect" expression just in time.

"Right on time as always." Jackson Tremayne wrapped his arms around her, the ice cubes in his Scotch glass clinking as he hugged her and kissed her cheek. "Does that thing ever let you relax?"

"Nope," Morgan laughed. "How are you doing?" She knew she should have arrived sooner, come by more often, but there never seemed to be enough hours in the day. Thank goodness her sister Sheila had moved home after the accident so her father wouldn't be left alone in the enormous house.

"I'm fine, Morgan. You worry too much." He gave her another squeeze. "Everything good with you?"

Little did her father know those four words held the potential to open a floodgate of panic.

The exhausted part of her wanted to say, "I've siphoned off charitable funds and left almost a quarter-million-dollar hole in the foundation's property purchasing account. I'll be lucky to make the property taxes this year. Your mother's old house needs a new water heater and copper pipes installed. By the way, I've accepted over one hundred thousand dollars from a thief stalking some of your biggest clients."

But instead she said, "Everything's great, Dad," with nary a trace of anxiety. "Where's Evan?" Morgan craned her neck to scan the crowd for Evan Marshall's telltale sun-streaked blond hair. To this day she thought the new D.A. looked more surfer-movie reject than politician. It was part of his charm, and while she liked Evan, she wasn't particularly invested in spending the evening playing tour guide to the rich and infamous of Lantano Valley. "Didn't you say he'd meet me inside?"

"District Attorney Marshall sends his regrets."

Morgan's head snapped around as Gage joined them, pocketing his donation receipt and bidding marker.

"Inspector Gage Juliano, Mr. Tremayne." He held out his hand. Jackson inclined his head as if trying to place him.

Inspector? Morgan's throat slammed shut like a bear trap as blood pounded in her ears.

"Evan hired me to oversee his new Special Investigations Task Force," Gage said. "I thought tonight was the perfect opportunity to introduce myself, touch base, and get your opinion on some of the cases we'll be working."

Morgan rubbed her hands down her suddenly chilled

arms. This distracting, disarming man was a cop? That hissing sound in her ears must be the burning fuse on a time bomb.

"Any case in particular?" Jackson asked, but Morgan already knew. Her skin went clammy. She felt her face grow cold as if every drop of blood had drained to her toes.

"The Nemesis burglaries," Gage stated as he gestured to a passing waiter and ordered a whiskey, neat. "Now that I've caught up on the investigation, I believe everything I need to catch him can be found right here in this house."

~

Most people assumed Gage's innate ability to read people was a result of his fifteen years as a cop. But they were wrong. While his mother claimed he'd been born with a bullshit detector, Gage, the oldest of six, had honed the ability on his energetic, opinionated, and determined siblings. As far as Gage was concerned, his brothers and sisters were the best training a cop could have when it came to exposing the truth.

"I wasn't aware Evan was establishing a task force." The trace of tension in Jackson's voice was what Gage expected given the turbulent climate surrounding Nemesis.

The Tremayne patriarch had become a trusted voice of reason in recent years, lending his expertise as the CEO of Tremayne Investment and Securities during the recent economic downturn. But Jackson had yet to be drawn into the continuing saga of the high-end burglar. Given the interest Agent Kolfax and the FBI had in the family—and it would take a lot more than a Post-it to convince Gage the Tremaynes were involved in anything untoward—a congenial relationship with them would be to his benefit. Beginning with Jackson Tremayne.

Tall and lean, his dark blond hair dusted with silver at the temples, Jackson carried himself with an air of sophistication that spoke of classic Hollywood glamour rather than successful business tycoon. But there was a sharpening in his gaze, as if Gage's uttering the name Nemesis had spun the tumbler on the criminal's secret vault.

"It hasn't escaped our notice that Nemesis is targeting a good number of Evan's campaign contributors," Gage fibbed. "Many of whom I'm sure are here tonight. We'd all like Nemesis stopped, which is why Evan is making this case our top priority."

"You don't strike me as naïve, Inspector." Jackson took a sip of his drink. "The national attention from capturing a high-profile criminal like Nemesis no doubt factors into Evan's political plans."

"It's no secret he's considering a run for Attorney General or even governor one day." Not that Gage cared about Evan Marshall's career plans. He only cared about bringing a criminal to justice. He owed that much to Brady Malloy. And if this case helped him decide on what his own future should be, he'd consider the information a bonus. "But you're right. I'm not naïve."

"I take it you don't subscribe to the belief that Nemesis is a myth." Morgan's lighthearted tone flipped Gage's frustration switch.

"Myths don't kill people." This wasn't the first time he'd heard Nemesis referred to as an urban legend. Some people didn't believe the string of robberies were connected despite Nemesis' proclamations to the press.

The crook loved to call out his victims in the media—online, print, didn't seem to matter how he reminded those who had more than most that they should be appreciative of their circumstance. He was a criminal giving morals lessons.

It appeared as if irony's depths of ridiculousness had no limits.

"I'm sorry." Gage didn't care for the mingled surprise and disbelief he saw on her face. "The Nemesis case is personal for me. The original investigating officer was a good friend. It's important I finish it for him." Not that Gage solving the case could change what happened to Brady. "But now isn't the time or place to discuss business."

"I agree. Feel free to call my office for an appointment," Jackson offered. "Enjoy your evening. Morgan, even though I know it's the last thing on your mind tonight, do try to have a little fun. You deserve a break."

"I will, Dad." Morgan gave his arm a squeeze before Jackson disappeared into the growing crowd.

The smell of aged money mingled with cigar smoke, over-sprayed perfume, and more than a hint of superiority set Gage on the edge of unease. The collective din from farther inside the house echoed of spinning roulette wheels and cheers amid bets won and lost on the roll of the die.

Everyone around him looked as if they'd been painted into the picture, comfortable, in their element. What he wouldn't give for a bottle of beer and a carton of Kung Pao. He gave Morgan a sheepish grin in the hopes of appeasing her.

"I hope you're not disappointed in the change of plans. I know I'm not an up-and-coming politician—"

"And here I thought you were intelligent enough to have done your homework, *Inspector*." Morgan's green eyes sharpened like brittle glass as color flooded her cheeks. "If anything, the fact that you're not a politician works in your favor. At least to me."

Ah, much better. Gage accepted the drink delivered to him and plucked a flute of champagne off another server's tray. His date was as quick as she was beautiful. And those legs. He'd be fantasizing about those for weeks. "Let's start over, shall we? Inspector Gage Juliano." He brought her hand to his mouth, brushed his lips over her knuckles. "It's lovely to meet you, Miss Morgan Tremayne." Her laugh threw his heart into an uneven tarantella. "You're going to be trouble, aren't you?"

Her smile tugged at the base of his heart. "Inspector, you have no idea."

∽

Karma had come calling and its name was Gage Juliano. *Inspector* Gage Juliano.

As if Morgan didn't need a record-breaking fundraising night already, the possibility of the cops circling her financial shortfalls only increased the suffocating pressure to succeed. While she appreciated Nemesis' dedication and donations to her cause, his anonymous and plentiful contributions came with a guilt-tinged price.

She—or rather the foundation—had profited from his crimes. The cash Nemesis had supplied over the last six months had kept the charity afloat. But something told her Gage wouldn't understand her actions no matter how desperate she was.

Come on, Morgan. Kick it into gear. She could soon be doing the prison two-step for ten to twenty if she failed to raise enough money to cover the deficit in the foundation's account. So she stalked the silent auction items like a predator.

Gage angled a curious look as she scribbled her name and bidding number down on a week's stay at an exclusive spa in Arizona.

"You don't strike me as the 'take a week off for the spa' kind of woman."

Morgan arched a brow, impressed and unnerved he read her so easily. She'd already bid on the private Mediterranean cruise, a Broadway theater package including transportation, and a tour of one of the most exclusive wineries in Napa. Then again . . . Oh. Her pen hovered over a well-known plastic surgeon's offering of twenty thousand dollars' worth of work. Gage grabbed her wrist.

"You don't need that." His tone was an odd combination of disapproval and disbelief, and the intoxicating compliment warmed her from the inside.

"I won't win." She crooked her finger and lowered her voice. "See that number? Yvonne Baker. She's due for her annual overhaul and she's already bid on it three times. Now that she's seen me scratch my name . . ." Morgan gave a quick glance over her shoulder to confirm the Jayne Mansfield clone was watching. "Yep. If her eyes could shoot poison darts, we'd both be dead. She'll reclaim it. Besides, she only bid eleven grand. It should go for at least as much as it's worth." It wasn't the first time she'd taken a chance by betting on people's greed. They had yet to disappoint her. "And Mitzi Chennault has had a honeymoon in the Mediterranean in her head for the last two months. Just making sure she gets what she wants."

"At a price that benefits the foundation. Impressive. Devious. I appreciate that in a woman." That smile of his could charm a cobra out if its basket.

"I'll do whatever I have to in order to raise money for my kids." Which was as close to the truth as the inspector was going to get.

"Your kids. Sounds personal."

Wanting to believe his interest was genuine, Morgan shrugged. "Do you know how many children are waiting for life-saving medical procedures their families can't afford? Experimental treatments their insurance won't cover? Thousands and those are just the ones I've heard about. I get calls and emails every day asking when the center is going to open, begging me to put their patients on our admissions list. I know every name, every disease. I've got pictures of each of them up here." She tapped the side of her head. "So, yes. They are my kids. Just as they were my mother's."

"It takes a strong person to build what you and your mother have."

Person, not woman. Because he didn't hesitate in the non-distinction, Morgan's tone softened. "We lost my little brother, Colin, when he was eight to a rare form of leukemia. The foundation, the center, they're in his memory. My mother was determined to save as many children as possible." Morgan blinked as if the lights were too bright. "She—we—didn't want another family to have to go through the loss we did. She dedicated her life to the cause. Now that she's gone, the mantle passed to me."

"I didn't realize the crusade was that personal." Gage's

voice rang with sympathy, and regret, as if he felt he should have known.

"My mother was the face of the foundation, but Colin is the heart. Don't you dare feel sorry for us." Her order earned a soft smile from Gage in return. "He was a gift we had for eight years. He changed my life. Gave me, gave my entire family, a purpose. I get the feeling you understand that, given your reaction to my myth comment earlier." Morgan took a deep breath, and stepped into the fire. "The Nemesis case. It's personal for you."

"It is." The coolness in his voice made her regret the comment, but she needed to know what she was up against. She still had a few hours to spend with the man and he'd asked about her work. She couldn't very well ignore the opportunity to reciprocate.

"The initial investigator was my training officer years ago." Gage swallowed the last of his drink. "Malloy got caught in the media and political cross fire, wasn't able to get anywhere with the victims. Drove him to an early grave."

Morgan's heart skidded to a halt. "You don't mean he committed suicide?"

Gage's gaze shifted to his empty glass. "If you mean did he eat his gun, no."

Morgan forced out a breath before the guilt could settle.

"But the media bubble was impossible to thrive under," Gage continued. "The stress, the pressure to close the case, the lack of assistance from anyone involved. It was a toxic combination when you add in his stubborn refusal to listen to his doctor and take a step back."

"But you blame Nemesis."

"Take Nemesis out of the equation and Brady Malloy might still be alive." Gage gestured with his empty glass as if toasting his friend. "Solving his last case seems the appropriate tribute."

Morgan bit the inside of her cheek.

If she'd had any doubts about Gage before, they'd evaporated. Gage Juliano saw the world in black and white, right and wrong. He'd never understand Morgan's world was a million shades of grey.

CHAPTER 3

"Bust. Dealer wins again."

Gage threw his cards onto the table, surrendering the last of his chips as Morgan scooped them toward her, then did the same with the other players at her table. Maybe she'd mesmerized him into forgetting how to play blackjack.

Or maybe he was just preoccupied. He'd come to the fundraiser tonight hoping to find a way into the Tremayne stronghold. He'd expected to loathe every minute of the evening. He didn't expect to find his escort intoxicating and intriguing, not to mention distracting, let alone enjoyable. He couldn't imagine the dedication needed to run a charity of this magnitude, or to hold children's lives in his hands like she did every day. Jackson had lived up to all Gage's perceptions and expectations, but Morgan Tremayne was definitely a surprise.

"Another drink?" Gage stood, gesturing to the young man hovering nearby that he could take Gage's stool. She smiled, shuffling and spinning the cards like a Las Vegas pro over and under with one hand. She'd cleaned him out. A few hands of strip poker and he'd be naked.

"Just water, thanks." She winked at him, surprising herself, it seemed, as her cheeks flushed again and she refocused on her players.

"Be right back."

Going in search of the bar made him feel like a bear stalking salmon upstream. The foyer had emptied of latecomers as everyone mingled their way through the enormous floor plan of the Tremayne house. The home he'd grown up in would have fit at least ten times over on the first level of the Tremayne's dwelling alone.

Floor-to-ceiling marble columns outlined the wainscoted hallway as he passed room after room offering everything from baccarat to roulette wheels. The Pai Gow tables were four deep with partygoers waiting to take their chances. All that was missing was James Bond ponying up his Aston Martin as bid collateral.

He found the bar situated in the solarium at the far end of the house, the glass-paneled walls allowing for a stunning view of the lighted and meticulously cared for rose garden.

"My mother's coping mechanism." The man who joined Gage at the bar followed his gaze and gave a smile that triggered the same twinkle, the same dimple in the chin that Morgan possessed. Same coloring, same vibrant green eyes, and a tall, lithe physique. "Can't tell you how many hours she lost herself out there, tending to those prickly bushes. Sometimes I think she's still tending them, just not in the same way." The man turned, held out his hand. "Nathan Tremayne. I'm head of security at the family firm."

"Gage Juliano. I was just getting your sister another drink."

"Water, huh?" Nathan nodded to the glass the bartender set in front of Gage. "She must be having a good night. When she starts guzzling the diet soda, watch out. Morgan on a caffeine high is both a wonder and a terror to behold."

Gage grinned. "I'll keep that in mind."

The back of his neck tingled seconds before a loud voice boomed, "Inspector."

Gage kept a casual elbow on the polished wooden bar as he turned to find a group of tuxedo-clad men watching him, their ages ranging from barely off training wheels to somewhere around Father Time.

"Gentlemen," Gage responded, determined to keep his expression and his attitude respectful. He'd memorized every Nemesis file and easily put victims' names to faces. "What can I do for you?"

"Nothing, my boy, nothing. Nathan, good to see you again. James Van Keltin, Esquire." A heavy hand slapped Gage's shoulder as the man who stood as wide as he did tall set his glass down. "Rumor has it you're reopening the Nemesis investigation. Dirty business, getting into the mud with that scoundrel."

Gage leaned away to avoid being assaulted by the high-priced defense lawyer's overabundance of bargain-basement cologne. Being called "boy" reminded him of his college days when he'd caddied at the country club for extra cash, and who used the word *scoundrel* these days?

"Can't reopen what was never closed." Gage kept his tone light. He knew flying under the radar and being underestimated was the best way to gather information. No need to change flight plans now. "But you hear correctly. We'll be starting from the beginning, going over every incident, every statement."

"Smart thinking." Nathan nodded. "Nemesis won't know what hit him."

Van Keltin chuckled. "That D.A. of yours has delusions of grandeur. No need to go poking into something that's going to blow over any day now."

"I don't think a stolen Picasso is something that will blow over, do you, Mr. Baker?" Gage peered around Van Ketlin's girth to the short, rotund man who looked like a young Truman Capote with thick bottle glasses and a pasty complexion.

"My w-wife was mistaken," Charles Baker stammered, blinking so fast it was like he was transmitting fake Morse code. "I sold that painting without her knowledge. There was no break-in." He cleared his throat, tugged at his tie.

"It's interesting," Gage said to Nathan. "You'd think a transaction like that would mean a trail of paperwork, and yet we haven't found a scrap." He felt as if he'd found a kindred spirit in Morgan's brother when Nathan hid his smile behind his glass. Gage returned his attention to Charles Baker. "But I'll be sure to make a special effort so we can eliminate your case completely. How about you, Mr. Swendon?" Gage addressed the tall, gangly man who looked more Lurch from the Munsters than a media mogul who'd made billions off the public's die-hard obsession with the cult of celebrity. "I suppose your wife's missing jewels were misplaced, which explains your retracted statement?"

"While we were traveling, yes," came the nasal response, even more appropriate given that Lance

Swendon was looking down his nose at Gage. "This task force is a waste of time and resources, something I intend to discuss with Mr. Marshall given the first opportunity."

"Mr. Marshall is always open to discussing his plans with his supporters. I find it odd, however, that so many of you are against this investigation. If, as you say, there were no crimes committed against you, then what we investigate hardly matters, and yet here you are." Gage could imagine the level of panic these men would achieve if they knew the FBI was sniffing around the case. "If you choose not to cooperate, we have all the communication between Nemesis and the press at our disposal." He made certain his smile stayed in place as he spoke. "Strange world we live in when the criminal responsible is more forthcoming about his crimes than his victims. I bet his records are meticulous."

"More like fictitious," Van Keltin boomed. Clearly he didn't appreciate Gage taking control of a conversation he'd started. "I'm sorry my wife and I are leaving in the morning for an extended stay in Europe and we won't be around to watch how you handle this first case."

"Then I'll make sure to have the case wrapped up before you return. For the rest of you, my office will be in touch. I'll be sure to give your regards to Mr. Marshall. I'm certain your enthusiastic response to his investigation will be taken in the spirit it was intended."

Nathan chuckled and finished his drink.

As he returned to find Morgan, Gage wrote the evening off as a success. Before tonight, he and Evan believed Nemesis' victims simply didn't want to be involved or were embarrassed with the case. They were wrong.

Nemesis' victims were protecting him. The question was, why?

～

"I've been looking for you all night."

Despite the multitude of guests milling about, the muted conversations, the clinking of glass and the rattling of poker chips, the world dropped away and Morgan covered her sister's hand as Sheila's arm encircled her shoulders.

Tears burned in Morgan's chest, searing, almost paralyzing as she gazed up at Catherine Tremayne's portrait. Their mother had been elegance personified whether in jeans and polo shirt—no T-shirts for Catherine—or the ruby red one-shoulder designer gown she'd forever wear in the oil painting mounted over the fireplace in the main sitting room.

"The dress is perfection on you, Morgan," Sheila whispered, tucking Morgan's head under her chin. Morgan closed her eyes, inhaled the gardenia perfume that had once been her mother's favorite scent. "Just as she knew it would be. She'd be so proud of you."

Morgan squeezed her eyes until she saw stars. "I'm not so sure." The confession slipped from her lips before she thought to stop it. She felt Sheila's arm tense.

In so many ways Sheila embodied Catherine—the same perfect figure; smooth, wavy blond hair; and stunning runway-model features. At times Morgan had felt like a very round peg in a tall and slender family, but she'd always felt loved, even when she didn't feel as if she belonged.

"What's going on?" Sheila had also mastered Catherine's piercing and quizzical gaze.

"Nothing." Dammit! What was wrong with her tonight? She wasn't used to not being able to keep her fears in check. "Sometimes I wonder how she did it, kept everything going. Gave equal attention to us and Dad and the foundation. How did she make it all look so easy?"

"Mom wasn't juggling a fixer-upper foster home for sick kids on top of everything else. Plus, she knew how to ask for help. Honestly, Morgan, I wish you'd let me do more with the foundation."

"You do enough." Morgan ran a finger under her eyes in case any tears had escaped and dragged her mascara along with them. Asking for help meant telling Sheila—telling her entire family—the truth, and she couldn't bring them into the mess she'd made. Besides, she couldn't risk tainting the foundation any more than she already had. "I couldn't do what you do, all this." Morgan gestured around the room.

"Yeah, party planning is a real challenge." Shelia retrieved a champagne flute off a passing tray and arched a perfectly plucked eyebrow. "I'm simply exhausted." Sarcasm rang like church bells in Morgan's ears, and while Morgan knew Sheila's intent wasn't to make her smile, she did.

"Parties are exhausting for some of us," Morgan said. "Believe me, knowing events like this are in your hands, that all I have to do is show up and pry open people's wallets, is a huge relief."

"I'm capable of more. All you have to do is ask."

"I know," Morgan said.

"Do you?"

Guilt tugged the corners of Morgan's mouth down. "Ladies."

Her heart tipped as Gage sidled up to them, despite knowing nothing good could come of her unexpected and inconvenient attraction to him.

"You ran off on me," he teased.

"Sorry." It didn't matter that Gage made her smile or that he made her heart pound as if she'd just swum the English Channel. It couldn't matter. "Sheila, this is Inspector Gage Juliano."

Given the way Sheila filled out her Barbie-inspired black beaded gown, Morgan figured she'd be the ideal distraction.

It wouldn't be the first time Morgan vanished in the afterburn that was a Miss California runner-up. But it might be the first time she cared.

Morgan sipped her water and wished she'd had him get her a shot of tequila.

"Nice to meet you, Sheila." Gage gave her a warm smile as Morgan looked away and bid his ego-boosting attention adieu. "Your brother was just telling me about your mother's rose garden. This must be her." He raised a glass to the picture. "She was beautiful."

Morgan didn't answer until Sheila elbowed her in the ribs. "Huh? Oh." Morgan found Gage watching her as if only the two of them were in the room. As if he barely noticed Sheila's presence. "Yes. Dad had that commissioned after"—it was still painful to say—"last summer."

"Inspector? Are you with the police?" Sheila asked, shooting Morgan a "what's wrong with you" look.

"D.A.'s office, actually."

"He's heading up the Nemesis investigation," Morgan

explained. Here she was expecting the vortex of her sister's male-attracting good looks to leave her in the shadows, but Gage Juliano appeared immune. Boy, her luck just kept getting better. "He's here in Evan's place."

"Something like that," Gage said, a quizzical expression on his face as he touched a hand to her bare arm. "Morgan?"

Sheila set her glass on the mantel and took their glasses from them. "I think my sister is suffering the aftereffects of too much work. Gage, why don't you take her for a spin around the dance floor? She could do with a break."

"Sheila." Morgan felt the humiliating blush start from her toes and erupt out the top of her head as Gage slipped his arm around her waist.

"I'd love to."

"Wait." Morgan shoved her purse and the envelope filled with checks and cash she'd collected throughout the evening into her sister's hands. "Add this to the count tonight?"

Sheila struggled to keep hold of everything in her grasp even as she glared at Morgan. "Good thing juggling is a family skill. Pile it on."

"So you dance, too?" Morgan asked as Gage led her through the crowd into the solarium, but before they joined the other couples on the dance floor, Gage bent down and lifted the edge of her dress. "What are you doing?" she asked.

A blush crept up her cheeks as she glanced around and offered a confused smile to the curious elderly couple dancing a few feet away.

"You've suffered enough for one night." He tapped her heel. "Up." He slipped off one shoe, then the other, and smiled as she let out an unladylike sigh of relief. Pins and needles the size of hypodermics shot through her feet as she stepped flat on the cool floor.

"My hero." She watched him shove her shoes into his pockets before he drew her forward and wrapped an arm around her waist. He captured her hand in his. Bringing it against his chest, he pressed her fingers against his beating heart, the heat of his body sinking into her.

Oh, this wasn't a good idea, but common sense had taken a much-needed vacation. She all but melted against him and tried to ignore the camera flashes from the media representatives circling the guests. "Vultures, but necessary ones," she murmured.

"They do have their purposes." Judging by the acrimony in his voice, it seemed Gage wasn't quite sure what those purposes might be. "I don't think you've stopped for two seconds since we walked in the door."

"Can't stop." But that didn't mean she couldn't enjoy the moment, or the fact that for once a man hadn't looked through her to focus on her sister. She rested her cheek against his chest, closed her eyes, and memorized every moment. "Too much to do."

She felt the chuckle rumble through his chest and smiled. He smelled head-spinningly divine—sandalwood with a hint of lemon. His arms made her feel as if he could shield her from the world's wrongs by holding her forever.

"You do know I'll be humiliated if you fall asleep on me."

"Noted." And for the next countless moments, Morgan let herself drift on the serenity that was Gage Juliano and an orchestra of comfort.

"Morgan?" Gage murmured she had no idea how much later.

"Hmmm?"

"I think your brother's trying to get your attention."

"What?" Morgan's eyes snapped open. "Where?" She turned around, saw Nathan motioning to them. "Oh." That expression on his face wasn't good. "I was wondering where he'd gotten to. Do you mind?"

"Yes, but lead the way." When Morgan stepped away from him, Gage captured her hand. Unsettled by the unfamiliar and caring gesture, once again Morgan was pushed off-balance. Tugging free would be rude, so she shifted her hand and held on, maneuvering through the gathering crowd awaiting the announcement of the evening's final tally. What was it about this man that put her on edge? She hadn't wobbled this much since she'd learned to walk.

She found Nathan and her father along with Sheila in their father's study. She inhaled the trace of tobacco lingering from the cigars he used to hide from her mother, the welcoming warmth of polished wood, and old books and family mementoes.

"I'll wait outside," Gage said as she joined her family.

"Please," Jackson motioned him inside. "Join us. Close the door. Nathan, I believe the two of you met earlier this evening."

"Nice to see you again, Inspector," Nathan welcomed him. "You handled that arrogant ass Van Keltin perfectly. Sure you're not interested in running for office?"

"I'd sooner set myself on fire."

Jackson nodded approvingly. "Morgan, we thought you'd want to know as soon as possible."

Morgan glanced at her father and, having seen that stricken look on his face before, Morgan's face went cold.

"Someone's dead." She stumbled and found Gage right behind her, steadying her. "Where's my phone? Did I miss a call? One of the kids—oh, God. Is it Lydia?" Her heart lurched as if she'd leaned over the edge of a thirty-story building.

"Oh, honey, no." Sheila handed Morgan's purse to her as Morgan fumbled to open it. "Your scheduling alarms have gone off, but no calls. I double-checked."

"Kids?" Gage asked.

"Um, four of them. I sponsor a group home for sick foster children," Morgan said.

"Of course you do," Gage murmured.

Morgan checked her phone. Sheila was right. No messages from the Fiorellis. Plenty of others though. Didn't anyone ever sleep? "I don't understand," Morgan looked to her father. "If it's not the kids—"

"It's Ralph Emerson." And then to Gage, "The foundation's accountant."

"Ralph?" Morgan echoed, relief and terror striking in equal measure even as she almost dropped her phone. He'd been with them from the start. Her mother's right hand. Ralph was the only person who could help Morgan fix what she'd done. "What happened?"

"Heart attack," Nathan said. "He and his wife were traveling in England. She called the office late this afternoon."

"Contact our office in London," Jackson instructed. "And make sure Edith knows we'll handle all the arrangements," Jackson said. "I don't want her to have to worry about a thing."

"Already done," Nathan said. "She's having him cremated there, wants to scatter his ashes before she comes home."

Morgan barely heard the words due to the buzzing in her ears. Her chest tightened, her hands trembled. Ralph was a friend, a confidant. She couldn't have stepped into Catherine's position without his support and guidance. His protection.

"We'll hold a memorial service when she's ready," Jackson said.

"Of course," Sheila said. "I'll take care of it. Morgan?"

"I'm fine." Aware that all eyes were on her, she swallowed the panic winding through her body.

It was Ralph who'd paved the way for her to make the deposits, to replenish the money she'd siphoned from the off-limits property payment account into the operating fund. It was Ralph who kept on top of how much she needed to fill in the hole she'd created—a hole that was currently at over two hundred thousand and counting. Money that, until recently, she'd been able to repay in doses thanks to Nemesis' "gifts." Even if she had been inclined to go to her father for help, Ralph had let slip the fact that her family's cash status had been glutted with Jackson's recent office building renovation.

She wouldn't put the stress of her mistakes on her father's shoulders even in the best of circumstances, and certainly not when he was still reeling from her mother's death, and now Ralph's.

"W-we should send flowers, once she's home," Morgan managed.

"Elliot Dunbar is going to take over the foundation's account," Jackson told her. "I've already been in contact with him. I'll have Corrine set up an appointment so the two of you can get things on track."

Morgan nodded. Was it cold in here? Oh, God. A new accountant. He'd want to see the books. The accounts. She'd have to triple-check the figures, make sure everything added up. She'd have to make sure she gave Elliot the right set of books. Her mind spun like an unmanned Ferris wheel.

Tonight was her last chance. They must have raised enough money to fill the gap.

A knock sounded on the door. "Mr. Tremayne." One of the waiters poked his head in. "They're finished with the count and ready for you to make the announcement."

"Morgan, are you up to it?" Jackson asked.

"Ah." Morgan couldn't seem to shake the feeling of doom barreling down on her. She looked to her sister, recalled their earlier conversation, and for once, surrendered. "Shelia, would you mind?"

Understanding and gratitude shone on her sister's face. Sheila nodded, took Morgan's hand, and gave it a hard squeeze. "I'd be happy to."

"Are you sure you're okay?" Gage asked as Morgan walked dazedly behind her sister, stopping to lean against the wall beside the main staircase.

"Yeah." She pressed a hand against her chest. "He was such a good man. It makes my heart hurt." All the good he'd done, the chances he'd taken to protect her, and now —now she'd have to do what she could to protect Ralph. It was the least she owed him.

Gage stood behind her, his presence both nerve-wracking and comforting.

"Okay, here we go. Almost done, Morgan." Nathan

patted her shoulder as he passed by, and Jackson took a place beside her.

Sheila stepped onto the piano platform in the music room just off the main hallway.

Sheila looked so much like their mother it was as if an arrow struck Morgan in the heart. Her father's hand closed around hers, as if he saw it too.

"Ladies and gentlemen," Sheila announced. "On behalf of the Tremayne family and the foundation started by my late mother, Catherine, we can't thank you enough for your attendance and generosity this evening. We hope this is only the beginning as we bring the final stages of the Pediatric Cancer Treatment Center to fruition." She opened the folded piece of paper in her hands and smiled. "I'm pleased to announce that tonight's event has raised a record breaking one million, one hundred forty-three thousand dollars. Thank you to everyone who participated."

Sheila's voice was drowned by the white noise erupting in Morgan's mind. Her head went light, as if she'd stepped out of a plane in midflight. She closed her eyes, let herself fall even as she plastered the practiced smile of happiness on her face and forced herself to breathe.

Over a million dollars and it still wasn't enough.

CHAPTER 4

Morgan felt like a fish on the end of a hook. The more she squirmed to survive, the less she could breathe. She inhaled in between handshakes and congratulations and thank-yous as the evening came to a close.

God. Her problems were multiplying exponentially the closer she got to the payment date. The money was there, on paper, but the second Morgan tried to pay off the property purchase for the center in five weeks, the check would bounce so high the International Space Station would spot it.

Morgan gnawed on her lower lip. Her hope not to have to use the last of the money Nemesis had left for her had just been blown into the afterlife. Dammit! With the new task force focusing on Nemesis, and with Gage overseeing the case, she was in big trouble.

Gage. Her mouth went as dry as Death Valley. She had to get away from him. Just a quick good-bye and then put one foot in front of the other.

"Looks like you could use a boost."

The stunned buzzing in Morgan's ears faded under the timbre of Gage's voice. She took the china plate he offered, her lips twitching at his thoughtfulness.

Not even chocolate-covered strawberries could ease the hollow pang clanging inside her. "I'm surprised there are any left." She managed a light laugh, grateful the crowd was thinning as obligations had been met and party-goers headed home to their blissfully uncomplicated lives while Morgan worked to find a way, any way, to stop the foundation from hemorrhaging.

Her mother's life's work, her family's legacy, depended on it.

Morgan couldn't be sure if her stomach was churning around too little food, too much champagne, or the nauseating combination of guilt and fear. She opted for the former and bit into a strawberry, the snap of dark chocolate cutting through the dread pooling in her chest. The sweetness of the plump berry exploded on her tongue, and for an instant, all was right in the world. A trickle of juice escaped the side of her mouth and she caught it with the tip of her finger. Gage's eyes darkened and locked on her lips. She swallowed, no longer tasting the fruit. The potent desire on Gage's face shook her resolve to walk away. But she didn't have a choice. Not if her life was going to stay intact.

"I'm afraid it's time to call it a night." Would she ever again be able to eat a strawberry and not remember that look on Gage's face? She set the remainder of the berries on a nearby table and picked up her clutch. "I have a full day ahead tomorrow. Thank you for a lovely evening, Gage." She couldn't have sounded more polite and dismissive if she'd walked off the pages of Miss Manners.

"Morgan, wait." Gage caught her arm as she turned to go. "You forgot something."

She should have known he wasn't going to make her getaway easy. "What?" More attitude than she intended slipped out. When she faced him again, she found him holding her shoes by the straps, an amused glimmer in his eye.

"Oh." The silent *ugh* that echoed in her mind didn't escape his notice and he grinned. "Thank you." Her feet had swelled too much in the last hour for her to even hope to get them on again. She reached for them, but he snatched them away, offering his arm instead.

"I'll walk you to your car."

Unable to think of a polite way to decline, she smiled and headed over to bid good night to her father.

"You did a beautiful job tonight, Morgan." Her father squeezed her arms and kissed her forehead.

Morgan's heart twisted. If only she could confide in him, to ask him for help, but she couldn't bear the thought of disappointing him. Or showing him the mess she'd made of what Catherine had so meticulously built.

"Tonight was Sheila's doing." But Morgan appreciated the sentiment.

"Gage, good to meet you," Jackson said. "Please do call my office for that appointment. Anything my firm can do to put a stop to Nemesis's prowling, we're happy to do. Thank you for looking out for Morgan this evening."

"I think she looked out for me, actually, but anytime." Gage shook Jackson's hand. "I'll make sure Evan knows he missed a memorable party."

"Say good night to Nathan and Sheila for me, would you?" Morgan tapped her phone. "I have some emails I need to return before I can even think of sleep." She saw the concern rise in her father's eyes like the evening tide, slow, predictable, but he refrained from reminding her yet again that there was more to life than work. Instead, he nodded, sending her on her way.

The cool night air swept over her, a christening of sorts, resetting her priorities, solidifying her resolve. One day at a time. One minute at a time.

The solution was there. She just had to find it.

Slamming car doors and rumbling engines accompanied them up the walk and across the street, the glare of headlights casting scraggly shadows as cars passed and drove out of sight. Morgan shifted her attention to bidding Gage good-bye.

"This was nice," Morgan told him as she removed her arm from his to get her keys out. *Nice?* Had her vocabulary been stunted in the last ten minutes? Nervous laughter bubbled out of her chest. "I hope your foray into our part of town—" She turned and found him close. Too close.

Her entire body went hot, as if his nearness flipped her internal temperature to high. Her face flushed, her skin tingled, and whatever air she had in her lungs evaporated as his hand cupped her cheek.

Morgan could only blink in time to the SOS stuttering her heart. This was so wrong for so many reasons, and yet . . .

Her tongue darted out to moisten her lips, and she couldn't help but smile as his jaw tensed, his eyes pinned to her mouth as if he couldn't wait to taste her.

"Gage," she whispered, nuzzling the hand that stroked her face. She closed her eyes, longed to lose herself. "I don't think—"

"Don't think," he whispered as she opened her eyes. He dipped his head, brushing his mouth so feather-light against hers she couldn't help but lean in for more. She braced her hand against his chest, felt the beat of his heart, more intoxicating than the champagne she'd drunk.

"I've wanted to do this all night." His lips skimmed hers, teasing until she whimpered. Her fingers curled into his shirt, gripping the fabric, wanting to push him away, needing to pull him closer.

She turned her head, trying to ignore the thrill the brush of his lips against her cheek sent racing through her. It would be so easy to give in.

"I have to go," she managed, hating the fact that there was nothing she could do except run. "Good-bye, Gage."

"Morgan," he whispered, the confusion in his eyes glimmering in the glow of the streetlamp above them. But when he moved toward her again, Morgan stepped away and pressed her lips together as if that alone could stop the regret stabbing her in the heart. "Don't go."

"I have to." She couldn't take the chance. Not with everything she had at stake. "I'm not good for you, Gage. It just wouldn't work."

She got into the car and closed the door. As she shifted into drive, she saw Gage move forward, but refused to look at him. She kept her too-dry eyes pinned on the dark road ahead and drove off into the night. Alone.

~

Darkness swallowed the car.

Gage watched the car's taillights vanish down the hill.

What just happened? Gage's mind cleared as doubt

crept in. Had he done something wrong? Moved too fast? Said something to offend her? Or was he overreacting, unable to take the hit to his male ego? Maybe she just wasn't interested. Not good for him? Who was she kidding?

No. There was something there. He'd felt it and there wasn't a chance she hadn't. But it had scared the hell out of her. The question was why.

A horn blared behind him and Gage jumped to the side of the road. When he lost his footing he looked down at her shoes, entwined in much the way he'd hoped to be with Morgan tonight. For the second time that night, he scooped them up, unknotting his tie as he walked backward to his car. It wasn't until he unlocked the door that he found the white envelope wedged into the seam along the driver-side window.

He tugged it free, pulled out the white floral-sized insert card with a solitary embossed gold *N* in the center. He turned it over.

Hope you enjoyed the party.

He swore, scanning the street even though he knew he wouldn't find anyone. His hand itched to crush the note. *Evidence.* His own personal Nemesis note, though. He must be making someone nervous. He slipped the note inside its envelope and tucked it into his pocket before tossing Morgan's shoes onto the passenger seat.

Finding and stopping Nemesis was what was important, the only thing that mattered. But as he glanced at the tangled shoes, he wondered if there shouldn't be more.

"Thank you, coffee gods." Morgan stumbled in the back door of the Fiorelli kitchen and dive-bombed the freshly brewed pot.

As exhausted as she'd been after the party last night, she'd lain awake for hours trying to find a way—any way—out from under the pile of mistakes she'd made. She was feeling as worn and tattered as the cutoff shorts and ratty T-shirt she'd tugged on moments ago. No sooner had she taken her first hit of caffeine than the doorbell chimed, followed immediately by an odd clunk. She dropped her head back.

Repair number two hundred eleven: fix the doorbell. That would go on the list somewhere between repairing the loose floor planks on the porch and replacing the moldings around the front windows. "Oh, Granny." Morgan stared heavenward. "I know you always wanted me to stretch myself, but we both know I was never meant to be thin."

Footsteps pounded down the stairs toward the front door. A warning to the kids not to run almost slipped from Morgan's lips, but the sound of active children lightened her heart. Sick or not, kids came with their own special power supply. Who was Morgan to switch it off?

"Morgan! It's Oscar with our delivery."

Morgan joined Brandon and Kelley at the front door, a smile curving her lips as she watched the twenty-something deliveryman bend down in front of Kelley.

"Your majesty." Oscar bowed his head as Kelley curtseyed in her bright pink princess dress, her small hand keeping her precariously perched tiara in place on her bald head. "As always, I am at your service."

Kelley giggled, beaming up at Morgan as Morgan

signed for the monthly package from the medical clinic. "Thanks, Oscar. Appreciate you bringing this out on a weekend."

Kelley and Brandon pushed the box along the floor and disappeared into the kitchen.

"She's looking better." Oscar's voice carried a familiar trace of surprise. "When will she be clear?"

"A while yet. One day at a time, right?" Morgan's insides felt as if a swarm of bees had taken up permanent residence, buzzing to life whenever worry took hold. Should be easy enough to shut down—worrying didn't do anyone any good, especially the kids—but these days she couldn't turn it off.

"One day at a time." Oscar grinned. "See you next month."

Morgan closed the door and joined the kids in the kitchen. "What's Lydia up to?"

"She's working on a secret project," Brandon said as Kelley climbed onto a stool and Morgan hefted the box onto the counter.

"I'm sure she'll be out soon. Shit." Morgan sliced her thumb with the scissors she'd been using to open the box.

"Dollar," Brandon announced, and bolted to retrieve the glass Mason jar off the counter near the pantry.

Morgan pinched her lips together. Damn. This no-swearing policy she'd instituted to stop the kids from cursing had bitten her in the butt. Not to mention it was costing her a fortune. The sad thing was she had learned to keep cash on her person at all times—like today, when she'd left her purse in her apartment behind the main house.

As she handed over the dollar and Kelley and Brandon

worked to stash it with the rest of the foul-mouthed cash stash, Morgan pocketed the medication invoice she knew Nico and Angela would fret over. Meds were expensive for one child. Meds for four seriously ill kids were ridiculous.

Morgan couldn't bring herself to look at the amount due. So far her personal finances kept her hovering above disaster, thanks to investments her father had made for her, but the way things were going, that wouldn't last.

The queen bee escaped and buzzed into her chest before Morgan squashed it with renewed determination. She'd find a way through this mess. She didn't have another choice.

Fighting the bitterness, she handed first Kelley and then Brandon their meds and they stashed them on their personal shelves in the far cabinet. She loathed these deliveries. She lived for the day when none of the kids needed more meds, but embracing the ritual had eased some of their fears over being sick. Making their lives as normal as possible, even while some of them faced a possible death sentence, was as important as the meds themselves. Positive attitudes. Hope. Normalcy. She'd seen the combination work miracles.

She'd also seen it fail.

Morgan pulled out a box of insulin and diabetic supplies and wrote the name *Drew* on the outside before setting them aside for when he got home.

"Why doesn't Drew like us?" Kelley dug her fingernails into the wood countertop. This wasn't the first time she'd voiced concern over the latest foster arrival.

"Drew doesn't like us?" Brandon's face reflected both shock and disappointment, and Morgan struggled for the right words.

"He likes *you*." Kelley rolled her eyes with such exaggeration Morgan thought they might fall back in her head.

"He's only been here a month, sweetie. It takes some people a while to adjust to new surroundings," Morgan said. "And I wouldn't say he doesn't like us. He just doesn't know us yet." Morgan wasn't about to admit that Kelley had given voice to yet another concern gnawing at Morgan.

She and the Fiorellis knew bringing the newly diagnosed sixteen-year-old diabetic into the house would be a challenge. Foster kids brought a unique set of issues to begin with. Adding a serious illness and an even more serious attitude problem into the equation would be a test for everyone.

Trust took time. If and when trust developed at all. Morgan straightened her shoulders, but her stomach lurched. Kelley was right. Drew did like Brandon, and that was something.

As she broke down the shipping box, she caught Kelley watching her, a frown on her face. "What's wrong?"

"Where's Lydia's medicine?" Her baby blue eyes widened with concern. "We always do her medicine first because it's the most important."

Morgan stooped down in front of the little princess. "We had to change Lydia's meds, remember? We'll take her in another few weeks to get them." Kelley didn't need to know that while her foster sister's new meds had stopped the growth of the tumor on Lydia's brain stem, the strain of AIDS continued to take its toll on her system as well. It was only a matter of time before Lydia's body couldn't take any more and the medication she was on did more harm than good. Morgan straightened Kelley's tiara.

Watching the two little girls together, fighting their medical battles with the valor of a Special Forces team, was part of what kept Morgan going.

Brandon, in his typical caretaker fashion, slung an arm over Kelley's shoulder and steered her into the living room, challenging her to a game of Monopoly. She heard the Fiorelli's van in the driveway and headed to the front door. "Let's help Nico and Angela with the groceries," she called as Brandon raced outside. Morgan stopped when she spotted Kelley staring at the front page of the morning paper, her tiny mouth hanging open as she looked up at Morgan.

She knew that look. "What's so interesting?" Morgan circled behind Kelley and nearly groaned at the photograph of her and Gage headlining the society page. "Kelley—"

"I told you. I told you you'd meet Prince Charming."

Too tired to fight eight-year-old fairy-tale logic, Morgan plucked the paper from Kelley's hands. "Things aren't always as they appear," Morgan told her as she put the paper on top of the hall table and pivoted the little girl out the door.

If there was one thing Morgan could be certain of, it was that Gage Juliano was no Prince Charming.

~

Gage took a final swipe with the fine-grit sandpaper and stepped back from the oak table that would soon occupy his kitchen.

He bent down, blew the dust away, and squinted, searching for any imperfections he might have missed, before tackling the varnish. He ran his fingers over the surface, feeling for bumps, ridges. A few. Tiny. Imperceptible to the naked eye, but if he didn't remove them now the flaws would gnaw at him like termites feasting in a lumberyard every time he sat down to dinner.

Jim Morrison tried to get his fire lit on the radio as Gage inhaled the calming combination of sawdust and lingering turpentine.

Some men drank to decompress; others obsessed over sports or women, or both. Gage preferred Sunday mornings in the detached garage, crafting furniture or refinishing antiques. For the last year he'd concentrated on refurbishing the craftsman bungalow he called home, but having completed the work last month, he'd had to find a new outlet. At the rate he was going, he'd furnish the house in half the time it took him to do the upgrades.

He'd spent countless hours like this after he'd come back to Lantano Valley. It was his version of physical therapy, he supposed, especially after he'd stopped taking the painkillers that turned his brain to sludge.

This was where he felt alive, where he could turn off all thoughts of work and recharge. He might not be happy, but here he was happiest.

Happy wasn't happening. Not much of anything was happening except that he'd burned through a year's worth of sandpaper, all the while thinking of a leggy, lush blonde with a hint of sadnes—or maybe fear—in her eyes. People were normally so clear to him, and yet Morgan was an enigma. And puzzles were impossible for Gage to ignore.

"Thought for sure I'd find you at the office." Jon

Juliano strode up the driveway, a frosty six-pack in one hand, his permanently attached laptop bag hitched across his chest like a Boy Scout sash. "Isn't that what usually happens after Nemesis makes a midnight visit?"

Gage glared at his youngest brother.

The bitterness lingering over that obnoxious note Nemesis left on his window Friday night reared again Saturday evening when the burglar made one of his unannounced visits and relieved a Hollywood producer of a recently discovered and rumored to be priceless Renoir. This meant Nemesis had forced Gage to abandon his skybox seats at the Dodger game and spend an unproductive and useless three hours at the scene.

Nemesis hadn't left anything new behind, and two hours after reporting the break-in, just like the previous victims, Tate Cunningham, recanted his statement and changed his story. He'd made a mistake, Cunningham declared, before ordering Gage and his team to vacate the premises. The painting was in their vacation house in the Cayman Islands.

Of course that didn't stop the *Lantano Valley Times* from reporting the break-in or running Nemesis' latest thank-you note to the Cunninghams for making a meaningful contribution to society. Tate Cunningham was having a hell of a week after just having been accused of raiding his employees' pension funds. Gage's head throbbed, the result of unending hours of teeth grinding and a lack of sleep.

Nemesis targeted the obscenely wealthy under the guise of helping the less fortunate—a Good Samaritan with a serious ego problem. Not that Gage gave a damn about Nemesis' motivations. Doing the wrong thing for the right reason was something Gage would never understand. Or accept.

What the hell did Nemesis have on these people that they refused to speak with anyone in law enforcement about the case? But none of that had to do with his brother's visit.

"I'll forgive the intrusion if you plan to share those bottles." Gage indicated the beer, then upon closer examination, cringed. "Christ, kid, root beer?"

Jon grinned. "I'm not twenty-one for another month and a half. Wouldn't want the cops to arrest me."

Gage grabbed a rag to clean his hands before giving his brother a hug and hard slap on the back. "Good to see you."

"You, too. Mom's been worried."

"Must be a day that ends in *Y*." Gage snatched up a bottle, twisted off the cap, and gestured to the step stool by the workbench.

"She's been calling you for three days."

"I am aware." Hence the not answering. "I'll call her today. But you didn't walk two miles to tell me to call Mom. What's up? Last semester before graduation, I'd think you'd be locked in the library cramming for finals. Don't want to lose that valedictorian spot for Lantano Valley U."

"That's a lock," Jon did the college student slouch as he took a seat and shoved his dark hair out of his face. "But I did want to run something by you. A kind of change in plans?"

"Whose plans?"

"Mine and Mom's. It's about graduate school."

"Law school, right? Going to add to the family fortune

and follow in Rich's footsteps?" Their brother, two years Gage's junior at thirty-three, was moving up in a law firm in New York. The fortune was a Juliano joke. Rich was heading up the pro-bono division and was lucky to make rent.

"Actually, I was thinking of following in yours." Jon gave him an "isn't that great news" grin.

Gage took care when swallowing as a tingle of dread wound its way up his spine. "Please tell me you're referring to my unrequited love of architecture."

Jon's grin widened, and Gage wondered if his kid brother was ever going to grow out of his baby face. Tall, a bit gangly, and with a face that had girls lining up from here to Tijuana, the entire Juliano family was waiting for him to pull his nose out of a book long enough to notice.

"If you apply to the academy, you'll kill mom. Tell me you know that." There wasn't enough adrenaline in the world to kick-start Gage's heart if his little brother was thinking about becoming a cop. Gage had learned the hard way that working for law enforcement wasn't all it was cracked up to be. He didn't wish his near-death experience —not to mention his subsequent trust issues—on anyone, especially Jon.

"Do I look suicidal to you?"

Gage let out a long, slow breath. Thank God. "Then what are you thinking?"

"I, uh, told Mom the other night that I was considering computer forensics, cold-case investigations, primarily. Developing new programs to aid in law enforcement. And before you say anything, I'm sorry. She blames you."

"Of course she does." Gage understood his mother's concerns. She hadn't been thrilled with Gage's plans to attend the academy after college. Her anxiety had increased the longer he served. He didn't want to recall the argument they'd had two years ago when he'd been asked to work on the FBI task force before heading off for special training at Quantico.

Gage rotated his left shoulder, the scar the bullet left on its way to his heart igniting the memories he wished he could erase.

"I've told her I wouldn't be working in the field that much, and that chances are I wouldn't have to carry a gun." Judging from the excitement on Jon's face, he was hoping that wasn't the case. "But I was thinking you could smooth things over a little with her? Let her know I won't be in harm's way like—"

"Like I was." Gage shouldn't have been surprised by Jon's enthusiasm or his shift in educational attention. Of all the Juliano kids, the youngest boy had always been the most curious with the deepest sense of honor. The examiner. The brains behind the mayhem. Well, until Gina and Liza came along. When it came to masterminds, the seventeen-year-old twins were one diabolical plan away from merging into a supervillain, with Gina most likely acting as the brain. Liza could design a kick-ass costume, though. "I'll see what I can do. But you have to tell me why."

Jon shrugged in that way that made Gage's temple throb. "Lots of reasons, but it's different. Rewarding. Besides, you make it look like fun."

Gage nearly shattered the bottle in his hand. Five exhausting months in the academy was anything but fun. After the years of riding with Brady Malloy, he'd spent the next four in a patrol car with a partner who was distracted by his personal life. Not fun. Another four bouncing from department to department never finding the right fit was definitely not fun. Getting shot and stabbed while undercover with the Feds was the least fun of all. Being thrown under the bus afterward, however, had been a hundred times worse.

"It's tough," Gage corrected. His family didn't need to know the extent of what he'd gone through. It should be enough that he'd come home to the less chaotic atmosphere of Lantano Valley where he could start over and find something. "Being a cop is rewarding. It's also all-consuming. But it's rarely, if ever, fun." And shame on him for ever making it appear to be.

"Not even this Nemesis case? Come on. He's the Robin Hood of my generation. Stealing from the rich, helping people pay their bills, save their homes, cover medical costs. I mean, yeah, you're trying to stop him, but still, tell me there's not a hint of fun in that. Like the Sheriff of Nottingham."

"Brady Malloy's grave is at East Lawn Cemetery. Feel free to run that theory by him."

The smile on Jon's face evaporated like water on a hot plate.

Damn. Gage felt as if he'd just sat on the kid's award-winning science experiment. "Sorry." He shook his head. "You didn't deserve that. It's been a crap couple of days." And nothing he wanted to delve into further. "I'll do what I can to smooth it over with Mom."

"Thanks." While Jon's smile wasn't nearly as contagious, his expression remained curious. "Can't have been all crap. We saw the picture in the paper over breakfast yesterday. Who's the new girlfriend?"

The root beer bubbles backed up as Gage swallowed

too hard. He covered his mouth as he burped. "What girlfriend? What picture?"

"The one that made mom stop grumbling about my ungrateful, selfish, and ill-advised career choice." Jon pulled out his phone and tapped a few buttons. "*Lantano Valley Times*, society pages. From the Tremayne fundraiser Friday night. You didn't see?"

When Jon turned his phone around, Gage stared at a photo of himself and Morgan dancing very, very close. That look on her face made Gage frown. She seemed happy, sultry. Why the hell had she run away from him? Not that it mattered. Except that it did matter, and the fact that it did bugged the crap out of him.

"No. I didn't see." Gage's chest felt as if it were suddenly overflowing with a troupe of Chinese gymnasts. Shit. He'd bet his mother was ordering wedding invitations online at this moment.

As if waiting for a cue, Gage's phone erupted into that obnoxious boy-be-bop song. He stared at it for a good ten seconds, considered using the rubber mallet to silence it for good.

"Answer it, man," Jon whispered from behind him, but when Gage looked over his shoulder, Jon stepped away, hands up in surrender. Or preparing to run for his life. "You know how she gets when we ignore her."

"Yeah." Gage turned his attention to the phone as Jon headed home. Police academy training, fifteen years on the job, and he'd rather walk unarmed into a drug den than answer that phone. "Coward." Gage winced as he snatched the phone and clicked on. "Hey, Mom."

"We made a deal after you got shot, Gage. I'm supposed to hear from you every two days, remember?"

Gage took a calming breath. Hard to forget any deal made with a tube down your throat and a catheter up your—

"I figured you'd be busy working on Stephen's birthday party." His life was never more peaceful than when Theresa Juliano was in event-planning mode. Thank God there were five other siblings to occupy her.

"I'm finalizing the menu as we speak." The edge of fear he'd heard in her voice when he'd first answered the phone was gone. Probably helped that she knew he wasn't lying dead in an alley somewhere. Not that Lantano Valley had that many alleys. "Are you going to invite Morgan Tremayne or should I?"

"Invite Morgan? Mom!" Oh, God. He'd just squawked. As bad as she'd been about his dating life before, she'd ticked up yet another notch on the crazy meter. "Mom, you have to stop doing this. My life is *my* life."

"Bah. Your life is mine as long as you breathe. It's either her or I'll call that darling Millie girl from the library."

"You do that and I'll head straight over to St. Augustus and take a vow of chastity." His Catholic upbringing reared its vengeful head and made Gage cross his fingers. Maybe he should spin three times and spit on the floor. The silence that followed carried an unfamiliar tension. "Mom?"

"You're alone. You shouldn't be alone."

How many times had they had this conversation? And it had become more frequent since the shooting. "Wounds heal. Memories fade." Maybe not as fast as he'd have liked, but they would. "I'm fine. I like my life the way it is." Despite the thoughts of Morgan skipping along the edges of his mind like a stone on a pond.

"*Fine* and *happy* are two different things," Theresa corrected. "We haven't seen you in weeks. You've buried yourself in work, in this new job, this Nemesis business. You need someone in your life and judging from what I saw in the paper, she's the perfect solution. Besides, I want grandbabies before I'm too old to enjoy them. So. Yes or no on the date?"

"Mom." Was he ever more exhausted than when he talked to his mother? "I love you. You know that. But the last thing I need is you hounding me about my procreation intentions. It'll happen when it happens, if it happens. Besides, wouldn't you prefer a nice legal daughter-in-law you could pester instead of me?"

"Legal, ha. At this point, I'll take what I can get, and I get what I want. I want that girl at my party."

"It's Stephen's party, and believe it or not I was working the other night. Meeting Morgan was business."

"Best job you've ever had, then. I've never seen that look on your face at the office."

There was no arguing with her. Especially since he knew she was right. "We can't keep doing this, you hounding me about my personal life. Please." There was a long silence, and for a moment he thought the phone had gone dead. "Mom."

"Bring her to the party and I will."

Oh, dear heaven. Gage frowned as a new set of alarm bells went off. "Wait. You'll what? Back off? What exactly does 'I will' mean?"

"It means." He knew that "I'm serious" tone and embraced the possibilities. "Bring Morgan Tremayne with you and I'll stop pestering you about getting married. I won't mention grandchildren. To you."

"For how long exactly?" He wanted details. Exact details. Carved in stone.

"Two weeks."

"Six months." He sensed freedom in his grasp.

"Two months."

"Three and I'll come for dinner once a month." Desperation made a man do odd things.

"Once a week."

"Deal." He scrubbed at his eyes. Something told him she'd made out better than she expected and he'd just gotten screwed. "Am I going to need this in writing?"

"Your father will keep you honest."

Yeah, that's what he was worried about. "I'll see you next Sunday, Mom. I'll call you tomorrow."

"I love you, Gage."

"Love you, too." He hung up the phone, sat down on the stool beside the workbench, and banged his head on the table. Then he popped up. Shit.

He'd traded one problem for another. How the hell was he going to convince Morgan to attend a family party with him? And then he remembered.

Gage slid open the bottom drawer of his workbench. He tapped a finger against his lips and grinned. What was it his sister Liza always said?

A woman could never say no to a pair of fabulous shoes.

CHAPTER 5

"You knew the rules from day one, Drew. Ditching school is unacceptable." Morgan shoved the washing machine in place, praying the new water hose would solve the leak issue. Not a good start to her over-scheduled Wednesday. "The answer is no. No movies. No basketball game. You're grounded for two weeks. Kelley. Brandon. Angela's waiting in the car."

"It was only gym and it was last period." Anger radiated off sixteen-year-old Drew in waves and Morgan steadied herself to ride the surf.

"Don't care. Ditching is ditching. You have responsibilities, beginning with your education. You don't like the agreement you made when you came to live with us, you know your options." Since those other options were limited to an extended stay in the juvenile detention center, Morgan considered the topic closed. "You're going to be late for homeroom if you don't leave now."

"This sucks," Drew blasted, and for the hundredth time Morgan had to bite her tongue to suggest he get a haircut.

She hadn't seen Drew's eyes in weeks, covered as they were with the too-long sandy brown bangs. His baggy jeans and T-shirts reminded Morgan of a Woodstock documentary reject and made her feel old for complaining about the clothes these young people wore today. More importantly, his attire made it difficult to see if he was maintaining his weight, or if he was showing signs of jaundice, something he'd been dealing with on and off due to the damage the undiagnosed diabetes had done to his organs.

What she wouldn't give to take that black leather jacket that never left his sight to the cleaners for an extended visit.

"I suggest you remember just how much this sucks the next time you let your so-called friends talk you into cutting class." Her phone chimed *Für Elise*, letting her know the bank opened in fifteen minutes. "Do you want a ride to school?"

"I'll walk."

Heaven save her from the hostile two-word teenage answer. "Okay, then. Don't forget to check your numbers before lunch. Kids, now!" Footsteps pounded overhead like a fleet of reindeer on the roof.

"Whatever." And with that, Drew grabbed his backpack and slammed out the door.

Morgan slumped against the washing machine. She knew how hard it was for him, a new school, dealing with his diabetes diagnosis, having to leave class every few hours to go to the nurse and be tested. It was hard enough to be a teenager these days without adding a medical issue to the mix.

There had to be some way to get through to him. At

least he'd bonded with Brandon. The little guy was Morgan's savior when it came to dealing with Drew, as the teen was incapable of staying mad with Brandon anywhere nearby.

She heard the zoom of Lydia's motorized wheelchair as the little girl buzzed into the kitchen, big brown eyes spinning like King Arthur's Carousel at Disneyland, her frail body swimming in the baggy jeans and Tinker Bell T-shirt she wore.

"Hey, kiddo." Morgan pulled herself together and dropped a kiss on the top of her thinning fawn brown hair. Her color was good, her eyes less cloudy. Hope that Lydia may have turned a corner battled against the reality of her illness. Today, however, Morgan chose to cling to hope. "Where's Nico? I thought you guys were going to make homemade pasta today."

"He's fixing the sink in the boy's bathroom. Brandon said there's something stuck in the drain. Nico started swearing so I thought I'd better leave." She grinned up at Morgan, chasing the aftereffects of Drew's attitude away. "You swear better though."

"Thank you very much." Morgan curtsied. "You hungry?"

"Got any bananas?" She stretched her chin up, searched the counter.

"Of course." She grabbed one out of the fruit bowl, started it for her, and handed it over. Not so long ago Lydia had been on a feeding tube because she couldn't keep anything down.

Morgan's phone chimed again, this time Beethoven's Fifth.

"You going to the construction site today?" Lydia's eyes widened as she peeled the banana and bit in.

"I'm meeting with Kent in about an hour." Morgan looked at her watch as Nico came in, stopped in front of Morgan, picked up her hand, and plopped a soggy orange plastic fish in her palm. Morgan peered closer. "Is that Nemo?"

"He was supposed to make it to the ocean," Brandon cried as he ran into the room, then he took Nemo into his possession and stuffed him to his jeans pocket. "How far did he get?" He turned excited eyes on Nico, who was putting the wrench in the toolbox.

"As far as the u-bend."

"Put it in your journal," Morgan called as they ran out to the car, managing not to laugh until they were gone. "Need me to check the sink?" Morgan asked him, knowing Nico wasn't as comfortable with plumbing issues as he was with other repair work.

"If you could, great." Nico washed up. "Lydia and I will take care of dinner. Angela and Kelley are going to make fruit salad for dessert. Will you be home in time?"

"Ummm." Morgan skimmed her schedule, added a note to double-check the sink. "I doubt it. Late meeting with Vanity Cleaners—I'm thinking they might be a good local source for linens and cleaning services once the center opens. Be nice to get more local businesses on board. Save me a plate?"

"It'll have your name on it."

"Great. I'm off." Morgan grabbed her purse from the kitchen table and headed out the back door, adjusting her Bluetooth. Once she was in her car, she pulled out the white envelope containing the checks she'd collected from various stores and individuals over the last couple of days, along with the bundle of cash she'd saved for a rainy day.

Except her rainy day was more like a typhoon.

All the more reason to get the money into the account and start whittling down the missing two hundred grand.

When she'd first siphoned money from the center's construction fund into the operating expense fund, it had been with the intention of repaying it as soon as possible, and for a while she'd been doing well.

But that was before construction delays set in. Before the bills mounted. Before money set aside to repay the "loan" had been gobbled up by Morgan's refusal to turn any patient away.

Within six months what had initially been one hundred grand had doubled and then exploded into the impossible.

She hadn't been able to fill the hole fast enough to keep up with the books. Until Nemesis stepped in.

And then stepped out.

She started the engine and turned on the radio as she did a final check of her calendar for the morning. The local news was spouting about the college basketball team and how they'd been pulverized by a neighboring community college during a practice game. Morgan couldn't remember the last time she'd gone to a game of any kind.

The local newscast blared its syncopated theme song as news personality Lara Stark's voice floated over the airwaves. Morgan withdrew the deposit bag for one final check.

"Sources inside District Attorney's office revealed the Nemesis investigation isn't running as smoothly as anticipated. Rumor is the D.A. is considering filing charges of receiving stolen property and/or collusion after the fact against anyone suspected of accepting money from Nemesis. As we've been reporting for the past few months, numerous individuals and businesses have publically thanked Nemesis for giving them large amounts of cash, money that has saved homes, paid bills, and in one instance, allowed for a life-saving medical procedure. But D.A. Marshall believes that while the public and media have embraced Nemesis, in doing so, they've goaded Nemesis into committing more crimes, as evidenced by the Cunningham burglary this past Saturday night. More details to come as this story develops. This is Lara Stark reporting."

Morgan's throat closed around the icy air in her lungs as her hand froze on the Nemesis cash.

Rumor has it. Nothing confirmed. It wasn't as if Morgan had taken out an ad on the evening news. She hadn't told anyone about the four "donations" she'd received from Nemesis. How could she when it meant admitting to shuffling money between the foundation accounts like she'd pilfered the cardboard Monopoly bank.

How Nemesis had gotten those envelopes onto her desk at the construction site was the question that gnawed at her most, but then that was what Nemesis excelled at, getting in and out of places without being seen. She wasn't going to question the gift.

Morgan dug into the bag and pulled out the bundle of twenty-five thousand she'd hoped to deposit today. Her pulse beat double in her neck. Better to be safe at this point, keep the deposit under the reportable ten grand. No red flags, no filings to the FBI or treasury. Not that large cash deposits were out of the norm for her for the foundation. But now wasn't the time to take chances, not when she still had four weeks and three days to find the rest of the money.

She'd done the wrong thing, she knew, but for the right reason. That money she'd taken had saved lives, and for that she would never regret her actions. But that didn't mean she wasn't desperate to cover her trail. No matter whose help she had to take. All the more reason to be relieved that Gage Juliano was out of the picture. She imagined he'd be the type of man she'd find herself wanting to confide in, and that wouldn't lead to anywhere good.

Morgan's ribs ached from her holding her breath. Blood pounded in her ears. Could be this stack of cash would be the last she'd receive from her not-so-anonymous benefactor. Which, given the D.A.'s pronouncement, was good news.

Wasn't it?

∽

The Tremayne Investments and Securities building revamp made Gage's office look like the turn-of-the-century factory space it was. The ultra-modern beveled glass of Jackson Tremayne's firm allowed for every ray of sunlight in the city to stream through and bathe its employees in a bright and positive atmosphere.

From a security standpoint, the design made sense to Gage. Nothing could be hidden in this open space. From a practical perspective, the lobby spoke of streamlined elegance and a down-to-business attitude. Any client would feel at ease both personally and financially.

As instructed by the sign posted just inside the rotating

glass door, Gage checked in at the security desk, behind which two uniformed guards kept watch on a bank of screens that rotated various camera angles every five to ten seconds.

A badge was printed out as soon as his name was entered into the system. Gage looked up after clipping it to his lapel and found Nathan Tremayne emerging from a closed door across the hall.

"Gage, good to see you again." Nathan greeted him with a warm smile and an open hand. "Hope you don't mind, but Dad asked me to sit in on your meeting. Just give me one second. Hey, Todd." Nathan slapped his hand down on the counter to get the young man's attention. "Go on home. Sawyer said he'll cover your shifts for the rest of the week."

"Thanks, man." The mingled look of excitement and relief on the second security guard's face told Gage Nathan had made the guy's year. "I was just venting before, about Courtney and the baby. I didn't expect—"

"I know. It's your first kid, give yourself a break. So go home, both of you put your feet up, watch some old movies, and wait for the baby to decide he's ready." Nathan tapped his knuckle on the counter. "And pick her up some ice cream on the way. Sorry, Gage."

Gage shrugged. "That was nice of you, giving him the week off."

"Poor guy's wife is a week over her due date." He led the way to the escalator at the far end of the lobby. "So you want to bounce some ideas off us about Nemesis?"

"Looking for some confirmation on some things. Appreciate your time." Truth be told, Gage had been surprised at how easy it had been to get an appointment. In his experience, being told to "call my office" was code for "I don't have time for this shit."

"If a meeting with you means putting a stop to Nemesis' reign of, well, terror seems a bit of an overstatement. He's a nuisance, but a diverting one at times."

"He does have a sense of humor." Albeit a warped one. "So the firm does enough business to warrant owning an entire building in downtown Lantano Valley?" As they moved toward the elevator, Gage noticed the subtle design shift from modern to paying homage to the historical attributes of the Romanesque, a transformation that finished once the elevator doors opened on the fifth floor.

"Dad took the firm global a little over ten years ago, which was when he made plans to buy the building. No financing, mind you. He waited until he had the cash in hand. Did the same thing when it came to the renovation. It was worth the wait." Then Nathan chuckled. "Too bad it means we won't be expanding for the next year or so, but hey, no debt. Always a good thing."

Sensible, confident. Gage could see a divide the size of the Great Barrier Reef between the Tremaynes and some of the other residents of Lantano Valley Gage had had the not-so-great pleasure of dealing with. Whatever Kolfax's interest, the agent was off base. As Gage had thought the other night, Jackson and his offspring destroyed Gage's perception of the wealthy elite.

Offspring. *Morgan.*

"Nathan, did you sign the birthday card for Beth Ann in accounting yet?" The fortysomething woman sitting behind a half-moon workstation aimed a warning look at Gage's escort when they stopped at her desk.

"Not yet, Corrine. Will do as soon as I'm done here. Inspector Juliano for Dad."

"Hello, Inspector." Corrine stood and held out her hand. She was tall, quite curvy, with pale blond hair draping down her spine in a graceful curtain. Her round face didn't carry a hint of stress despite the lights flashing on the phone at her side. "It's a pleasure to meet you. Jackson is still on that call with Kurisan in Japan," she told Nathan. "Should be another ten minutes."

"Gives me time to go sign that card then. Be right back."

"Where should I—?" Gage glanced around the spacious floor plan.

"There's a waiting area to your left," Corrine told him. "Would you like something to drink? Coffee, perhaps?"

"Thank you, I'm fine."

"Gage." Sheila pushed out of a nearby office, file folders clutched against the front of her pale yellow dress. A flouncy skirt danced around her knees as she strode toward him on what he could only describe as needle-thin stilts. Her blond hair bounced in airy curls around her shoulders, framing a picture-perfect face he suspected was responsible for her run on the pageant circuit. "What brings you by? Corrine, would you mind?"

"I'll leave them on your desk." Corrine accepted the files and disappeared around the corner.

"So." Sheila gave Gage a slow smile, linked her arm through his, and guided him to the waiting area Corrine had pointed out. "How did you enjoy the fundraiser the other night?"

"I had a very nice time, thank you."

"Mmmm. I think Morgan enjoyed herself." She

blinked her lashes faster than a hummingbird's wings. "Have you spoken to her since?"

"Subtlety is not your strong suit." Gage tried not to laugh. But he shouldn't be surprised at her interest. After all, he was the one who had mingled business with pleasure. "No, I haven't spoken with your sister since the party. But that's something I plan to remedy by the end of the week."

"Excellent. I think you're just the man to remind her she's a woman and not a walking appointment book." Gage felt his face flush as Sheila veered him down the hall. "And in preparation for that, um, *conversation*, there's something you should see. We'll be showing this to the public at the next foundation event in August, but you've earned the right to a sneak peek."

She turned into a room so bright he thought about pulling out his sunglasses.

"I thought you might like to see the object of Morgan's obsession," Sheila said. "This is what we hope to open by the end of the year."

The quarter inch scale replica of the Pediatric Cancer Treatment Center stole the breath from his lungs as effortlessly as a morning breeze. The mix of grey stone and glass surrounded by lush serene walkways and water features reminded him of the Japanese Tea Garden in San Francisco. The cold, sterile environment one associated with a medical facility didn't exist in Morgan's creation. No, this place was one of comfort. Softness in the angles and curved lines of the windows and walls belied natural elements and features he couldn't recall seeing in another Lantano Valley project.

"It's remarkable," he told Sheila. "Nothing like what I expected."

"Before he died, our brother would draw pictures of what made him feel better." She gestured to the framed drawings on the wall behind the display: crayon-imprinted images of waterfalls and moss-covered stone houses. Sunlight. Lots and lots of light. "Morgan kept them in a scrapbook for when Mom was ready to talk design. They worked on it together, then with Kent Lawson. He's a general contractor but he dabbles in architecture."

"That's not dabbling. It's genius." Gage bent down, circled the model. "And what's this going to be over here?" He pointed to the expanse of grass behind the structure.

"She can't decide. Exercise and fresh air is an important part of the program Morgan wants to implement, something along those lines."

"So this is all Morgan? You don't have any say?"

Sheila shrugged, and for a moment Gage thought he saw resentment flash across her features. "I have some ideas, but she hasn't asked. She doesn't ask for anything." She wagged a finger at Gage. "You need to be aware of that up front if you're going to be *speaking* to her again."

"I'll remember."

"And also remember that this"—Sheila pointed to the center—"has been her life ever since she was a teenager. She lives it, breathes it. She will do what she has to in order to make it happen. As a concerned big sister, I'd like her to see there's more to life than a building, no matter its intent."

"My mother said something similar to me recently,"

Gage murmured, then realized he'd spoken out loud. "Just that—"

"There you two are." Nathan popped his head in. "Dad's ready for us. Ah, you're looking at Morgan's baby."

"I thought I should warn him about what he's up against should he try to eke out some time in Morgan's schedule," Sheila said with a too-wide smile. "I'll let you get to your meeting. Good to see you again, Gage."

"You too, Sheila." As he followed Nathan to Jackson's office, Gage pondered how interesting and baffling the sister relationship could be. His own were either plotting together or trying to verbally kill each other. Did Sheila and Morgan associate in the same way?

"Jackson, I appreciate you seeing me." He greeted the senior Tremayne just inside Jackson's office.

"No trouble. Corrine?"

"Coffee?" His assistant nodded. "Of course."

"Thank you. So, Gage, how's the case coming along and how can we help?"

Gage heard the question as if from under water. He tried not to gape at the wonder of this room. Stepping into Jackson Tremayne's office was like walking into the pages of a Jules Verne novel. Brass and wood intermingled in paneling and shelving that housed everything from antique books to a collection of spyglasses.

"Pretty impressive, right?" Nathan said as Gage bent to examine a patina sculpture, an artist's rendering of the Greek gods surrounding what appeared to be the Arthurian Round Table. "Dad's been collecting for years."

"My late wife indulged my obsession of certain types of antiquities," Jackson explained. "History's always been an interest of mine. There's something about drawing from the power of what we were that makes me less cynical about what we've become."

Nathan cleared his throat as he took a seat at the small conference table in front of the paned window. "So, what's on your mind, Gage?"

"I have this list." Gage pulled a sheet of paper out of his jacket pocket and handed it to Jackson as he continued to scan the endless shelves of items. "I was hoping you could tell me what these names have in common."

Jackson scanned the list, passed it to his son. "To start with, they've all been targets of Nemesis."

"Despite what they claim now." Was that a Remington? "Sorry. I could stay in here for hours." Gage shook himself free and refocused on the case. "Yes, Nemesis has paid them each a visit. Anything else?"

"They're Tremayne Investment and Securities clients," Nathan said before placing the sheet on the table. "Or they were at one time. But you knew that before you walked in the door."

Gage had expected some hostility, but he needed to get Kolfax and the FBI out of his head and out of his case. Proving the Tremaynes had nothing to do with Nemesis was his best bet.

"Nathan." Jackson patted his son on the shoulder. "Gage is doing his job just as you would. We've worked with each of these families, Gage. Lance Swendon and his wife chose to take their business elsewhere about a year and a half ago after one of my brokers refused to alter some financial records for his taxes."

"And we discontinued our relationship with Van Keltin

in January when he accused us of making irresponsible investments on his behalf," Nathan said.

"Investments he requested," Jackson clarified.

"In writing, the idiot," Nathan scoffed. "He threatened to sue us for his losses until we sent him a copy of the email he sent to Dad."

"And yet both men attended the foundation fundraiser the other night," Gage observed.

"Appearances are everything in Lantano Valley, Gage," Jackson said. "James Van Keltin was one of the first to donate to the foundation's funds for the center. He can't very well withdraw his support of a charity he helped establish without raising some eyebrows and feeding the rabid rumor mill."

"Not that his wife would ever let him," Nathan interjected. "She and my mother were tennis partners for over a decade. Appearances," Nathan added with a quirk of his lips. "Equal parts entertainment and irritation."

"Doesn't sound to me as if you're fans of these two." While Gage wasn't surprised by Jackson's genial tone, he found Nathan's sarcasm and honesty of more benefit. "What about the others on the list?"

"Charles Baker is a spineless weasel," Nathan observed. "But other than that he's okay. Grant Alvers, Josiah Fitzgerald." He shrugged. "Nothing comes to mind other than they're all more interested in expanding their profit margins than anything else."

"There is one interesting commonality, but I'm not sure it means anything," Jackson trailed his finger down the list again. "If you check court records, I think you'll find a number of these people were represented by James

Van Keltin at some point. Corrine, thank you. The table will be fine."

Corrine offered a polite smile as she carried in a shellacked tray filled with cups, a decanter of steaming coffee, and a plate of cookies. "I brought in oatmeal cookies for the birthday party this afternoon and set a few aside."

"Best oatmeal cookies in the county," Jackson pronounced as he plucked one off the plate. Corrine withdrew from the room. "Lest we forget, Nemesis was the Goddess of retribution and vengeance. Nasty fellow in the myths, but then none of them were particularly likable, I suppose."

Brady Malloy had also made mention of the origin of Nemesis' name in his notes. "You think Nemesis is avenging something or someone?"

"Getting into Nemesis' head is your job, not mine," Jackson said. "I was merely pointing out it's an interesting choice of moniker for what is essentially a glorified thief. While I can appreciate the idea without agreeing with it, vengeance doesn't get anyone anywhere in the long run. Most times it comes around and bites you in the ass. Does any of this help?"

"Yes, it does." Gage took an offered cookie, drank his coffee, and felt the case open in a new direction. "It most definitely does."

CHAPTER 6

Since taking over the foundation, Morgan had mastered many skills, but the one she used most often was biting her tongue while she spoke. "Yes, I understand you believe the delay isn't your fault, Doug. But Mother Nature's hissy fit and your warehouse getting flooded in the last storm wasn't my doing. If the supplies had been delivered by the date on the contract, we wouldn't be having this conversation. For the *third* time."

The tires of her Mustang ground over loose rock and dirt as Morgan pulled into the construction site's cordoned-off parking area, killed the engine, and downed the last of her coffee.

Once upon a time she couldn't blink for hours after drinking her triple-shot latte. These days her Monday fix had as much kick as an arthritic donkey. Appropriate given the paint supplier she'd been dealing with for the last two months was an ass.

"I'm not paying for supplies we haven't received," she stated. "And if you need confirmation of that, check the contract I signed with your boss last fall." Just to make sure, Morgan tapped the PDF app on her phone and opened the Johnstone Paint Supplies paperwork.

Vindicated, she set the business bitch loose as Doug Vallard issued another barrage of excuses. "You know what, Doug? You can stop there. Here's what we're going to do. Either you have our order on site by five tomorrow afternoon, or we're going with another company." Morgan rolled her eyes at his inept panic-induced sputter. If only someone would invent a death-ray app so she could zap incompetent idiots out of her universe. "Tomorrow at five is impossible?" Hallelujah. "I'll fax a copy of the cancelled agreement to your boss's office within the hour." She clicked off the call, leaned her head against the headrest, and closed her eyes.

So this was what a car running on empty felt like.

At least her meeting with Elliot Dunbar, the foundation's new accountant, had been pushed to next week. She'd take good news wherever she could get it, and not having to turn over her books just yet? Definitely good news.

Morgan yelped at the knock on her window. After pressing a hand against her hammering heart, she shoved the door open, got out, and glared at her general contractor.

Even in the middle of a construction site, Kent Lawson made jeans and a button-down blue flannel shirt look as tailored as a Savile Row suit. Dark hair and equally fathomless dark eyes completed the handsome picture.

"So I cancelled our contract with Johnstone." As expected, Kent's grin exposed his molars. "You were right. I should have listened to your recommendation from the start. Get me a contract you can live with and—" Wait a minute. Morgan stood up straight from having gone into the car for her purse. "I know that look." Kent's eyebrows rose so high they almost touched his hairline. She crossed her arms over her chest, narrowed her eyes. "You already got a new contract, didn't you?"

"Last week. Paperwork is on what you laughingly call a desk in the office." He sniffed the air. "Do I smell donuts?"

"You smell Wednesday, which is when I always bring donuts for the crew." She shoved her phone in her back pocket, slung her bag over her shoulder, and opened the trunk to expose four pink bakery boxes from Ignacio's 24-Hour Doh!Knot Stop.

Kent opened the top box, snatched a chocolate old-fashioned, and stuffed it in his mouth as he lifted the boxes out of the car.

"You keep scarfing those, you won't make it down the aisle," Morgan muttered, hoping her willpower stayed intact and she refused the call of the lemon-filled. She really loved the lemon-filled. Kent grinned around the cake as she followed him to the construction trailer and the snack table he kept for his crew. "How are the wedding plans coming along?"

"You'd have to ask Craig." Kent swallowed. "Let's elope, I said. Just the two of us, no fuss, but no. He wants a party. With both our families. We're still arguing about the band, so he booked both."

"Yeah, a real tragedy." Morgan laughed at the gleam in his eye. "Happily ever after with the man of your dreams. Poor you." Kent was one of the few friends she'd kept in touch with after high school. Quarterback, star of the debate club, and class president. He'd also been out for as long as she'd known him. Having become one of the most sought-after general contractors in southern California, he was Morgan's first call when the final plans for the center were approved. "Seven weeks and counting until *dum-dum-da-dum*."

"You're coming, right?"

"Wouldn't miss it." Not that she relished attending without a plus-one. The thought of Gage and his taut torso-accentuating tux came to mind.

Dangerous, dangerous, dangerous. She'd been unable to shake the thought of him since she'd left him in the middle of the street. She shook her head as if her mind were an Etch A Sketch. Didn't work. No matter how many times she tried.

"I thought maybe you'd want to change to a plus-one now that you made a new friend." Kent waggled his eyebrows as he filled a paper cup with coffee.

"What new friend? What are you— Oh, God." Morgan rubbed her eyes. "You saw the paper. I thought print was dead."

Kent chuckled and tossed her a copy of the *Lantano Valley Times*, which she attempted to deflect into the recycling bin. Instead it plopped on the table in front of her.

"It was one dance, Kent. It wasn't anything." But it could so easily have been.

"Are you seeing the same picture I am?" He let out an attention-grabbing whistle. "Break!" He gestured to the boxes. "I always suspected there was a social butterfly lurking beneath that Joan of Arc facade," Kent teased over his shoulder. "Glad to see you had a good time."

Morgan could almost feel Gage's arms around her and

hear the echo of the string quartet as she gazed at the picture. "Too bad there's no time."

"Make the time, Morgan. You can change the world all you want, but it doesn't mean anything if there's no one to share it with."

Cranky Morgan reared her head like a horror movie jack-in-the-box. "Anyone ever tell you you're an irritating combination of Dr. Phil and Yoda?"

"Surprisingly, yes." The grin returned. "That last permit we were waiting for came through. Let me grab the paperwork and I'll show you what's been done since your last visit."

Morgan pulled out her phone and scanned her calendar. "I can give you until one, then I have to hit the road for a pickup in L.A." And hopefully miss crush-hour traffic both ways. "Those new fixture and tile samples came in but they want to charge us two arms and a leg for delivery. I'll drop them by here on my way home."

"I could have had one of the guys go get it." Kent headed up the three stairs into the trailer.

"I had to go in anyway. No need to take one of your people off the job." She marked off the three phone calls she'd scheduled, along with her drop-off at the bank and the meeting with Kent. That left two pickups for fundraisers from Los Angeles schools, the samples and the meeting with the linen suppliers. Just in time to get home and check the bathroom sink for Nico. "I'll wait for you in the lobby." Or where the lobby would be once construction was completed.

"Thanks for the donuts, Morgan." Morgan glanced up at the swarm of workmen passing by on the way to the snack table, clueless as to who had spoken, so she smiled at all of them.

"You're welcome." The faces were familiar to her, having seen them at least once a week for the past eight months, but trying to put a name to any of them was futile. "You're doing a great job. Oh. Thanks." She caught the fluorescent yellow hard hat as it sailed through the air. "Almost forgot."

And then everything around her vanished except for the center.

Hour by hour, day by day, her dream, her family's dream, was coming to fruition. She loved these once-a-week visits, loved seeing the meat go on the bones of the skeletal structure.

This was what mattered. Getting the center built, opening the doors, bringing patients in, and giving them their lives back.

Nothing, not new accountants, not construction delays or legally questionable financial situations, was going to stop her.

And neither was Gage Juliano.

~

Had Gage not spotted Morgan's Mustang parked in front of the three-story house he might have thought he had the wrong address. Finding dilapidated chic where he expected pristine Victorian was yet another reminder Morgan Tremayne was anything but predictable.

Wedged comfortably between the bustle of Los Angeles and sedate Santa Barbara, Gage considered Lantano Valley an eclectic conglomeration of businesses and culture-rich neighborhoods—a throwback of sorts, with zoning restrictions on big-box stores and an economy that thrived on independent movie houses and yoga studios, cafés, and art galleries.

Days like this, when the sun had burned off the clouds and a cool breeze bathed the city, he was glad he'd come home. Days like this, he was glad for an excuse to get out of the office. He'd be happier if Agent Kolfax would stop sniffing around the D.A.'s office like an over-hyped bloodhound. Twice Gage had seen Kolfax lurking in the lobby trying to play invisible secret agent man. As if Gage wouldn't notice him wearing the same appalling suit Evan had caught on film.

Irritated, Gage had called a contact at the Los Angeles FBI office, asked on the QT if the Tremaynes or their foundation were on anyone's radar, and while he had yet to receive a direct answer, no red flags had gone up. Hearing that Kolfax had more enemies than friends in the agency perked him up considerably.

The "leaked" story about the D.A.'s office pressing charges against anyone accepting Nemesis' help was a long shot. When it came to scaring people into proper behavior and sharing information, if it meant endangering their wallets, silence was the more predictable outcome. Still, the threat wasn't a bad notion to have floating around. If anything, it might make Nemesis think twice before putting those he wanted to help at risk of jail time.

Not that Gage expected Nemesis to stop his midnight visits. Nemesis had invested an armored truckload of ego and was having far too much fun to stop now.

Then again, a crime scene at just the right time—say, Sunday afternoon around one—would solve his present social dilemma. Gage let out a long-held breath and stared out at 947 Tumbleweed Drive.

He hadn't been to the historic section of Lantano Valley since he'd come home last year. Odd, as his parents' house was less than a mile away. But while the Juliano residence was two-story brick modern, the Tumbleweed house looked as if a plastic surgeon gave up halfway through a facelift. It was, however, in far better shape than the other houses in the area, a number of which were in foreclosure or for sale.

Gage reached for the paper bag that held the gift-wrapped shoe box. Janice had saved his sanity by wrapping the shoes in purple and silver and topped it with a glitter-edged fabric hydrangea—a special touch, she'd said with a wink. He'd been tempted to delay leaving the office to postpone her inevitable call to update his mother on "The Morgan Situation."

As he crossed the street, a Ford minivan rumbled into the driveway and parked beneath the shade of one of the two enormous oak trees in the front yard. No sooner did it stop than the side door slid open and two little kids tumbled out, squealing and laughing, racing around the lawn as if the game of tag had become an Olympic sport.

A tall, slender woman in her mid-fifties climbed out from behind the wheel, thick grey hair pulled away from her windblown face as she circled to pop the hatch. He knew when she spotted him. She cast a cautious glance to the children as she watched him approach. "Can I help you with something?"

"Inspector Gage Juliano," Gage introduced himself. "I'm looking for Morgan Tremayne."

Her face broke into a smile and her face flashed recognition. "Oh. Of course. I'm Angela Fiorelli. Kelley. Brandon. Come get your bags. Sorry. School holiday. Only time I had to take them for new shoes. Morgan's in the garage. I'll show you around in a minute. Kids, now, please." Gage shifted Morgan's gift under his arm and took some of the bags as Brandon and Kelley skidded up beside him.

"Hello," he greeted them and was rewarded with a skeptical step away by the towheaded boy and a comical double take by the sprite-like girl.

Dressed in a bright yellow dress and sparkly purple sneakers, the girl's baby-doll blue eyes blinked up at him from beneath an enormous floppy hat big enough to protect the pale skin of her face and arms. Her smile tugged at his heart. "It's him," she whispered, stepping closer, only to be stopped by the boy's hand on her shoulder.

"Excuse me?" Gage asked, but the boy spun her away and grabbed the next bags Angela held out, and they disappeared into the house.

"Sorry about that." Angela laughed. "Kelley's been preoccupied with fairy tales and with that picture of you and Morgan in the paper—"

"Ah." Good thing he wasn't working at the precinct any longer. He didn't want to think about the torture his fellow officers would have conjured up.

Angela closed the hatch and gestured for him to follow. "Appreciate the help. Can I get you anything? Something to drink?"

"No, thank you. I have to get back downtown but I wanted to get this to Morgan." He cocked his arm, indicating the package. Gage glanced up at the front of the house and saw a second-floor window curtain pulled to the side. A teenage boy stared down at him with a combination of curiosity and suspicion, radiating hostility like an overheating furnace. "It's a gift." Of sorts.

Angela held the front door open. "Women love to get presents."

He was counting on it.

As Gage headed inside he noticed a number of porch planks and posts had been replaced, but work wasn't close to complete. While the outside still needed work, most of the attention had been paid to the interior.

The house welcomed him with the addictive aroma of fresh-baked bread and hot brewed coffee. The spacious foyer was divided like a multipronged fork. The woodwork and crown molding along the ceiling must be original to the house. The floors had been refinished, accentuating the aged dings while giving them a modern shine. Quality work, too. The house would be a real showplace once it was finished if the attention to detail continued. The carpenter in him itched to be set loose on the house.

So much potential here. Absolute paradise.

"Morgan gets the same look on her face when she comes in." Angela laughed, gesturing for him to follow her into the kitchen. "Bringing this house to life again is one of her passions. Any spare minute she has is spent working on it. I think that's why her grandmother left it to her. She knew it would be in good hands."

"This is Morgan's doing?" Despite her penchant for surprising him, Gage had a difficult time picturing the woman he'd met the other night staining antique floors or cutting baseboards.

"She's a whiz on home repairs, thank goodness. Saves

us a fortune. Just not enough hours in the day to keep up with it all. You can set those on the counter. Nico, Inspector Gage Juliano. Inspector, my husband, Nico Fiorelli."

"Nice to meet you, Inspector," Nico said as Gage caught sight of Kelley peeking around the pantry doorway. Gage winked at her. She brimmed with the energy of an overloaded pixie as she giggled, her cheeks tinting bright pink.

"Gage, please." Gage wondered how such a bear of a man made a kitchen feel so welcoming. Taller and much wider than Gage, like a clean-shaven Santa, but jollier. "These look amazing." The kitchen counters and table were filled with racks of cooling bread, pastries, and muffins. "Where do you sell?"

"Sell?" Nico let out a bark of laughter. "I don't. It's what keeps me sane since I retired. What we don't freeze or eat I give to family and friends, although I think by now they consider me a carbohydrate dealer."

"Do you mind?" Gage gestured to a blueberry muffin that would dwarf a softball.

"Help yourself." Nico tossed flour on the butcher block island and started rolling out a large rectangle of dough. "I tend to lose track and get carried away."

"You should see this place at Christmas," Angela joked. "It looks like a cookie factory exploded."

Gage split the muffin and felt steam release against his fingers as he bit into the moist cake. The mixture of tart berries and crumb topping made his stomach growl in greedy response. "Amazing. There's something different though—"

"Nutmeg." Nico grinned. "My secret ingredient."

"Gage brought Morgan a present," Angela all but sang. "Must be a special occasion?"

"Just returning something she lost the other night."

Angela's not-so-innocent tone clanged a familiar warning bell in Gage's head. In that instant he vowed she and his mother should never meet. Gage glanced at the clock as he polished off the muffin, thinking Nico could make a small fortune if he went into business. He'd told Janice he'd be back by one and it was twelve fifteen now. "You said Morgan's in the garage?"

"She is," Nico said, aiming a warning look at his wife. "Instead of interrogating our guest, Angela, why don't you show him the way?"

"I'd love to," Angela grinned and took a swig of coffee. "I'm sure she'll be surprised to see you."

∾

Morgan pulled out her wrench just as someone banged on the side of the car.

"What?" Morgan shouted from under the carriage of her latest pride and joy.

"Company, Morgan." Angela called.

"Tell them I'm busy."

"I can see that." Morgan tucked her chin down in time to see Gage grinning at her. "'67 Impala. Nice refurb. How's it coming?"

"Sh-ugar!" Morgan whacked her forehead on the oil pan. "Oh, ow." Pain shot through her skull as she was dragged from under the car by her ankles.

"You okay?" Gage's grin faded under the concern clouding the blue eyes that had haunted her dreams all week. He picked up a rag as she shoved herself up, pressing oil-slick fingers against the sore spot.

"I'm fine." Oh, God. What was he doing here? Had the D.A. found something? Had there been a break in the case?

Morgan slammed her foot on the mental brakes. Gage had no way of connecting her to Nemesis that she knew of, and if he had come because of the case, he wouldn't have done it with a wink and a smile. *Get it together*.

"Your eyes are spinning." He pushed her back until she leaned against the car door. "Sit still for a minute. Let me get you some water."

"I don't need water." What were the odds that as soon as she vowed to extricate herself from Nemesis, Inspector Juliano stopped by for tea? "Where's Angela?" She could use a buffer between them about now.

"She went inside. Probably to grab one of those muffins Nico made."

At the mention of muffins, Morgan realized she'd forgotten to schedule in breakfast again and then lunch, which baffled her because Nico made the best blueberry muffins in the county.

"Here." Gage pushed a bottle of water into her hands, squatted down next to her, and dragged a semi-clean rag across her forehead. "Damn. That's going to bruise. I didn't mean to startle you."

Holy. The man wore simple dark slacks and a blazer as perfectly as he had the tux. "What are you doing here? I didn't think I'd see you again after the other night."

"Hmmmm." He pressed gentle fingertips against the sore spot on her head. "How do you feel? Nauseated? Dizzy?"

Not from the knock on the head. "I've had worse. Help me up." He grabbed hold of her hands and pulled, but before she toppled into him, she detoured and leaned on the workbench. The last thing she needed was to be in Gage Juliano's arms again. Dammit. What was she supposed to say? She opened the water and took a long drink. "It's Friday. Shouldn't you be at work?"

"I am at work."

Morgan's mouth went dry and she drank again, trying to swallow the panic. "You are?"

"Well, lost-and-found isn't in my job description these days, but I thought you might like these back." He reached back for a paper bag she hadn't noticed before and pulled out a beautifully wrapped shoe box. He placed the gift on the trunk of the Impala. "I don't know much about shoes, but they didn't look as if you got them at the Salvation Army."

"Oh." Morgan pressed a hand against her heart as gratitude swelled within her. "Oh, I didn't think I'd see them again. My, um, my mom bought them for me to go with the dress." She hadn't wanted to dwell on the loss, not when there were more important things to worry about, but the dress looked lost hanging alone in her closet.

She grabbed hold of his shoulders and kissed him on the cheek, startling them both.

She stepped away, tried to laugh, but his hand came up to cup her cheek like he had after the party. Her entire body ignited as if he'd turned on a blowtorch. So much for hoping the fireworks between them had been her imagination.

"What happened the other night?" He rubbed a thumb

against her lips. She shivered, unable to pull her gaze from his. "What scared you away?"

What didn't scare her about Gage? The way he made everything else vanish? The way her mind turned to hot, steamy soup whenever he touched her? Or maybe that with very little effort he could rip her life apart?

"The other night was a fairy tale, Gage. Make-believe. You see this?" She shouldn't want him touching her, but she did, even as she gestured to her grungy, grease-stained cutoffs, and ripped T-shirt. "This is me, my life. I fix cars, repair water heaters, and paint siding when I'm not working, which is pretty much all the time. I'm helping to raise four foster kids and trying to keep this roof over their heads. I'm not that glamour girl you met the other night. I don't get prettied up and go to parties and eat at the tennis club. I am not my sister." Not that that didn't work for Sheila. It just didn't for Morgan.

"Did it ever occur to you that I might think that's a good thing?"

"No." Because no man ever had before. Not that there had been many interested. "Look, Gage, the other night was wonderful." *For the most part.* "But there isn't any room in my life for this. Besides, you're a cop. That isn't the safest profession in the world, and, no offense, I can't take on someone else to worry about." She flailed her hand between them, gasped when he caught it and tugged her closer. "Forget what scares me, Gage." She tried a different tactic because nothing, no good at all, could come out of what he made her feel. What he made her want. "Everything around me should scare *you*. You need to run."

He ran his thumb over the sensitive skin at her wrist,

jump-starting her pulse beneath his touch. He smiled, watching her as if she were a mirage in the middle of the desert, commanding every bit of his attention. "I was a cop for fifteen years, Morgan. It'll take more than 'all this' to scare me, and trust me when I say I've learned to be extra careful. But there's more. Something you're not telling me." He inclined his head, those piercing blue eyes shooting like lightning into her soul.

Anger sliced through her, sharp, irritable. She didn't like being read so easily, which was even more reason to stay away from him. He might see too much. "Did it ever occur to you I'm just not interested?"

"No." Gage grinned and brought her grease-covered fingers to his lips. "Fairy tales don't work that way."

"You've met Kelley." Morgan let out a small laugh, and for a moment, rested her forehead against his chest. Big mistake. He smelled fresh, clean, and she caught a trace of . . . sawdust? Her head spun. She patted a hand against his arm, lifted her head. "She's eight, Gage. She still thinks bedtime stories are real. Besides." She needed to put some distance between them. "I don't need any man riding to my rescue. I manage on my own."

"I wouldn't presume to rescue you. But work can't be everything. There has to be more to life. Crap." He frowned, his eyes narrowing as he shook his head hard. "Crap. Crap. Crap. Dammit, she broke through after all." He rubbed fingers across his forehead as if trying to erase a thought. "Why is she always right?"

Morgan looked around for a hidden camera. "Who are you talking to?"

"Talking about, actually." Gage blew out a breath and dragged a hand through his hair. "Okay, I'm just going to do this. Not that this will be humiliating at all. I'm hoping, praying, actually, that returning your shoes has earned me a favor in return."

Morgan felt a labyrinth erupt around her. No clear way out, dead ends at every turn. A Minotaur lying in wait wasn't as dangerous to her as Gage could be. So she went with, "What kind of favor?"

"What's that calendar of yours look like for Sunday?"

"Sunday? I spend my Sundays here working on the house unless I have brunch with Dad, which I don't." Why, oh, why hadn't she arranged for brunch with her father? Better yet, why hadn't she just lied? "Gage, I know you think you're being charming and that this is fun, trying to seduce me into a date, but—"

"Morgan, please say you're free on Sunday because you are the only woman who can help me out of a situation with my mother."

Morgan stared at him. Blinked. Blinked again. "Say again?"

"One afternoon with me, at my parents' house. Family birthday party. Your presence has been, well, requested."

"By your mother?" Morgan clarified.

"She saw that picture—"

"In the paper." That damned picture. First Kelley, then Kent, now Gage's mother? "And your mother is . . . ?" She waved her hand, urging him to explain.

"Obsessed with me getting married and giving her grandchildren." He grinned, held out his arms in exaltation. "Tag. You're it."

"Seems like a lot to expect from one afternoon."

"You think this is funny."

Morgan laughed and held out a hand as he advanced on

her, which made her laugh harder. "Of course I think this is funny. The big, bad inspector's afraid of his mother. Don't!"

Strong hands gripped her arms, freezing the laugh in her chest as he hauled her against him.

"Gage, I—" Her voice lost its strength as his gaze fell to her mouth. A whimper escaped her lips as his face dipped toward hers. Her hands skimmed the front of his shirt, grazed the taut muscles of his chest, fingers tingling against the buttons as she considered exploring further. "You can stop," she whispered. "I'm not laughing anymore."

Please stop. Please stop. Please . . .

Don't stop.

And then his mouth was on hers. Doubt became vapor. Desire and passion entwined as his tongue swept over hers, teasing, exploring, tempting. Gage was all there was, all she wanted, the heat of him, the strength of him. She drew him closer, felt his leg wedge between hers as he pushed her against the workbench and pulled her higher against him. Her body pulsed, hot, ready, to the point of overheating, and still she clung, not wanting it to end. She was on the brink of surrendering to this man who had invaded her thoughts and dreams from the moment they'd met.

Her cell phone chimed, the blaring alarm cutting through the Gage-induced fog. His mouth lifted, but only enough for him to press his forehead against hers. His fingers continued to stroke her face, his breath hot against her face. "Time's up." Except, for the life of her, she couldn't remember what was next on her calendar.

"Is that a yes to Sunday?" His question brushed against her cheek, against her heart.

The only excuse she had for saying no meant confessing to a felony. She nodded.

"Thank you." The relief in Gage's voice did nothing to quell the hammering of her heart. A date. With a cop. What the hell was she playing at? "I'll call you tomorrow with the details."

And then he was gone. Morgan raised her hand to her mouth, touching her swollen lips.

The back door banged open. Tiny feet ran down the stairs.

"Morgan, what did he give you?" Kelley slammed into her side, her arms wrapping around Morgan's waist as the little girl bounced on her toes. "The bag. I heard it's a present. Ooooh. Is that it? What's in the box?"

"Th-the what?" What was it about the man that left her stammering? She dislodged Kelley from her person and walked over to the car, then stopped before she picked up the package. "My hands are dirty. Would you like to open it?"

Kelley scrubbed her eager hands down her dress.

Morgan pressed her lips into a silent smile as Kelley scooted the ribbon and bow off, then plucked each corner of the paper free.

Kelley huffed out a breath as the paper released and she lifted the lid and rose up on tiptoe to peer inside. Morgan moved in behind her. "It's your shoes."

Kelley lifted them out and twirled around the garage, prism rainbows erupting against the car as the light caught the beaded straps.

"Can I have them please?" Morgan asked.

"Nope." Kelley hugged them against her chest and shook her head with such defiance that Morgan frowned.

But then the wonder erupted on the child's face. "You really are Cinderella."

"I'm really not." Morgan held out her hands. "Give me the shoes."

"Uh-uh. I need to keep them safe for when Prince Charming needs them." She dashed toward the back door.

"Kelley—" This little fantasy of hers was getting out of hand, but it was too late. Kelley was gone.

So were Cinderella's shoes.

CHAPTER 7

"Pizza's on its way." Officer Hallie "Bouncer" Thorne piped up from the far end of the conference table. "Who's doing the coffee and soda run? I'd volunteer, but . . ." The one finger gesture she aimed at the thigh-high cast on her right leg made Gage grimace.

"That's what you get for playing chicken with an '89 Cutlass." Rojas, edging toward retirement after thirty years on the force, got to his feet and stretched. "Peyton's turn."

"Peyton's turn for what?" Peyton, as stick thin as Rojas was round, carried yet another file box into the room and dropped it on the already overloaded table.

"Caffeine." Gage set down the file he'd been skimming. How many times could he look over the same information before something popped? Not only were they sorting through the mess that was the Nemesis case, they had at least a dozen boxes of case files from additional closed cases they were expected to reopen in the next few weeks. They were running out of time when it came to keeping their focus solely on Nemesis. "Please tell me that's the last of the boxes from storage."

"I sure as hell hope so," Peyton grunted. "I recognize Brady's scrawl on the outside, so I'm thinking this—" He flipped the lid off, coughing as a plume of dust erupted. "Yep." He sifted through papers and notes, looking for anything that might be relevant to the Nemesis case. "That's Brady's filing system. More Nemesis scribbles interspersed with his other open cases."

Gage's frustration meter ticked up ten notches. No wonder Malloy's boss had been urging him to retire. What was a notation about Grant Alvers and Nemesis, a case that had been active for a few months, doing in a closed homicide investigation from five years ago?

"Guess this means our Friday night just went into lockdown." Gage would be lucky to get home before midnight, but he couldn't stop wondering where his once meticulous training officer had gone astray.

There were piles of handwritten scribbled notes, some unreadable, others seemingly nonsense. Not one of Brady Malloy's three boxes of reports and photographs had been structured. Which explained why this case, or any case, hadn't gone anywhere under Brady's supervision. He'd known Brady wasn't in the best of health, but had he been this far gone?

"We live to serve," Bouncer muttered, her lips turning down in disgust as Peyton dropped the box on the chair beside her. "I'm going to need more room and maybe a bottle of Scotch."

As if she could buy a bottle without getting carded. At twenty-four, Bouncer was whip smart, balls-to-the-walls ambitious, and willing to do whatever it took to get the job done. Requesting her addition to the team while she recuperated from her injuries was logical. Having worked with her twice since he'd returned to Lantano Valley, Gage knew what to expect, knew how she worked. He could say the same about Rojas and Peyton, who had both known and worked with Brady.

He trusted them. They'd get the job done.

But Bouncer wasn't kidding about the lack of space or the need for a drink. If there was an inch of table showing from beneath the stacks of files and papers, Gage couldn't see it.

"Let's get anything that's not Nemesis related moved to the side tables." As far as he was concerned, no other case mattered for the foreseeable future. By the time the pizza arrived and Peyton made a run to the quick mart across the street, they were in better shape and began filling up the six whiteboards they'd pilfered from other offices in the building.

"Heads up," Bouncer said as she crutch-hobbled into the conference room after a bathroom break. Gage glanced around the edge of the whiteboard he was making notes on and saw the D.A. step off the elevator.

"And here I thought it was Gage who couldn't leave this place at a decent hour," Evan said.

"Opera in town?" Gage took in Evan's tuxedo, sans jacket that was draped over the D.A.'s arm. The poor guy looked as if his tie might strangle him.

"Don't I wish. Fundraiser dinner for Representative Hollis."

"Representative Douchebag," Bouncer muttered, then realized who was in the room and added, "Sir." She bit her lip.

"Man, I wish I could have said that," Evan grumbled. "I saw the lights on up here and thought I'd see how things are going."

"Got grilled by the constituents on the Nemesis case, huh?" Rojas flipped open one of the pizza boxes and shoved it toward Evan. "Hungry?"

"Starved, thanks." He tossed his jacket over a chair, grabbed a slice with mushroom and olives, and popped open an orange soda. "And Rojas is right about getting grilled, but it was Agent Kolfax turning up the fire. Creepy little guy was waiting in the parking lot like a stalker."

"What is this guy's fascination with this case?" Gage asked, back to wondering if it wasn't about Nemesis at all. Then again, his distrust of the FBI could be coloring his judgment. "We haven't found any indication that Nemesis has committed crimes outside the state. It's not federal. Besides, Kolfax is white collar, not treasury."

"I wish I had an answer for you." Evan reached for a second slice before polishing off his first. "But he did ask if you had a good time at the Tremayne Foundation event last week."

Peyton covered his snort of laughter behind a well-timed cough. Bouncer grinned over at Rojas, who looked as if keeping a straight face was an effort.

"Good God, is there anyone who didn't see that damned picture?" Gage asked. "And since when do the Feds oversee someone's personal life?"

"Those of us with a personal life," Bouncer quipped. "How the hell do you manage that?"

"By making it about *business*," Rojas joked.

"Didn't look like business to me." Peyton gestured with his own slice of pie.

"Any idea yet why the FBI would be looking at the Tremayne Foundation?" Evan wandered the perimeter of the room as if taking inventory of the information on the whiteboards.

"They aren't a cover for terrorist activities, if that's what you're asking," Gage said, not liking where the conversation was headed. "I checked with some old contacts and there's nothing on file about the foundation being investigated. Hell, Evan, they're building a hospital for sick kids. It would take a pretty warped mind to use that as a cover for a crime syndicate. Trust me, Morgan might be many things, but deceitful isn't one of them." Although she did seem as if she kept things to herself more than most.

"I've met Morgan on a couple of occasions, and her father was a big supporter of mine during the election. But that's two times the name has come up around Kolfax. That's no coincidence."

Sensing there was more to this conversation than his team needed to hear, Gage grabbed the half-full pizza box. "Let's finish this in my office. Guys, head home. Hopefully I won't need you until Monday." He waited until Evan was inside before he closed the door. "What's going on?"

"Exactly what I asked. Kolfax is sniffing around the Tremaynes, and no, this isn't me worrying about future campaign contributions. I like Jackson. I admire what his wife built, what his kids continue to build. The center can put Lantano Valley on the national map, provide jobs, be an example for the standard of care children can and should get. It's a win for everyone in this city, and I don't want the Feds fucking it up."

"I agree," Gage said. "Which is why I ran every possible check I could. I've looked at their incorporation papers, their financial status, and there is nothing off that I can find." Which had been a huge relief. "Kolfax is seeing something that's not there."

"Maybe. But he's not the dolt he pretends to be. I finally heard back from my connection in the agency. Kolfax has a reputation for not being able to let certain cases go, even after they're closed. About three years ago he went after a career con man named Mac Price, took too many steps over the line, lost the case and the collar. Price pled guilty without revealing the location of most everything he stole. Kolfax was convinced he had a partner, someone still working on the outside even while Price serves the better part of twenty years. He's spent the last few years trying to prove a theory no one in the agency believes."

"And what?" Gage frowned. "You think that's why he's so keen on Nemesis? He's trying to redeem himself? Or is there some connection between these thefts and this Mac Price guy?"

"Not that anyone's found, not that Price is admitting to. When I asked my guy about Nemesis, he looked into any connections between Price and Lantano Valley. The only thing he came up with was Price had made some investments with Jackson Tremayne just when his investment business was getting off the ground. Other than that?" Evan shrugged. "You and I both know what obsession can lead to. Kolfax might not be the most popular agent, but he's good enough that they're keeping him on the job. Or at least he was valuable until about eighteen months ago. Something about him screwing up some big investigation he was running. But I don't want him bringing his vendettas here, especially at the expense of one of our own."

"I can't see where there's anything for Kolfax to latch onto," Gage said as he pounded a knuckle against his desk. "If something odd was going on with the Tremaynes, there'd be a hint of it somewhere." But dammit, he didn't like the doubt creeping along the periphery of his mind. "The entire family is devoted to finishing Catherine's work. None of them would do anything to jeopardize that. Especially Morgan." And Gage definitely didn't like the idea of Kolfax focusing his attention on her.

"Know her that well already?" Evan arched a brow. "Look, I agree with you, but Kolfax thinks he's got something and the fact that he's hinting about it to us tells me we should be paying attention. Or at the very least be on the lookout for whatever damage he wants to do. All the more reason for you to stay close to Morgan." Evan grinned. "If you need an excuse, that is."

"We can end this now and just flat-out ask them. No offense, Evan, but I thought our focus was supposed to be on Nemesis."

"It is. Just . . ." Evan shrugged. "If something presents itself, if there's an opportunity to find out more about what Kolfax is really interested in—and that could very well be Morgan and the rest of her family—look at it as an opportunity to get yourself in with the Feds. If that's what you want."

"They should be trying to get in with me." Gage walked over to the window, stared out into the black sky and regretted, not for the first time, accepting Evan's job offer. The chaos that had ensued from his time working with the FBI had left the foundation of his life in shambles. He hadn't known who to trust, where to go. His only choice, once he came out of the fog of pain meds, was to come home and attempt to regain some semblance of solid footing and figure out what he was meant to do from here. Finishing what Brady had started—the case that had literally been the death of his friend—seemed the ideal solution. Except . . .

Sometimes he felt so damned tired and he wished he could just turn his brain, his suspicions, off. Then he wondered what the hell he was still doing on the job. "I don't think there's anything to Kolfax except the inability to let go of the past. He's digging where there's nothing to be found and then he saw that picture of me and Morgan in the paper. He's using her, using his suspicions to get into my head, into our investigation. This is about Nemesis. It has to be. What better way to restore his reputation than to bring down a criminal that would be a coup for any law enforcement agent."

"Then might I suggest you close the case before Kolfax burrows any deeper. I don't want that guy in my town any longer than necessary."

"Oh, don't worry." Gage set his jaw, imagined Kolfax's head as the center of a bull's-eye. "He can play whatever games he wants with me, but I'm not letting him near Morgan or her family."

∿

"Can you put that phone down for ten seconds and at least try to relax?" Sheila kicked Morgan in the shin and sent the bowl of lavender water on the manicure table sloshing onto the towels. "Sorry."

Morgan tapped her phone. Shit. Elliot Dunbar had an opening in his schedule sooner than expected. She added the appointment to her calendar.

Sheila smiled at the nail technician, who looked irritated as she swiped the smudge of pink polish off Sheila's thumb. "Morgan, please. You promised."

"Okay, you're right." Although it felt like amputating a limb, Morgan dropped her phone into her overstuffed purse, settled in the chair custom made for the Winstead Salon and Spa, and lowered her feet into the swirling sea salt–infused water. Ahhhh. Okay. Yeah, that was better. Wait. She gripped the arms of the chair. Did she reschedule that conference call with the board of directors?

"If you didn't switch that thing to vibrate, I'm going to smother you during your seaweed wrap."

"My what? Sheila, I don't have time—"

"Excuse me." Sheila pulled her hands free and held up a finger, and the technician sat back with a sigh. Next thing Morgan knew, her sister's fingers gripped her chin and turned her face so she could glare into Morgan's eyes. "One day a month is not a lot to ask. It's four hours out of your overscheduled life. So turn. Off. Your. Brain." She offered her hands back to the tech.

"It's not just four hours," Morgan argued. "I'm losing tomorrow, too." That meant this weekend's tasks were going to roll into next week and snowball from there. She was never going to catch up.

Sheila rolled her eyes. "Cry me a river. A gorgeous man wants to take you to meet his family."

"I'm a means to an end," Morgan tried to explain

again, but the more she tried to downplay the date with Gage, the more ridiculous she sounded. "He's trying to get his mother off his back."

"Boo-freaking-hoo. I bet he's a scrumptious kisser."

"Sheila." Morgan caught the smile on the manicurist's face before the young woman ducked her chin and refocused on Sheila's cuticles.

Sheila turned her head and arched an expertly shaped brow. "Well?"

Morgan accredited the sudden heat in her body to the steaming water at her feet and not the oh-so-tempting memory of Gage's magic mouth on hers. "It didn't mean anything." But it could have, should have, meant everything.

Sheila smirked. "About damn time."

Morgan had to admit she liked the mixture of envy and curiosity on her sister's face. "This feels weird."

"Then clearly you weren't doing it right."

Morgan snorted, picked up her cucumber-laced water, and took a nauseating sip. A triple-shot latte would taste so much better right now. "No, I meant having this conversation with you. Shouldn't our positions be reversed? When was the last time you had a date?"

"I banked them ahead of time. Summer party season and all."

Morgan envied how Sheila could tune out. But then party planning wasn't as all-consuming as running the foundation, or maintaining a stagnating bank account, or keeping a roof over four kids' and two adults' heads. "I've been meaning to ask if you had time to help plan Brandon's tenth birthday party." She'd learned a long time ago not to take birthdays for granted. When birthdays were a gift, as they were for all sick children, parties should be as big and boisterous as possible.

"The twenty-seventh, right?" Sheila rolled her head to the side and smiled like a pampered Persian cat. "I've already been in touch with Angela. We're doing a cowboy theme, BBQ and a rootin'-tootin' bouncy house, handicapped accessible of course so all the kids can enjoy it. Mark that off your list of things to worry about. It's taken care of." When Morgan didn't respond, Sheila sighed. "You're welcome."

"Oh. No, Sheila, I'm sorry, thank you. I just—"

"Don't get to play overworked Superwoman now?"

"That's not fair." It hurt that Sheila thought she was somehow playing the martyr.

"I just hope Gage will fit into that overextended calendar of yours. Ten minutes here, half hour there. Puts a lot of pressure on a man to perform."

"It's not like he doesn't know what I do for a living."

"You don't work *for* a living, you work *instead* of living. The other night you wondered how Mom did it? She knew what to make a priority. We, the family, always took priority."

"The family is my priority." Why else would she have gone to such extremes to protect them from what she'd done? And maybe if Sheila knew, she'd stop complaining about Morgan's unavailability. But then the disappointment would set in and the media would pounce and dig and stalk everyone involved. "And this isn't the place—"

"When the hell else are we going to talk about it?" Sheila's voice lowered to dangerous levels, evidence of her boiling temper. "We never see you anymore, Morgan. We rescheduled today four times in the last six weeks and I'd bet my next trust-fund payment you almost cancelled today. So don't sit there and tell me your family comes first for you."

Morgan couldn't argue. Sheila was right. She did almost cancel. As if recognizing a challenge when issued, Morgan's phone chimed the theme song from *COPS*. Sheila arched her brow again and angled her gaze to Morgan's bag.

"I'm not answering it," Morgan said quickly.

"You're incapable of ignoring a ringing cell phone. Even with me threatening you with certain death if you tried. What gives?"

"It's, um . . ." Shit.

"Oh, wow, do you need therapy. It's Gage, isn't it? Give me the phone."

"Absolutely not." The last thing she needed was for Sheila and Gage to gang up on her.

"Now seems like the perfect time to remind him what he's getting into."

"All done, Miss Tremayne." The nail technician got to her feet, did a quick cleanup, then wheeled her table away, leaving Morgan and Sheila to do battle alone.

"Girl knows when to get out of the line of fire. Give me your phone, Morgan."

"Feel free to get it yourself."

"You underestimate my concern for a pink passion manicure." Sheila snapped her fingers just as the phone went silent.

Morgan snuggled into her chair and closed her eyes.

"You've spent most of the morning talking to contractors and landscape engineers," Sheila said. "Not to mention threatening great bodily harm to a hospital administrator who filed a protest against an insurance claim for one of your future patients. Yet somehow you won't talk to one of the most beautiful men I've ever seen in my life. You, dear sister, are seriously messed up."

Messed up. Excited. Nervous. Terrified. "One date and that's it. Just enough to get his mother to stop hounding him, and then both of our lives can get back to normal." *Normal* meant that Gage Juliano was as far away from the foundation and the center as possible.

"Oh, honey." The sympathy in Sheila's voice had Morgan turning her head, lifting heavy lids so she saw the piteous expression on her sister's face. "I saw the way Gage looked at you the other night. He's not going anywhere."

∼

Not answering Gage's call was the perfect impetus Morgan needed to ignore her phone for the rest of the day. Well, enough of the day that she and her sister enjoyed a sedate and uneventful lunch next to the pool.

That didn't mean Morgan's insides didn't do the antsy dance whenever she heard the vibrations of her cell. She did, however, manage to resist temptation until she pulled into her driveway and shut off the engine.

She didn't expect to find five more missed calls in the last three hours, all from Gage. He hadn't left a message. Maybe he needed to cancel and didn't want to do so in a voice mail?

Morgan's stomach dipped as if she'd taken the first plunge on a roller coaster. She pressed the phone to her forehead, closed her eyes. Not having to go tomorrow would be good news. Right?

Her phone buzzed again and Morgan flipped the vibrate switch off and answered with a tight breath in her chest. "Gage, I was just going to call you back."

"Way to scare a guy, Morgan. I was about ready to put out an APB. I thought you always answered your phone." The relief in his voice made her smile. He'd been worried about her.

Not that she cared.

"Sheila bet me I couldn't put the phone away for the afternoon." She glanced at her watch. Five p.m. Close enough. "I understand if you have to cancel tomorrow."

"I'm not cancelling." Before Morgan's dread could take root again, he continued, "I totally forgot I'm in charge of my brother's birthday present for tomorrow. *The* present. From all the kids. It has to be spectacular. It's his thirtieth."

"I'm guessing that panic in your voice means you excel at choosing gifts, right?" Sympathy and amusement mingled in her chest and Morgan covered her mouth with her hands. She laughed, hoping he couldn't hear. This poor guy with his family. "Calm down, Mr. Inspector. I take it a gift card is out of the question?"

"Stephen gave Jon a gift card for his birthday a few years ago and has yet to get his Christmas stocking privileges reinstated."

"Wouldn't want you to lose your Christmas stocking." And still she laughed. She could not wait to meet Gage's mother tomorrow. Anyone capable of inflicting this much mental stress on their oldest son was worthy of worship. "How can I help?"

"Help me pick out the best birthday present ever. I will owe you. Forever."

There was a sobering offer. "We'll figure something out. Tell me about your brother." Morgan gathered her stuff and locked up the car and headed to the garage apartment.

"He manages my parents' grocery stores."

"Which stores?"

"J & J Markets. All seven locations."

Morgan turned and sat halfway up the stairs. "Are you kidding me? There's one a few blocks from here. I can't tell you how many times I've stopped in for a late dinner. The lasagna makes me cry."

"Mom's secret recipe. Wait until you try her eggplant parmesan."

Note to self, wear pants with an elastic waistband tomorrow. "So that tells me he's organized, efficient. Responsible. What are his hobbies? Interests? What were his favorite toys as a kid?"

"Hobbies, women. Interests, women. Favorite toys—"

"Don't say women."

"*Girls*. And cars. Anything with wheels. That give you any ideas?"

"Sure does." She got up, unlocked her door, and went inside. "Grab a pen. Don't panic, but you'll need to do some shopping on your way to pick me up tomorrow."

CHAPTER 8

"He's been shopping."

Gage had barely popped open the trunk of his car before Kelley raced down the walkway to greet him. Morgan followed, tugging her turquoise sweater across the matching tank top, hoping she hadn't underdressed for the party. Jeans and sandals were casual to her, and Gage had said casual.

Kelley, on the other hand, didn't know the meaning of the word. Today's princess dress was Rapunzel purple, but the shiny shoes were definitely Wizard of Oz red.

"They aren't for you, sweetie." Morgan called as she joined them on the sidewalk. "It's a present for Gage's brother. You can help though. If the kitchen is cleaned up."

"I'll finish. But I can help carry bags." Kelley swung from side to side and blinked her big eyes up at Gage like a cartoon cat demanding affection. She held out her hands, flexed her fingers. "Gimmie. Please," she added at Morgan's warning look.

"Actually, there is something you can help me with."

Gage squatted down and rifled through one of the bags. "I was told every pretty princess needs one of these." He pulled out a long lavender glitter embossed stick with a giant light-up star at the end. Ribbons and glittered beads cascaded from the tips.

Kelley's mouth formed a silent *O*, the expression firmly tethering Kelley's and Gage's hearts before Kelley launched herself at Gage. He held her close as tiny arms locked around his neck. As she heard Kelley whisper "thank you," Morgan turned away.

She should have realized bringing Gage into her life would risk the kids getting attached.

Stop fooling yourself. You're the one getting attached, and that damned magic wand isn't helping.

Morgan turned around and caught Gage watching her. "Okay, Miss Pretty Princess, grab a bag."

"Wonder where she learned to overdo?" Gage asked Morgan as Kelley grabbed the biggest bag and tried to drag it on her own. "This one's more your size." He held out one of the smaller ones. "Trade?"

" 'Kay." She raced ahead, slamming into the house with the force of a tiny tornado.

"Beautiful day for a party," Morgan said as they walked up to the house and then she stopped. Sniffed the air. Looked up to the second story. "Son of a—"

"What?" Gage followed her gaze and saw the telltale sign of cigarette smoke drifting out of one of the windows. "Oh."

"I'll meet you in the kitchen." Morgan slapped the bag she'd been carrying against his chest and stomped into the house. "Drew."

Gage cringed in sympathy. Poor kid was in for it once she reached the top of the stairs.

"Where is everyone?" Gage joined Kelley in the kitchen.

"Nico's delivering leftover bread downtown and Lydia and Brandon are drawing pictures for his birthday party. Angela's working in the garden. We're going to grow tomatoes and zuchinnini. Here." She handed him a still-damp cereal bowl and pointed to one of the cabinets. "I'm too little."

She was indeed, but together they put away the last of the breakfast dishes. Only then did Kelley peer into the bags. "What did you buy your brother?"

"What Morgan told me to. Let's see." Kelley helped him unload the wooden shadow box and a variety of Hot Wheels cars. "Any idea what she has in mind?"

"She got out the glue gun. Could be anything," Kelley said then winced when she heard Morgan's raised voice upstairs. "Drew's in trouble."

"Sounds like."

"Brandon would like these. Lydia, too." She plucked at the edge of the packaging of a Porsche 911. "Can your brother come over and play?"

"Stephen's a little old to be playing." All evidence to the contrary. "I haven't met Lydia yet. Is she your age?"

Kelley nodded. "And my bestest friend. She can't play like she used to but she likes to draw and read and she plays video games better than the boys. But not so much lately since her eyes don't work so good." She stopped, took a deep breath and then said, "I heard Morgan and Angela talking about how Lydia's really, really sick. They don't know I heard." Her eyes filled. "I don't want her to die."

Gage pulled Kelley into his lap, needing the comfort of this child as much as she needed him to tell her everything was going to be okay. But would it be the truth?

Until this moment he didn't realize how lucky his family had been. How would they have coped with a situation like Lydia's? Or Kelley's? Thinking of his own brothers, his heart broke for the one Morgan had lost.

How could anyone, even someone as ambitious and callous as Kolfax, think she would do anything to put her kids or the foundation at risk? No. Seeing her again, being with her like this, he was more convinced than ever that whatever plans Kolfax might have for them, for her, he needed to be standing in the way. Even if Morgan didn't want him there.

"It must be very scary that someone you love is sick." Gage held Kelley close and found solace in the little girl's presence. "I'm sure Morgan and Lydia's doctors are doing everything they can."

"I know," Kelley leaned against him. "Just like she did for me and Brandon. We got better. Maybe Morgan's wrong. Maybe Lydia will get better, too."

Gage hugged her close, amazed at how easily the little girl fit. He hadn't held a child like this in a long time, not since his sisters had been this age.

"Wanna meet her?" Kelley asked.

"Meet Lydia?" Gage tucked in his chin and looked down at her. "Sure. If you think it would be okay."

Kelley nodded her head. "Lydia loves meeting new people. Come on. She's in our room. I'll take you."

She jumped off his lap and took his hand in her tiny one, leading him out of the kitchen and past a motorized wheelchair at the base of the staircase. As they turned left at the top of the stairs, Gage heard definite raised voices from down the hall and wondered if he should intervene.

Kelley knocked on a door covered with drawings and a smattering of Tinker Bell and Hello Kitty stickers. "Lydia?" She pushed open the door. "Morgan's new friend is here. Wanna meet him?"

Special care had been taken to make the room feel as normal as possible. Gage might not have known the children who occupied the space had medical issues save for the fact that the wood floor was bare of rugs and carpet to make a second motorized wheelchair beside the bed easier to maneuver.

Two raised beds sat against opposite sides of the room, one tall enough to see out the enormous bay window overlooking the patiently tended flower and vegetable garden. Everything in the room was bathed in bright colors, especially the portion of the room he assumed was Kelley's, as her princess wall denoted every hue of pink ever created.

The short round table in the center of the room was piled with crayons and markers and stacks of drawing paper and was occupied by the boy he knew was Brandon and a stunningly pretty albeit thin and drawn Hispanic girl.

"Brandon, Lydia, this is Morgan's friend Prince Ch—" She looked up and grinned. "Gage. Gage, this is Lydia. She's my foster sister and my bestest friend."

"I thought I was your bestest friend?" Brandon frowned at her.

Kelley tugged Gage closer to the table. "You're my bestest, too."

Brandon's smile lit up his entire face. "I knew it. Hi." Whatever suspicion he'd held the other day was gone, replaced by a welcoming smile on his face. His features were slightly emaciated, but his eyes were so alive, so charged with sapphire light, he slid right into Gage's heart.

Gage let go of Kelley's hand and bent down between Brandon and Lydia. "It's nice to meet you." Gage crossed one arm over the other and offered them each a hand.

Lydia looked down, hesitated for a moment. "I'm sick," she said matter-of-factly. "I have AIDS."

The word sucker-punched Gage, stole the breath from his lungs, but he pulled his other hand free of Brandon's and picked up Lydia's. "It's nice to meet you, Lydia."

Lydia glanced over to Kelley, then to Gage. "You don't care?"

"I care that you're sick, not about what you have. We all have things we don't like about ourselves, right?" he asked the three of them.

"I didn't like my leukemia," Kelley said, nodding vigorously. "But I don't have that anymore." She knocked against Brandon as if telling him he was next up at bat.

"I don't like—" Brandon scrunched his face as he thought. "That I had to have chemotherapy and it made me so sick. Does that count?"

Kelley nodded as if she were leading a group therapy session. "I didn't like it either. Gage, your turn."

Well, he'd walked into that one. Given what they were facing, Gage didn't have one thing to complain about. "What's that you're drawing?"

"Pictures for my birthday party." Brandon announced. "We're having a cowboy barbeque. You can help if you want."

"I haven't colored in a long time, but I can give it a try." He grabbed the chair across the table and settled between them. The second he sat down, Kelley wedged herself under his arm and grabbed some paper and a thick black crayon.

"Here," she announced. "This color's easiest to outline with."

Gage held her around the waist and leaned over, trying to think of something amazing to illustrate. He looked over the finished drawings, noticed the number of men in uniform Brandon had drawn.

"Looks like someone likes police officers and firemen and . . ." He leaned forward, narrowed his eyes. "Is that a lion tamer?"

Brandon rolled his eyes as Kelley and Lydia giggled. "Vet-er-a-nar-ian," he said incorrectly, and Gage hid his smile. "But I like police best. I want to be one when I get big enough."

"I'm going to be a princess and a ballerina and a doctor," Kelley told him as she waved her new wand over all of their heads. "Like Morgan always says, we can be anything we want. Lydia?"

But Lydia shook her head, her long, thin hair draping over her shoulders as she continued to color.

Gage's hand tightened and he snapped the crayon in two. "I used to be a policeman."

Brandon's eyes went huge at Gage's announcement. "You were?"

"Yep." He picked up the blue crayon and shaded in some sky.

"You're not anymore?" Kelley asked, tilting her head to look at him.

"I'm a special kind of policeman now. I work to find special criminals. Extra tricky ones." He pulled out his ID folder, flipped it open, and handed it to Brandon.

"That's so cool." Brandon's eyes went wide as he traced his finger over the numbers and shield. "I've never met a real policeman before."

"Well, now you have." Gage said.

"What was it like? Being a policeman?" Brandon asked, abandoning his current project as he continued to stare at the badge. "Did you catch lots of crooks? Do you have a gun? How many were there in your squad? Do you still talk to them about cases?"

Gage smiled and hoped none of them would see the traces of regret. "It was a good job, and yes, I did catch a lot of bad guys. I have a gun, but don't carry it unless I want to. I don't remember exactly how many there were, and yes, sometimes."

Morgan's voice flew through the house like the Wicked Witch on her broom. Gage looked toward the door.

"Drew's in biiiiig trouble," Kelley sang.

"What did he do this time?" Brandon sighed, looking more like a little adult disappointed in his child.

"He was smoking," Lydia told them. "And boy is Morgan mad."

Given what Gage was hearing, *mad* was an understatement. Gage set Kelley on her feet and picked up his badge. "Stay here."

He closed the bedroom door and walked down the hallway toward the voices. The door was ajar so all he could see was Morgan's back. He was about to step inside when he realized she appeared to be handling things okay.

"I will not have you jeopardizing anyone's health,

including your own, while you're in this house. Do you understand me?"

"It was one cigarette," came the young man's response, and Gage heard the attitude of youthful immortality in his voice. "One fu—"

"Don't you use that language with me," Morgan blasted in a tone Gage was certain he wouldn't want to be on the receiving end of. "I might not be a shining example in that area, but watch how you speak. I'm going to tell you this once. Smoking will kill you. Not because it's stupid and addictive, but because your system can't handle it. We're still figuring out what works and what doesn't, and you smoking will make our job harder in controlling your diabetes."

"I'm not a job." Drew yelled. "And it was one cigarette."

"It was your last. Give me the pack." He heard shuffling and the sound of a lid slamming. "Is that all of them?" Morgan asked, and Gage noticed her tone had softened considerably.

The kid hesitated too long.

"Every last one, Drew. I mean it."

More rustling and shifting about the room, and Gage decided now might be the right time to poke his head in. "Everything okay?"

The door creaked under his touch and Morgan spun around. "Gage, I'm sorry. I'll just be another minute."

"Not a problem. Kelley introduced me to Lydia and Brandon." He looked at the teen.

Drew was the same boy he'd seen in the window the first time he'd visited. The kid had a lot going on under the surface: anger, resentment, and, if Gage wasn't mistaken, a sliver of fear. His guess? The sagging clothes and long hair was more a defense mechanism than a desire to stand out. He'd seen enough kids from the system to recognize one who knew to protect himself.

Gage met the suspicious glare aimed at him and arched a brow in silent challenge.

"Who's the cop?" Drew asked.

"How do you know he's a cop?" Morgan asked sharply.

"Walks like a cop." He smirked at Gage. "Acts like one, too."

Gage slid his hands into the pockets of his jeans and rocked on his heels. He sized the boy up in the same way Drew was looking at him, with restrained irritation. "You're half right. I used to be a cop. I'm not anymore."

"Once a cop, always a cop." Drew snorted and tossed another pack of cigarettes at Morgan. "That's the last of them."

"This was your warning." Morgan crushed the package in her hand. "Think about the other people living in this house. Brandon and Lydia are especially at risk from secondhand smoke, and I know you don't want to put them in harm's way. And before you try to wiggle around it, that does not give you permission to smoke outside the house. If I ever catch you smoking, hear of you smoking, or suspect you're smoking, you will be incredibly sorry."

Drew had the good sense to look chastised.

"You'll do both yours and Brandon's chores tomorrow, and tonight you're on dish duty. It's the least you can do for putting everyone's health at risk."

"That's not fair." Drew's eyes flashed and his fists clenched he took a step toward Morgan.

Instinct moved Gage between them.

"I'd say you were getting off easy, kid." He felt Morgan's hand on his arm and eased up. "My father had me mowing lawns every Saturday for two months when he caught me."

"So?"

"So." Gage inclined his head. "A few dinner dishes seem a small price to pay for being irresponsible with your family's safety."

"Gage." Morgan moved around him. "Thank you, but I think Drew understands. Don't you?"

"Whatever."

Gage ground his teeth together. Was there a more irritating word in the teen vocabulary than the *W* word?

"We'll work on your communication skills next," Morgan told him. "I'm not here for long. I'd appreciate you keeping an eye on the little ones until Angela is done in the yard."

Drew dropped onto his unmade bed, sulking, Gage thought as the two of them left his room.

He waited until they were downstairs before he spoke. "You're good with him."

"I should win a fucking Nobel Peace Prize for not strangling him." She held up the crumpled cigarette packs in her hand. "Remind me I owe a twenty to the swear jar. Damn stupid thing to do, smoking like that."

"Teenage boys are stupid. It's a prerequisite for the job."

"Teenage girls don't corner the market on intelligence. I can attest to that personally."

Gage grinned. "I'd love to hear about that sometime."

"Never going to happen." Ah, there was the smile. "Let's get this present going. What time are we due at your parents?" She headed down the stairs.

"Mom said noon, so probably one?"

Morgan looked over her shoulder. "Is that some sort of Juliano code?"

"Mom calls it Gage time. I tend to run late so she ups my arrival time by an hour to be safe. I caught on about five years ago."

"No wonder she thinks you need a keeper."

"She thinks I need a wife."

"Mmmm. So you've said."

"You're not going to make me do this myself, are you?" he asked as they returned to the kitchen.

"We'll help." Morgan plugged in the glue gun.

Footsteps echoed on the stairs as Kelley bounded into the room. She reached for the display cabinet that dwarfed her and tried to heft it onto the counter. "Lydia wants to take a nap and Brandon's playing Angry Birds, so I can help."

"Hey, hold on," Gage said as he took it out of her hands. "You aren't Wonder Woman."

Kelley scrunched up her face. "Who?"

Gage staggered, a hand over his heart. "Who's Wonder Woman? Only the coolest female superhero ever."

The look of skepticism on Kelley's face had Morgan laughing.

"Girls aren't superheroes," Kelley told him.

"Where are the DVDs when you need them?" Gage muttered to Morgan. "What about Buffy? Black Widow? Veronica Mars? Okay, so she's not a superhero, but—"

Kelley shook her head. "Buffy who?"

"She's too young for Buffy," Morgan explained. "And she hasn't seen Wonder Woman yet."

"Wait a minute." Gage leaned against the kitchen sink and folded his arms over his chest as he addressed Kelley. "You know all these princesses, but not Wonder Woman or Buffy? Has no one taught you about girl power?"

"Are they like James Bond?"

Gage angled his head down. "How do you know about Bond?"

The sheepish look on the little girl's face told Gage he'd just entered tricky territory. She looked up at Morgan as if to ask permission. "I spied during movie night."

"*Casino Royale*," Morgan clarified. "Nico has a movie night with each of them during the week and Drew chose James Bond."

"I take it James Bond isn't suitable for six-year-olds?"

"I'm eight and a quarter." Kelley planted her hands on her hips. "I'll be nine in nine months."

"Of course." Gage held up his hands in surrender. He'd forgotten how much fun little girls could be.

Morgan snapped off the plastic covering from the cabinet. "We need to get this finished if we're going to be on time for the party."

"Another party?" Kelley whined. "You always get to go to parties."

"I know it seems that way, but I really don't. Go get me the glue sticks out of the craft barrel, please. I want to make sure we have enough. The plain ones. No glitter."

Pouting, Kelley left the kitchen as Morgan discarded the packaging. The glossy black finish looked sleek and stylish. He hoped he'd chosen the right one with three shelves lining the inside. "Okay, mister. Get to organizing your brother's new car collection."

As she tapped her finger against the tip of the glue gun, he grasped the counter on either side of her and locked her in.

"Gage, stop. This wasn't part of the deal." She tried to move away and it was all he could do to resist the urge to cup her hips in his hands, to nuzzle her neck. He did, however, inhale the soft fragrance of her hair and skin, springtime and summer, flowers and sunshine. "Please don't," she whispered, and moved her head away as his lips skimmed the side of her throat.

"I can't thank you enough for coming to my rescue. You fix cars, can use power tools, and now, you find the perfect present and save me from familial humiliation. What don't you do?"

He felt her stiffen in his semi-embrace and wondered what she was thinking. Was she thinking about the way his arms felt around her? Did she realize how much he liked holding her? Touching her?

He lifted one hand and pulled her hair to the side. He leaned in and brushed his lips against the side of her neck. She sighed and he smiled against her petal-soft skin. Now this he understood.

She spun around, nearly knocking her head into his chin. Instead of moving away, however, he took a step closer and had the satisfaction of seeing her eyes cloud over as his body molded against hers.

"Gage, we talked about this. One date. One and done. That's all this is." She kept her voice low, planted her hands on his chest. He felt her fingers curl under, grip his shirt, and scrape his skin, and he wished she'd show him what those fingers were capable of. When she continued her thought, he wondered who she was trying to convince. "This can't happen. I know you think it should and it will, but I just can't— Gage, there's so much you don't know. About me, about my life. More than you could ever understand and deal with, believe me."

"Maybe I want to try," he murmured, dipping his head, a whisper of caress against her lips. "And this Woman of Mystery stuff? It only makes me more determined."

"Gage—"

He swallowed her protest with his mouth, diving in before she could stop him. She tasted so sweet, so perfect, like strawberries and sunshine and the promise of the world. He couldn't get enough of her.

"Got 'em." Kelley announced as she ran into the room.

Morgan shoved him away before she took the opaque glue sticks from Kelley, not looking at him even as her cheeks flamed bright red.

He stepped away, watching from a distance as the two of them put their heads together and began arranging his brother's gift.

What was stopping her? What did she see standing between them that he didn't? Why couldn't she admit there was something strong, something special within reach? She was just scared. Of change. Of trusting someone. Of loving someone.

Whoa. Gage shifted as if a swarm of ants crawled up his spine. Where did *that* come from? Walking into this house was like playing make-believe, as if the real world faded outside the front door. But playtime, as Morgan reminded him, was over.

Whatever Morgan thought he wouldn't understand, it didn't matter. She was as honorable a woman as he'd ever met. Nothing could change the way he was starting to feel about her.

Nothing at all.

CHAPTER 9

"How sick is she?" Gage asked as he waved at Kelley, who waved from the porch, her cracked tiara back in place on her head, her princess dress drooping off one shoulder, magic wand circling the air.

Had Morgan's heart not already been tilting in Gage's direction, it would have tipped all the way over when he insisted that Kelley sign Stephen's cabinet along with him. They'd dated it together, putting her mark, a crooked smiley face, beside his blocky script of initials. Now it seemed whenever she looked at Gage, her insides kickstarted like a Harley Davidson after a year-long stall.

She set the overflowing bag of dinner rolls and freshbaked bread Angela had insisted she take into the trunk beside Stephen's gift. "Kelley was diagnosed with stage three leukemia, but her prognosis is good." Anytime Morgan doubted the decisions she'd made, all she had to do was look into Kelley's joyful eyes. Or Brandon's. Or Lydia's. Morgan closed her eyes and let the sadness pass over her like a silent fog.

"What happened to Kelley's parents?"

"Gone," Morgan said. "Her father was never in the picture and her mother brought her for her first treatment at the hospital, went out to get something to eat, and never came back." Morgan saw Gage's jaw tighten. "Part of me hates her for abandoning Kelley. But then I think if she hadn't, I wouldn't get to see that beautiful face every day or watch her thrive and explode into every morning she sees. We've all tried to get her to talk about it, asked if she misses her mom, but . . ." Morgan shrugged, wishing she had the resiliency of a child. "I think she's handled the abandonment better than we have. Besides, chances are if she'd stayed with her mother, Kelley wouldn't be alive."

"I've seen my share of monsters on the job, but I can't imagine anything worse than abandoning a child. Except maybe abandoning a sick child."

It wasn't until they were in the car that Morgan remembered. "I didn't see a birthday card in the bags."

Gage swore. "I forgot it at the office. Quick stop?"

"Sure." She was already playing with fire; might as well walk into the inferno that was his office.

"What about the other kids?"

"Brandon survived stage two kidney cancer thanks to an experimental chemotherapy drug. Although if you ask me, the treatment was worse than the disease. His mother had drug issues, surrendered her parental rights when he was four, but his previous foster family couldn't take on the burden of the medical expenses."

"They all seem well adjusted."

"Most of them, anyway." She couldn't shake the feeling that she'd lit the fuse on time-bomb Drew this morning.

"And Lydia? I thought they'd made significant progress when it came to children with AIDS."

"They have. She has a particularly voracious strain. Her mother was five months pregnant with Lydia before they found out Lydia's father had contracted the disease from a blood transfusion when he was working overseas. But it's not Lydia's T-Cell count that's the problem right now. It's the tumor on her brain stem. Three months ago I couldn't have kept up with her if I'd tried." Morgan looked out the window as they headed into downtown, watched people strolling between cafés and stores. What it must be like, not to have to worry about, well, everything. "Her mother met with me and the Fiorellis and surrendered her parental rights before she died. Greatest gift she could have given us and, wow, doesn't all this sound maudlin." Morgan laughed then pressed her lips together when Gage covered her hand with his. "Kids constantly surprise you. As much bad as there is, it's far outweighed by the good. I don't know what I'd do without them."

Gage nodded. "You love these kids as if they were your own. Anyone who spends any time with you can see that."

"They are mine," Morgan said without hesitation, grateful for the chance to make him understand why she did what she did, even if at this point he didn't know why she had to. "They were given to us in one way or the other. When my brother Colin was sick, he had us, a support system, and while it didn't make him better, it made his passing easier. At least that's what I tell myself. Instead of parents having to worry about hospital bills or whether they're going to lose their house or their jobs, they should be able to focus on their child. That's why the center can't get finished fast enough. Every day we go over schedule, we could lose another life." The list of potential admissions was already overflowing and they didn't even have the facility completed yet.

Gage pulled into a parking space outside the renovated office building.

"Where do your parents live?" she asked as she got out of the car and walked through the lobby door he held open for her.

"Fallen Oak Lane."

"Then you'll still surprise your mother by being early."

"I bet we give her a heart attack." Once they stepped out on the second floor, Gage gestured to the corner of the loft. "I'll just be a minute."

Morgan strolled around the spacious loft, her soft-soled sandals silent against the hardwood floor. The office space was welcoming. Neat, tidy, streamlined, and comfortable. A good environment to be productive in. Lots of light thanks to the giant-paned windows inside the conference room. She braced her hand on the doorframe, leaned inside, and saw the lineup of file folders, laptops, and smatterings of notes. The whiteboards displayed photos and lists.

Morgan took a tentative step inside, as if she might trigger an alarm. This must be what it felt like to walk into the Bat Cave. Some secret sanctum she shouldn't be trespassing in.

Each of Nemesis' victims up to the most recent, the Cunninghams, had their own section of whiteboard with dedicated bullet points and pinned photos. A list of what had been taken from them, another notation in red below each of the dated report of the burglary: charges withdrawn.

The reality of seeing all the information in one place, like a snapshot of Nemesis' action plan, wedged like a stone in the bottom of her gut. She'd known the names, even the people involved, but it was easy to forget lives had been affected by what Nemesis—and by extension what she—had done.

There was nothing romantic about stealing. There wasn't anything romantic about accepting money from a thief. It didn't matter that the money had been put to good use. Morgan wasn't a character in a fairy tale searching for a happy ending. That stack of Nemesis cash hiding in the bottom drawer of her desk didn't just feel tainted—it felt poisoned.

She hadn't just skirted the edge of the law. She'd crossed it months ago.

But what else could she have done? Turned away those patients who needed the money for treatment? Sure, she'd taken the money she'd set aside to pay off the balance of the property payment, but it had just been sitting there, waiting while children died.

Even with the evidence staring her in the face, she knew she wouldn't have made a different choice. The kids she'd helped were leading healthy or healthier lives. Most important, they were alive. But there were always more kids, more diagnoses. More demands on her for help, and she couldn't say no.

"Finally found where I put the card." Gage joined her in the conference room, followed her gaze. "If you see something we've missed, let me know."

"I wouldn't know what to look for," she whispered.

"Neither do we, otherwise I'd have Nemesis locked up by now. Hey." Gage caught her chin between his fingers, turned her face toward his. "You okay? What's wrong?"

"I'm fine." Morgan wrapped her hand around his wrist. "I shouldn't be in here."

"You're welcome to stop by any time. Ready to head into the lion's den?"

Morgan smiled. "I don't think your mother would appreciate you calling her home the lion's den." Besides, it couldn't be more dangerous than where she was already standing. "Let's go."

∽

The pristine manicured lawn and giant oak tree sheltering the front walk of the Juliano home were dotted with late spring color.

An unruly garden hose wound around the front of the two-story brick house while a comical stone cat stretched a curious paw toward a smattering of violet and pink pansies. A happy birthday sign placed like a for-sale sign peeked out of the hedges, blue and white balloons sagging in the breeze.

"You have a tire swing." Morgan pressed her fingers against the car window.

"Dad's been trying to take that down but Mom won't let him." When she didn't respond, Gage touched her shoulder. "Want a ride?"

"Are you kidding?"

"It's not there for decoration. Go ahead."

Morgan headed up the walk and dropped her purse on the thick grass. She walked over and ran her fingers down the length of the aged rope as it swayed against her touch. She smiled, grabbed on, and hoisted her feet up and through the tire, situating her butt on the edge. She leaned back as far as she could, closed her eyes, and pushed off with her feet, spinning and swinging, feet dangling in the air until her shoes dropped off.

A moment of perfect, of nothing. Everything. The wind rushed against her ears, clearing her mind, invigorating, bracing. Wondrous.

The tire froze.

Morgan lifted her head, opened her eyes, and found Gage holding the tire still, an odd look in his eyes. "What?" She sat up as his hands covered hers, and he moved closer as she leaned up. "Gage?"

He kissed her, soft, slow, his hand moving to cup the back of her neck as she smiled against his lips. The shade of the oak embraced them, the early-afternoon breeze bathing them in spring warmth, and the world dropped away. She clutched his wrist, felt his pulse beneath her fingers, heavy and strong. When he lifted his mouth, he pressed his forehead against hers, and her doubts, her fears, melted beneath his touch.

"Told your father we weren't done with that swing." Morgan felt rather than saw the heat rise in Gage's face as she caught sight of a petite dark-haired woman walking barefoot from the back gate toward the front door, a box of soda cans in her arms. "When the two of you are done, I could use some help in the kitchen."

Morgan laughed and couldn't resist. She kissed Gage again before ducking free of the swing and grabbing her shoes.

"Precious, isn't she?" Gage muttered as he retrieved the bags he'd set down by her purse.

"Actually, she's pretty much what I expected." Morgan loved how easily his mother flustered him. "I'm going to want another go at the swing," she told him as they headed in the front door.

"I don't anticipate a problem with that. Geez, Mom. We need to put a bell around your neck."

His mother popped around the door the second they pushed it open and Morgan locked gazes with the older woman. Her round face was open and warm and she stood a few inches shorter than Morgan. A stained apron was draped over her jeans and T-shirt, and her jet black hair was pulled into a snug ponytail.

"Morgan, my mother, Theresa Juliano. Mom, as requested, Morgan Tremayne."

Morgan hefted her purse up on her shoulder and held out her hand. "It's nice to meet you, Mrs. Juliano. I hope you don't mind, but I didn't want to arrive empty handed. Compliments of Nico and Angela Fiorelli." Morgan gestured to the second bag in Gage's arms.

"It's Theresa, please." She returned the greeting. "No one calls me Mrs. Juliano unless one of my kids is in trouble."

"Something tells me you were called a lot over this one." Morgan gave Gage a wink. "Did you say something about needing help in the kitchen?"

Theresa tucked the dishtowel she'd been holding through the apron string around her waist. "I knew I'd like you. My son is rarely on time, let alone early. Come inside." She linked her arm through Morgan's and led her into the home that welcomed her with the aroma of tomatoes, basil, and onions.

The Juliano home was part showplace, part comfort and practicality. Magazines and photo albums lay scattered on the enormous coffee table situated between two large upholstered sofas. Two recliners sat nearby, angled toward the flat-screen television against the far wall. The walls were painted a soft gold, giving a feel of old-world charm mixed with modern comfort. The paintings made Morgan think of driving through the endless golden fields and blue skies of the Italian countryside.

A large staircase curved off to the upper floor. Morgan peered into the dining room that housed a table which could no doubt fit up to sixteen people. The scene looked as if it had been drawn from the pages of *Kitchen Design* magazine, an observation Morgan confirmed once she saw the amazing kitchen that lay beyond.

"You must be a serious cook." Morgan marveled at the pots and pans and the six-burner gas range situated beneath a copper hood. The cabinet space alone promised to feed an army, which, with six children, was no doubt what Theresa had done most of her life.

"My husband let me design the kitchen of my dreams for our thirtieth anniversary," Theresa said. "I've always believed this to be the heart of the home."

"And here I thought it was the stomach." Gage set his brother's gift on the counter, along with the bag from the Fiorellis.

Theresa waved her hand. "Ignore him and put that present in the living room with the others. Do you cook, Morgan?"

"I zap a mean microwave dinner." She ran fingertips

along the gold-speckled marble counter top. "I loved helping Ella. She was my parent's housekeeper when I was growing up. I would spend hours helping her knead dough and chop vegetables. Half the time I'd end up covered in flour and spices."

"I'd have paid to see that," Gage said when he returned and earned an appreciative look from his mother. Morgan took a deep breath. Damn it. Encouraging his mother, making Theresa think there was more than today, that there could be more between her and Gage, felt deceptive and somehow cruel.

"Stop embarrassing the girl, Gage," his mother ordered. "Or I won't make your favorite."

"Would that be the eggplant parmesan he's raved about? Can't be any better than the lasagna you sell at J & J." Morgan decided to pretend Gage wasn't in the room as Theresa glowed.

"And since the parm is Stephen's favorite, and he is the birthday boy, I'm safe," Gage countered. "As I said, Mom makes the best."

"Mothers usually do," Theresa agreed, walking around the center island and opening a cabinet.

Not in Morgan's experience. Her mother and the kitchen had been a frightening and smoke-alarm-triggering combination. But the memory made her smile without the usual pang of sorrow.

"Where is everyone?" Gage asked, heading over to the industrial-sized wood-encased refrigerator and grabbing a bottle of beer.

"I banished your father and the boys to the backyard until we're ready to eat."

Morgan glanced outside and caught sight of a man who

was as tall and blond as Teresa was dark. She could see both mother and father reflected in the faces of their children.

"And the terrible two?" Gage's question came with a slight grimace.

Morgan frowned at the reference.

"They'll be down momentarily."

The second the words left Theresa's mouth, Morgan heard footsteps on the stairs that were soon drowned out by the sound of raised teenage voices.

"It's a family party, for crying out loud, Liza. Nobody cares if your eyebrows are even."

"You'll forgive me if I don't take advice from Sasquatch."

"Bite me."

"Not even if you paid me."

Gage grinned at Morgan and shook his head as he took a long drink of beer. "Welcome to the show."

"Girls, please fix the salad," Theresa said as if she hadn't heard a word of bickering between the two young women rounding the corner. "And cut up extra vegetables for a platter. I made the dip last night. It's in the fridge."

Judging from the conversation, the lithe blonde with razor-straight hair and outlined bright blue eyes had to be the eyebrow enthusiast. She was stunning and, despite the sharp sarcastic wit, greeted Morgan with a warm smile that mirrored her mother's.

"Hi. You must be Morgan." She held out her hand. "I'm Liza."

"Nice to meet you." Morgan's gaze fell on the shorter, rounder young woman beside her. "Hello."

"I'm Gina." Shoulder-length chocolate brown curls

framed her full face, which lit up as she greeted Morgan with a wave. "I can't tell you how great it is to meet you. I've read all about you."

"You have?" Surprised, Morgan looked to Gage, who straightened as if he'd heard a warning bell she'd missed.

"Gina," he warned.

"What?" Gina cast him a quick dismissive glance. "I've been reading about the center and the foundation. I've applied to get on as a pediatric volunteer at Lantano Valley General, but they won't take me until I'm eighteen."

"They have certain guidelines, especially for young people," Morgan explained. "Working with seriously and terminally ill children takes a certain mind-set. But I'd be happy to see if they might make an exception if you're that interested."

"Please don't encourage her," Liza pleaded. "She's already insufferable."

"Or *you* could hire me." Gina flashed wide, excited eyes on Morgan.

Gage choked on his beer. Theresa gasped.

"Too late." Liza rolled her eyes. "There she goes."

"Gage told us about your foster kids and all the work you do with the foundation," Gina plowed on, tucking unruly curls behind her ears. "I bet you can use an assistant, right? What?" Gina didn't look apologetic in the least as she glanced at her horrified mother. "Didn't you and Dad teach us to take advantage of every opportunity? Morgan being here today is a serious opportunity." She pulled out a file folder she'd stuffed in the back waistband of her jeans. "My resume." She tapped the top page. "I've also done some research on advances other pediatric medical centers have been making. I wrote up a report with some ideas you might want to consider that include some additional events I think would work in downtown Lantano Valley. Rich people are great, but they can only get you so far, right?"

"Honest to God, Mom, please make her stop." Gage plucked the file out of Morgan's hands and slapped it against his sister's T-shirt that stated "sarcasm is my gift to the world." "Not the time."

"Hey." Gina frowned.

"Now, wait a minute." Morgan pushed Gage aside and grabbed the folder before it fell. Granted, she couldn't involve Gina with the center or the foundation, at least as far as working with her. She had enough trouble keeping details to herself as it was. But she'd be stupid to ignore someone as enthusiastic as Gina, for however long it might last. "It takes guts to do what she just did. I want to hear her out. What are your plans for college?"

Gina's face lit up as if a flare gun had exploded in the room. "A business degree with a concentration in charity management. I'm working toward a scholarship at Lantano Valley U, like Jon got. I want to do something worthwhile, something good. You know, like him." She stuck her thumb at Gage. "Even though he can be a dick—"

"Gina Marie Juliano!" Theresa grabbed a wooden spoon.

"—tator." Gina finished in a rush.

"I'm touched." Gage wiped invisible tears from his eyes. "Such sentiment."

"I'll tell you what." Morgan chuckled as she flipped through the information Gina had compiled. Impressive was an understatement. This girl made Morgan look like a slacker. "Let me talk this over with my sister. She handles the social aspects of the foundation, decides on events, parties, and she's been thinking about hiring an assistant. Is that something you'd be interested in?"

"I'll take whatever I can get." Gina bounced on her toes. "And it sounds amazing."

"I'm not promising anything," Morgan insisted. "But yeah, let me see what we can do. I'm keeping this." She pushed the file into her purse, then remembering the reality of what she dealt with on a daily basis added, "You do know what you're getting into, right, Gina? Emotionally speaking, it's not easy. You'll be dealing with serious issues, and you'll meet kids who might not get better. They'll die. No matter what we do."

"They're alive now, aren't they?" The fact that there was no hesitation on her face or in her voice struck a familiar chord inside Morgan. "Isn't that what matters? Making things better for them while they are here?" Morgan nodded. Gina squealed and launched herself at Morgan, hugging her tight. "Thank you."

Morgan couldn't help but notice the pride shining in Theresa's eyes as she covered her mouth with the wood spoon. Morgan gave her a smile of approval and Theresa's face lit up as bright as her daughter's had moments ago. "Just make sure I have your cell number, okay?"

"You won't be sorry. I promise." Gina turned around and stuck her tongue out at her sister as if she'd regressed to the age of five. "Told you I could do it."

Liza just shook her head. "Just promise me you'll get some decent clothes for work."

"The babies of the family are always the most entertaining." Gage grabbed a stalk of celery from the pile.

"I don't think one should be called a baby once one is old enough to *have* a baby." Gina slapped his hand away.

Gage turned an odd shade of green. "That's not funny."

"It kind of is." Morgan took the apron Theresa handed her. One second she had the cream-colored fabric in her hands, and the next, Gage snatched it from her. He shook it out, opened it up and whipped it around her waist, pulling her against him as he pulled the strings tight.

Morgan closed her eyes even as she felt his mother and sisters looking on. His hands slid around her hips, dragging the string along. He took his time tying the bow, lowering his head to skim his lips against the side of her neck. He seemed particularly enamored of that part of her anatomy.

"Stop that." She tried to dislodge his hands. "One and done."

"We're not done yet." He nipped her ear before stepping away.

"Go play with your brothers," Morgan ordered, brushing her hands down her body as she tried to shake off the effects of his touch. "Leave the beer." She grabbed his bottle and took a giant swig. Because alcohol was going to help the situation. He tossed them one of his disarming grins as he headed to the sliding glass door. The second the door closed behind him, Liza and Gina collapsed in a fit of giggles.

Theresa turned around, hands on her hips, and pinned Morgan with a look that made her feel like an amoeba under a microscope. "I want grandchildren."

Morgan set down the beer. "Before or after dinner?"

CHAPTER 10

Given the number of photographs lining the staircase wall, Morgan figured Theresa and Daniel, Gage's father, must have spent at least eighty percent of the last thirty-plus years taking pictures of their children. On her way out of the bathroom, she found herself pulled into the family's history. She traced Gage all the way to infancy, including the obligatory naked baby on a rug. Is this what his son would look like? Would his boy gaze out with wide-eyed curiosity at everything around him?

"God forbid fire ever strikes this house, but if it does, everyone's under orders to grab pictures first." Theresa joined her on the staircase and leaned against the railing as she watched Morgan observe her family. "I was sorry to hear about your mother."

"She loved taking pictures of us." Morgan ran her finger along the edge of a wood frame. "We thought it was annoying, even gave her a bad time about it, particularly when she demanded we all get into one together. What I wouldn't give for just one more."

"She raised a wonderful daughter."

Morgan gave a sad smile. "You don't know me well enough to say that." Wonderful daughters didn't put their mother's legacy at risk.

"I see how my son looks at you when he thinks no one is watching. Especially when you aren't looking. Plus, you're the first woman he's brought home."

Morgan angled her head. "You blackmailed him into inviting me."

"Ah, but he asked and you said yes. That means I was right. You'll be good for each other." And now sadness appeared as she focused on a more recent picture of Gage surrounded by his brothers and sisters. "He almost died last year. Did he tell you?"

Morgan's skin went clammy. She shivered. "No." He hadn't said a word. "What happened?"

"Joint operation with the FBI. He was so excited." Theresa shook her head. "I was terrified, of course, but it's what he'd always wanted. Law and order, justice. Catch the bad guys. Then the operation went bad, his backup went to the wrong address, and Gage's cover was blown. The gunshot missed his heart by less than a centimeter." She held her fingers apart. "That much closer and he wouldn't be here. As it was, he lost one of his kidneys when the second man stabbed him."

Morgan's pulse flatlined. That much closer and they never would have met. The idea of never having seen him, touched him. Kissed him. The need to see Gage's face felt as urgent as the need to breathe.

"I've been waiting for him to see there's more to life than his work, than his job. Now, thanks to you, he has."

"He still only sees his job," Morgan corrected. "And he's not the only one."

"But you also see each other. This Nemesis business has been hard on him. Brady Malloy was a good friend for a lot of years, and I think Gage sees closing the case as a way to make up for losing touch with him." Theresa brought a hand up to Morgan's cheek. "You make my son smile, and for that alone I can never thank you enough. Now come, it's time to eat, and then presents. I can't wait to see what you came up with for Stephen." She took Morgan's hand and led her down the stairs.

"Oh, no. It was all Gage—"

"Oh, Morgan, please. I know my son. You got a last-minute panicked phone call, didn't you? He forgot to get the present? Had no idea what to get? The entire family was depending on him?"

Morgan's mouth twisted. She should have known.

"Don't feel bad," Theresa laughed. "It's the one con he can pull off. Means he trusts you and that he didn't have to rely on me to bail him out this time." She patted a hand against her heart. "Makes my heart happy."

∽

"Best present ever," Gage whispered into Morgan's ear as he came up behind her and slipped his arms around her waist. They'd taken the party outside along with the gifts, and as the sun began to set, a raucous game of badminton ensued pitting, sisters against brothers, husband against wife. "I don't think any of us will forget the look on his face when he saw that car collection. You were right—the personalized license plate was an inspired touch."

"You're just glad you didn't have to ask your mother for help this year."

"I knew she'd rat me out." Gage laughed and hugged her tighter.

Sadness swept through her even as her body tingled. The evening was coming to an end. Their "one" was nearly done. But she leaned against him, covered his hands with hers, and enjoyed the moment. Men like him didn't come around for women like her, and while she'd be lying to say she hadn't developed feelings for him, it was better to break this off now before things went too far. The longer this went on, the harder it would be to keep secrets—keep the truth—from him, and Morgan was so tired of lying. Besides, it wasn't just the center and the foundation and the kids she was protecting. She had to protect her heart.

She had to protect Gage and his family.

"Your mother told me what happened last year. With the shooting."

His hold on her stiffened, as if his bones had been replaced by iron. "Ancient history."

"Not for her." She turned to face him, linked her arms around his neck. "Not for you, either, I think."

"Is this your way of asking me what happened?"

"If you want to tell me, I'll listen."

"Nothing to tell, really." But his shrug was anything but casual. "Eight months of undercover work and when it went wrong, they blamed me. Said I didn't follow procedure even though statements from other agents proved otherwise. I was an easy target because I'd been on loan from the L.A. police. By then it was too late. I was pulled from the task force, and since my old position with the department down south had been cut for budget reasons—"

"You came home." She stroked her fingers through the hair at the nape of his neck.

"Seemed a good place to start over, get my footing back. Figure out what I wanted for my life. Well, that and there aren't as many drug shootouts in Lantano Valley." His smile didn't quite reach his eyes.

Morgan couldn't help but wonder how things between them might be different if he'd stayed a cop. "Do you like your new job?"

Gage shrugged. "Sure. It's nice to trust the people I'm working with. People I knew wouldn't throw me to the wolves if something went wrong. Besides, now I'm the one in charge." He angled his head, tapped a finger against her lips. "And look where that's taken me."

How she wished she'd never heard of Nemesis.

"You two need to get a room." Gage's brother Stephen grabbed another beer from the cooler, swiping the frosty bottle over his forehead as he grinned at them.

Of all the sons, Stephen most resembled his father, but she'd noticed each of the Juliano kids had a certain glimmer in their eye that continued to sparkle, especially when they were teasing one another. "We're taking odds on when Mom starts looking at bridal magazines. Want in?"

"I do not." Gage turned and came face-to-face with his mother. "Um, hi?"

"Jon wants to be a cop."

Morgan squirmed to get away, but Gage held on, no doubt planning to use her as a shield.

"Not exactly. He's a geek, Mom. A talented one,

although don't tell him I said so." Theresa's accusatory glare softened. "He'll get all the training he needs. He's smart. He'll adapt and he'll learn from his mistakes. It's what he wants. If it matters, I think he'll be good at it."

"You'll watch out for him." Definitely not a question.

"As much as I can. He's his own man. Took guts to tell you when he didn't have to. He could have waited until it was too late. Like I did."

"My children do have guts," Theresa said, and winked at Morgan. "First you, then Jon, now Gina. A mother likes to see her children's lives falling into place. Now, if we can get Liza to settle on something . . ." And with that, Theresa buzzed over to her husband for a kiss.

"Your poor sister." Morgan looked over to his sisters. "It's like she's a walking target."

"Liza's not as unfocused as mom thinks. Although not as determined as Gina."

"I don't think Attila the Hun was as determined as Gina is. Um." She peeked up at him. "Any chance there's any chocolate cake left?"

"I was just thinking the same thing. I know where she stashes the leftovers."

"Just let me check my messages." Morgan retrieved her purse, pulled out her phone, and felt her mouth go dry. Nine text messages. Seven voice mails. All from Angela. Her entire body flooded into ice. "Oh, God." Her hand trembled as she tried to remember how to access her phone book. "Oh, God, what is it?"

"Morgan?" Gage set down two plates of cake on the table as he passed through the dining room. She heard the sliding door open and close. The look of concern on

Gage's face shifted to controlled cop the instant he saw her. "What's happened?"

"I don't know? Voice mails, messages. Angela said she'd only call if there was a problem with one of the kids." She never should have let herself get distracted. She should have had her phone with her. She dialed the house, wrapped an arm around her waist as the phone rang.

"Morgan, thank God. I've been trying to reach you for over an hour." Angela's normally calm voice rang with barely controlled panic. "It's Drew. He's been in an accident."

∼

"You can just drop me off."

Gage leaned over and pulled the door closed to prevent Morgan from dashing out of the car and into the hospital before he'd stopped the car. "You need to stop."

"Gage, I need to get in there. I need to see for myself he's okay."

"You're not going to do anyone any good in the state you're in, so just take a minute. Let me find a parking place. You just sit there and remember how to breathe." Aside from calling her sister to ask if she could stay with the kids, Morgan hadn't uttered two words since they got into the car, but he could hear the wheels in her head grinding. He wished she'd just scream and get the fear and frustration out of her system instead of stewing in it. "Kick the anger, Morgan. It won't help the situation."

"What the hell was he doing out? He was grounded."

"As a former teenage boy, I can tell you that's exactly

why he went out. He's a typical kid, Morgan. Try treating him like one."

She didn't give any indication she heard him.

"I never should have put my phone away. Another few minutes, another hour—"

"Stop feeling guilty because you took some time for yourself."

"I didn't take it for *myself*. I took it for *you* and look what happened. There—" She pointed ahead and to the left. "There's a spot. Park there."

He took the verbal blow because she needed to swing at someone, but that didn't make the words sting any less. What he wanted to do was shake some sense into her. Heading in to see Drew in her current state of mind was going to make the situation worse. Getting between Morgan and one of her kids, however, could be as dangerous as stepping in front of a barreling freight train.

"You don't have to come in." She pushed out of the car before he could turn off the engine, but he caught up before she hit the emergency room entrance and grabbed her arm, spun her around.

"Forget the fact that my mother would flat-out kill me if I let you go in there by yourself. You need someone to yank you off the ledge." He gripped her arms until he saw her wince, confirmation he had her attention. "Get your head on straight and go in there and talk to him."

"What did you think I was going to do?" Disgust dripped from her tone.

"Talk *at* him." A glimmer of acknowledgment flickered in her green eyes. "You're scared, Morgan. Hell, you're terrified, and you have every right to be. But don't take that into the room with you. Rail at him later, ground him for life next week, but for right now, he's a hurt and scared kid."

"Easy for you to say. He's not your kid." She tried to wrench free.

"If you're not careful, he won't be yours either." Now he did shake her. "For God's sake, Morgan, why won't you let anyone help you with him? Why won't you let us help you with anything?"

"I don't need anyone's help. My debt's been paid in full, you got your one. Now go away." She twisted her arms with enough force to break his hold.

My debt's been paid in full. The words ricocheted against his ears like a hollow-point bullet. Damnable, frustrating, stubborn.

What was *wrong* with her? Why couldn't she see he wanted to help her? To show her she didn't have to take everything onto her already overburdened shoulders.

She didn't want his help; hell, he'd all but become invisible the second she'd gotten the call about Drew. Understandable, sure, but why was it that whatever angle he tried to take with her she, deflected him?

What the hell was he still doing here?

Because whether she knew it or not, wanted to admit it or not, she needed him.

Embracing the anger she'd leveled at him, he followed her through the double doors, pulled out his cell phone, and dialed his father, who answered on the first ring. "Hey, Dad. I need your advice and help with something."

Morgan thought he was in her way? She hadn't seen anything yet.

"And you said smoking would kill me." From his prone position on the gurney in the emergency room and the dazed look in Drew's eyes, his comment didn't carry the humorous punch Morgan figured he intended.

His handsome young face was cut; the butterfly bandages across one cheek and over his right eye told her flying glass had been involved. His left hand twitched where it lay on the bed, attached to beeping monitors and an overhead IV.

But it wasn't until then that she felt as if she could breathe again. "Thank God you're okay." The tightness in her chest and throat eased. "I haven't talked to your doctors yet. What did they tell you? Did they remember to test your blood?" She indicated the Medic Alert medallion around his neck.

"Yes." The venom in his voice made her cringe.

"Yes, they tested my blood."

"Drew—"

"Accident destroyed my pump." He jerked the hospital gown free and exposed the tube dangling from his side, but kept his face turned away.

"I don't care about your pump."

"Since when?"

"I—" Morgan's mind went blank.

"Since when do you care about anything other than this fucking disease?" When he did look at her, she saw what she described as anguish on his features.

"Drew—" She moved closer but he swung his arms wild and sent the water pitcher and vomit tray flying against the wall.

"I'm not this damned disease. Why don't you ever see me?" Tears pooled in his eyes and she saw him struggle to keep them from falling. "Why don't you see *me*?"

Just as fast, the stoic taciturn Drew returned. His face closed as if he'd slammed a door. He swiped at his face, as if the thought of tears was abhorrent. "Just go away."

The three words struck like arrows in her heart. The same words she'd said to Gage moments ago. Except now she understood what Gage had been trying to tell her. Now wasn't the time to chastise Drew for his reckless behavior or even rail at him for being an irresponsible teenager.

What he needed, what he'd always needed, was for someone to listen to him.

She set her purse on the floor and sat on the edge of his bed. "Tell me what happened." His clenched fists relaxed, his gaze darted to her and away, as if afraid to believe his words had had an impact. "I promise, I won't be mad," she said. "Just tell me what happened." And because she needed to, she brushed the hair out of his eyes.

He shrugged and avoided her probing gaze. "We were just going to go for a ride in some guy's car. Jonesy had the keys. But then Ruffo brought out this bag with beers and I wanted to get out. I know smoking is bad enough—no way am I going to mess with booze. You know that."

"I know." Morgan nodded.

"Jonesy reached for the bag, took his eyes off the road and slammed the car into a telephone pole. I was pinned, felt my pump break. There was beer everywhere. I couldn't get free from the seat belt—"

"Thank you for wearing one," Morgan interrupted.

"Yeah. Like I don't hear about it every time we get into the car. Next thing I know, I heard sirens and Ruffo and Jonesy were gone, and then I woke up here." Another shrug, only this one seemed less forced, as if he didn't feel quite so heavy. "They're going to use this to take me away from you guys, aren't they? That CPS chick."

"If that CPS *woman* is Deanna Crawford, she's here."

Morgan spun on the thin squeaky mattress as Gage came in. Regret washed over her as she thought about what she'd said to him, how she'd treated him, and yet here he was.

What was wrong with the man? Didn't he see she didn't deserve his loyalty? His concern? And yet, seeing him made her feel more in control. More importantly, he'd just proven how much he cared.

"They aren't going to take you from us. Not if we can help it," Morgan told Drew as she covered his hand with hers. "I need to go talk to her and your doctor, okay?"

"Don't move," Gage warned Drew, but without the heat she'd have expected. Drew must have sensed the shift as well because he frowned.

"Man, where would I go? Do you know what they stuck up my—"

"I have a pretty good idea." Gage nodded seriously. "Angela and Nico are waiting."

Morgan stood, then planted her hands on either side of Drew's hips and leaned over. "We both have some making up to do. We can both do better with each other. But you need to make up your mind, Drew. Do you want to stay with us, yes or no? No." She shook her head when he opened his mouth. "No. You need to think about this. I'll promise to do better. When you're ready, you tell me. And Drew?" She waited until he met her gaze. "I do see you. Maybe I didn't before, but I do now."

Morgan followed Gage to where Nico and Angela

waited at the nurse's station. A petite, dark-haired woman with a tablet computer snug under her arm was nearby.

Even from a distance, Morgan knew the conversation wasn't going well.

"Tonight's events leave me no choice, Mr. Fiorelli. I've redrafted my letter of protest on Drew's placement and plan to file it with the juvenile court in the morning."

Whether it was the woman's choice of words, her superior tone, or the disdain with which she looked at Morgan as she approached, had Gage not draped an arm over her shoulders, Morgan might have pounced on the Child Protective Services chick like a puma on a rabbit.

"I was just reminding Ms. Crawford that Drew's situation is a sensitive and unique one," Angela said, the tension and worry beginning to show on her strained face. She clung to Nico with white knuckles.

"Every case is sensitive," Ms. Crawford dismissed Angela's argument. "Like the other cases in your house. I don't believe Drew is an appropriate influence on them—"

"Children," Morgan cut in. "They're children, not cases." A lesson learned she wasn't about to forget.

"With the other *children* in residence, the attention Drew needs isn't available," Ms. Crawford said.

"And another foster home . . . What would this be, his sixteenth in seven years?" Morgan asked with an arched brow. "Would another foster home be able to give him what you think is lacking?"

"Of course, nothing can be guaranteed," Ms. Crawford admitted.

"Drew's home is with us. We're his family," Nico said, and Morgan heard in his voice how he'd taken this attack on his ability to care for his kids personally.

"Surely removing Drew from the house at this point is going to do more harm than good," Gage said.

"Who are you?" Ms. Crawford angled her pointed nose in Gage's direction.

"Inspector Gage Juliano from the District Attorney's office. I'm also a friend of the family."

"Well, Inspector," Ms. Crawford said. "I'm sure as a law enforcement representative you'll agree that Drew's reckless behavior sets a poor example to the other children in the house. For him to disregard his condition and be drinking to the point of intoxication—"

"Drew wasn't drinking," Morgan snapped, and while she understood Gage's attempt to silence her with a squeeze of his hand, on this topic she refused to be silent. "He wouldn't. He was trying to get away from the boys who were."

"A teenage boy out without permission, an open six-pack of beer found in the car, and you expect me to believe—"

"They ran his blood, right? Those results should be in by now." Gage signaled to one of the nurses, took out his ID. "Can I speak with Drew Palmer's doctor or nurse when they have a moment? Tell them we'd like to see his latest blood work results."

The nurse scampered away as Gage drew Morgan tighter into his side.

"You have read Drew's file, right?" Morgan felt like snapping her fingers in front of Ms. Crawford's face to regain her attention. "Because if you have, then you know his parents were killed by a drunk driver when he was seven. He wouldn't drink, and if he did, he wouldn't drive or be in a car with someone who did. Maybe if you spoke to him instead of relying on files and paperwork, you might see Drew is where he needs to be."

"Morgan," Gage whispered over her head. "Enough. Let's see the test results."

"She wants to take my kid." Morgan couldn't keep the tremble out of her voice. "Our kid. He belongs with us. So he's stupid at times. Who isn't? He's a teenage boy, for crying out loud. They're all stupid." As Gage had pointed out.

"Until I see proof that Drew wasn't drinking—" Ms. Crawford said.

"Because his word isn't good enough," Morgan spat.

"Okay, give us a moment, would you, Ms. Crawford?" Gage pulled Morgan into a faraway corner and leaned over her. "Antagonizing her isn't going to help your case. Drew made the choice to go with the boys. He has a history of delinquency. You have a house filled with impressionable kids. This isn't going to be a cake-walk. He's not a saint, so stop overcompensating for your mistakes with him and work with her. You think she wants to go to all the trouble of moving him?"

Morgan snapped her mouth shut, glared at him. Did he always have to be so damned right? "He goes to another foster home, he'll be lost, Gage." Morgan hugged her arms around herself and squeezed. "It'll be my fault. I failed him. I didn't see him through all the shit I pile on myself, and because of that his life might never be what it could be."

Dammit, she hated the tears and she would not let them fall. As long as she could keep them inside, she'd be okay. As long as she kept control.

"Of all the—" Gage took a deep breath. "Why is everything that goes wrong your fault?"

Because as far as Morgan could tell, everything was her fault. Everything she'd tried to do to protect her kids, to protect her work, was falling apart. If only she could tell him the truth, tell anyone the truth, then maybe she could put a stop to the hemorrhaging that had become her life.

"You just can't help but take the entire world on your shoulders, can you?" Gage asked. "Okay, we tried this your way. Let's try mine. But you keep these"—he tapped a finger against her lips—"shut."

"But—"

"Shut it, Morgan." Gage's warning glare stole the words from her lips as they returned to the Fiorellis and the social worker. "Ms. Crawford, the crux of your argument is that you think Drew needs more supervision, more responsibility."

"I—yes. He needs something to keep him occupied. Obviously that isn't an option while he's residing at this residence, and with summer coming there's no telling what trouble he might get into."

"Then we don't have a problem. As soon as his doctors give their approval, Drew will start his new job as a stock clerk at the J & J Market a few blocks from the Fiorelli house. Part-time, of course, to start with, and then after classes during the school year. He'll be under the direct supervision of the owner, Daniel Juliano, my father."

Nico, Morgan, and Angela all stared at him, but Gage continued as if this revelation was common knowledge. "And just in case you're worried about his weekends, he'll be getting a crash course in home repair and garden maintenance from either Morgan or myself. Plenty to do around the Fiorelli's, and if not there, my father can use some help and my yard has seen better days. I can assure you, from tonight on, Drew will not be wondering what to do with his free time because he won't have any."

Doubt still hovered on Ms. Crawford's face. "You're willing to put yourself, your reputation, your family's reputation on the record as assurance? You could be called to testify on any future hearings regarding the boy's placement. You'd also be subject to interviews and visits to assure compliance."

"As I'm all about rules and regulations, I understand the commitment I'm making," Gage said, but Morgan heard an undertone of annoyance in his voice.

"Inspector Juliano?" A young man in a white coat approached them. His wire-rim glasses and pale complexion made Morgan wonder if he'd just walked out of the frat house and was playing doctor. "I was told you were interested in Drew's initial blood results? I'm afraid I can't release them without his legal—"

"That would be us," Angela jumped in, silently daring Ms. Crawford to state otherwise. "Can you just tell us what his blood alcohol level was?"

The doctor blinked as if he misheard. "Zero. He hadn't been drinking. The trauma of the accident sent his blood sugar sky high, so we need to admit him so we can repair or replace his insulin pump, but other than that, I'd say he's very lucky."

Morgan didn't realize until the balloon of pressure burst in her chest how important that bit of information had been.

"Thanks, Doctor." Gage shook his hand. "Appreciate the information."

Without saying another word, Gage returned his attention to Ms. Crawford, who cleared her throat, made some notes on her tablet computer.

"Given the developments, I suppose I can amend my protest regarding the child's—"

"Drew's," Gage said.

"Drew's placement. But we'll be following up, Inspector. With all of you."

"Great. Give Kevin my best. Tell him he still owes me fifty from the Dodgers game."

"Kevin?" Morgan asked as Ms. Crawford left looking as if a bomb went off in her face.

"Kevin McMahon." Gage grinned. "Her boss at CPS. We went to high school together."

Nico laughed and hugged Angela. "Gage, I don't know if we could have come out of that without your help."

"Do you want to tell Drew he's coming home with us or should we?" Angela asked Morgan.

"Go ahead," Morgan squeaked, her heart so full she couldn't breathe.

The only thing she could think to do was turn into Gage, link her arms around his neck, and hold on to him as if only he could anchor her to the ground.

Feeling his arms around her, letting the heat of him, the strength of him seep into her in ways she hadn't thought possible, made her feel safe yet utterly terrified.

"Just one downside that I can see," Gage said, lifting her off her feet. "Afraid you aren't getting rid of me just yet." He pulled his chin in, dropped a kiss on her forehead.

Morgan attempted a smile, and when she failed, hid her face in his neck. Now what was she going to do?

CHAPTER 11

"Is Drew okay?" Gina asked once Gage and Morgan returned to the Fiorelli house.

"He will be." To Gage it looked as if the energy it took for Morgan to smile drained her power reserves. "Thank you so much for coming over to help Sheila with the kids. How are they?"

"Kelley and Brandon are watching a movie with Mom and Sheila. I stayed with Lydia until she fell asleep. She was telling me about her new protocol. I felt like I was an extra on *House*."

Gage leaned around the corner. Sure enough, Sheila Tremayne and his mother were cozied up on the couch, heads together as Kelley and Brandon laughed along to the closing credits of *A Bug's Life*.

"Lydia is not your typical eight-year-old," Morgan confirmed.

"Brandon invited us to his birthday party. I hope you don't mind."

"Of course not." Morgan dropped a hand on her shoulder, smothered a yawn. "It's going to be quite the celebration. I want to peek in on the kids," Morgan told Gage as she headed into the family room. "Sheila, I owe you."

"Hey," Gina whispered to Gage. Recognizing Gina's conspiracy-inspired urgency, Gage cast a cautious glance in her direction and followed her into the kitchen. "Have you seen this?" She plucked a clipboard off the wall and handed it over to him. "Morgan's insane, right? Thinking she can fix everything that's wrong with this house by herself."

While it was on the tip of Gage's tongue to chastise his sister for snooping, he appreciated the fact that he wasn't the only person who thought Morgan thrived on living on the edge of sanity.

"This list of repairs and upgrades has to be five pages long." He flipped through the paper and a ripe combination of anger and frustration crept over him, batting against his rib cage as he tried to remind himself that this was who Morgan was. Every minute of the day had to be filled, scheduled, or planned for. But damn if she wasn't heading for a crash of epic proportions.

"Seven and a half. Single spaced." Gina glanced behind him as if Morgan walking in on them would spell their doom. "Seriously, Gage, a lot of this is pretty easy to do but it's going to take her forever. These kids need a safe house. There are rooms they've locked because they need work. Morgan needs some relief. She shouldn't have to spend whatever free time or money she has fixing dry rot or the leaking pipes in the basement. Sheila told me she hadn't taken a day off for months before yesterday."

"You got the job with her sister, didn't you?" Gage

looked up to find Gina grinning like a fool. "As long as you heard what Morgan said. It won't be easy."

"We're Julianos. We don't do easy."

From the list Gage was looking at, neither did Tremaynes. Gage returned the list to her. "Take a picture of those and send them to my phone."

"Already did. Check your email."

Gage smirked. Typical. "How long do you think it would take to get that list taken care of if we rallied the troops?"

"If we plan out our strategy, and everyone on the list I'm making comes through, we could knock out at least half of what she wants to do on Saturday, more if we come back on Sunday. Getting people to help won't be the problem."

"What is?"

"Convincing Morgan to let them."

Gage wrapped an arm around Gina's neck and pulled her in for a hard hug. "Kid, you truly are the wisest of us. I'll take care of distracting the dragon at the gate and hereby put Operation Morgan in your hands. We shall commence first thing Saturday morning."

The second he returned to the living room and sat down, Kelley jumped to her feet and propelled herself onto his lap, settling into the crook of his arm as if she'd been born there. He caught Morgan's sleepy smile as she leaned her head on her sister's shoulder. Either she was too tired to be worried about, well, anything, or she was getting used to him being around.

Either worked for him.

"Sheila, I hear you're planning the birthday party of the century," Gage said.

Sheila crossed her ivory pant suited legs and tightened her ponytail. "It's not every day Brandon Monroe turns double digits. We need to celebrate properly."

"We're going to have a bouncy castle that looks like a sheriff's station." Brandon scooted forward, peering at the DVD player. He pushed the button to eject the disk, pushed it again. Then he pushed it again. "Morgan, how—"

"You don't need to know how the DVD player works." Morgan groaned and pushed to her feet.

"That reminds me," Sheila said, angling a look at Brandon. "I think your washing machine is broken."

"I just replaced the hose on Wednesday," Morgan said, casting a look at Brandon, who was paying far too much attention to a snag in the rug. "What's wrong with it?"

"I think you need to see it to believe it." Sheila grinned.

Gage hid a smile behind his hand. The effort it was taking for Sheila not to laugh must have been killing her. She'd turn blue any second.

With a stern look in Brandon's direction, Morgan left the room. By the time she returned, Brandon had gotten to his feet and stood with his hands behind his back as he swung back and forth, pursing his lips over and over. "Brandon?"

"Yes, Morgan?" He turned wide eyes on her.

"Why are there coins in the washing machine?" Morgan asked.

Gage snorted then covered with a cough.

"I wanted to wash my money." He dug his hands into his pockets. "Like on TV. You know, like they talk about on the news?"

"Do you mean laundering money?" Gage asked.

Brandon's face lit up. "Yes." Morgan groaned as Brandon clapped his hands. "I couldn't remember the word, but I knew it had to with cleaning. Did it work?"

"It did not. How much—" Morgan shot a shut-up look to her sister, who couldn't control her laughter any longer, and triggered Gina and even had Theresa joining in. "Exactly how much money did you attempt to wash?"

"All my piggy money." The pride with which he announced this erased the irritation shining in Morgan's eyes. "Seventeen dollars and ninety-six cents."

"Most of it was pennies," Kelley added. "I bet they're shiny now."

"Let's check." Brandon attempted to race past Morgan, who caught him in mid flight and hoisted him into her arms. "I broke it, didn't I?" He flattened his palms against her cheeks, looked into her eyes. "Sorry. I'll help you fix it."

"I'll handle this one, bud. Why don't you head on up to bed." She kissed him and set him down. "But the next repair is coming out of the swear jar money. Bed," Morgan told Kelley. "Now."

"I can take them," Gina offered from where she was perched on the arm of one of the sofas.

"Yes, please." Brandon sprang forward and grabbed Gina's hands. "Come on, Kelley. I bet Gina will read us two stories."

"You're only obligated for one," Morgan called after them as Kelley scrambled off of Gage's lap, snatched up the wand she'd left on the floor, and scooted up the stairs after them.

"God, I love that kid," Sheila said as she wiped tears

from her face. "What other nine-year-old would come up with that?"

"Yeah, it's all fun and games when you don't have to fix his experiments," Morgan muttered, triggering a pang of sympathy in Gage's chest.

"So, I have a new assistant." Sheila aimed a look at Morgan, who acted as if she had no idea what Sheila was talking about.

"I have her resume, if you want to see it," Morgan offered.

"Oh, she had a copy on her phone." Sheila looked at Theresa. "Something tells me my life just got very interesting."

"One's life becomes so once you've met a Juliano," Theresa confirmed. "Speaking of which—"

Gage's phone buzzed against his waist. After having been blessedly silent for most of the day, he'd almost forgotten he had it with him.

"Someday I hope he realizes there's more to life than work." Theresa aimed a look at Morgan.

"Maybe they both will," Sheila agreed.

"We are both in the room with you." Gage would have rolled his eyes but wasn't in the mood to be smacked with a wooden spoon. He didn't want to have to admit to his mother he was coming around to her way of thinking. "Bouncer, what's up?"

"Boss, you near a TV? Channel seven news."

"Turn on channel seven," Gage said softly, scooting to the edge of the couch as Morgan grabbed the remote.

As the picture came into focus, he saw the "Breaking News" chyron skim across the bottom of the screen.

"Nemesis Strikes Socialite's Estate" was in bold yellow against the bright blue banner.

Gage clenched his jaw so tight he was afraid he'd shatter his teeth. Media choppers circled a crime scene that looked like something out of a pumped-up episode of *Dexter*. Squad cars with lights blazing, news crews staked out down the street, uniformed officers milling about and stretching yellow caution tape across the metal gate to prevent anyone else from crossing onto the property.

"What the hell is that?" Gage demanded of Bouncer.

"Forty minutes ago Clarice Bell tweeted she'd been robbed by Nemesis. It's gone viral. She's already had her face in front of three different local news cameras and has her press agent scheduling interviews."

"Call Rojas and Peyton in," Gage told Bouncer and tried to ignore the fact everyone in the room looked transfixed by the story. "Looks like Nemesis just ended our weekend early. Run Bell through that new system you're working with. I want every detail you can pull, so you'd better grab another whiteboard."

"Got it."

Gage squeezed his eyes shut, pinched the bridge of his nose. "I'll head over to the scene right now. I'll see you at the office in a bit."

"Donuts and coffee?" She sounded as hopeful as a five-year-old asking for a new box of crayons.

"Yeah." The front door opened as he hung up. "I need to go to work."

Morgan stood frozen in front of the television, her eyes glazed as if she couldn't believe what she was seeing. "Nemesis? You're sure?" she whispered as she started chewing her thumbnail.

"Looks like." So much for a reprieve from his real life. But the concern in her eyes when she focused cut through the bitterness of having to deal with a new crime scene. "Don't worry, I'll be careful."

Morgan nodded. "I know."

"I'll head out with you." Sheila gave Morgan a hug and trailed behind him. "I can't believe Nemesis would target a media whore like Clarice Bell. Seems beneath him."

"I have no idea what Nemesis would consider beneath him," Gage said. "Mom, I'll call you in a day or so. Oh, hi, Nico. Drew all set for the night?"

Angela and Nico came in looking both worn out and relieved. His mother appeared instantly, as if she'd been waiting to pounce. Gage frowned. He knew that look. He'd seen it on Gina's face a few minutes ago.

"He's good to go," Angela told him. "They were able to repair the pump and his numbers are evening out. Should be able to come home tomorrow."

"Give Drew a day to get used to the idea of his new job, then my dad will be in touch. I'll walk you to your car, Sheila." Once they were on the sidewalk, Gage said, "You have any trouble with Gina, you let me or my mom know. She can be pushy when she wants something."

"You're talking to someone who grew up with Morgan, Gage. I can handle your sister. I might work her to exhaustion, but I'll also make sure she has some fun. Did I see her with Morgan's clipboard of death?"

"We've deemed Saturday Operation Morgan Day."

Sheila arched a brow, her lips curving. "Will we need body armor?"

"Grubby clothes and a paintbrush, I'm thinking. We're taking on the house and Morgan's monstrous to-do list."

"I'll bring a flak jacket just in case." Morgan's sister chuckled. "You're good for her, Gage. I hope she sees that."

She wasn't the only one.

She hit the fob for her Mercedes coup, but hesitated before she climbed in. "You don't think Nemesis is dangerous, do you? He's never hurt anyone."

"Maybe not intentionally." An image of Brady flashed in Gage's mind, but the sting had lessened. The longer he was on the case, the more he understood the pressure his friend had been under. "But I don't think he considered collateral damage. Good night, Sheila."

"Yeah." She got into her car and Gage waited until she drove off before returning to the real world.

And Nemesis.

~

Given the chaos he'd watched on television, Gage didn't even consider parking near the Bell estate. Besides, the three-block hike in the cool evening breeze got his mind off Morgan and on the job.

Clarice Bell. New money. Some would say obnoxious money if the rumor mill could be believed, cash earned by flaunting stupid antics along the west coast with her buffoon-like entourage. An uber-reality star who made the Kardashians look like posh British royalty.

Which was why Gage wasn't the least bit surprised to find Clarice standing in the middle of the street with a rabid-looking Pomeranian tucked under one arm. Fifty pounds of extensions tumbled down her back like compost worms gone wild as she blinked tearfully into the cameras, exalting her "terrifying" tarrying encounter with Nemesis.

God, he was getting sick of this shit.

"Gage." Evan called out to him from the other side of the crime scene tape where he stood with a short, rotund man in his dress uniform.

"Chief Randall." Gage held out his hand, keeping his expression blank as he greeted his former superior.

Randall's face relaxed to the point that Gage let out the breath he'd been holding. While the chief hadn't tried to talk Gage out of taking the inspector position, he hadn't been encouraging on the matter either. "Got your hands full with this one, Inspector."

"Yes, sir."

"Have to admit, I wasn't thrilled with the mayor's order to turn the Nemesis case over to D.A. Marshall here, but I'm glad you'll be the one dealing with the fallout from this."

Gage managed a weak smile, all too familiar with the chief's sense of humor. Chief Randall had at one time been Sergeant Randall and had been the one to assign Brady Malloy as his training officer. "Glad to be of assistance, sir. Okay to head inside?"

"It's your case." The chief turned to address the two uniformed officers by the gate.

"The last thing we need is a media presence at one of these scenes," Gage muttered to Evan as they headed inside. Gage took in Evan's attire. "Nemesis doesn't need the added ego boost. You going incognito tonight?"

"I was out for a jog when I got the call from the chief. This case is starting to piss me off, Gage. Bringing out the crazies."

"Right there with you." Gage nodded to the officer by the door and followed the line of police through the first floor. This much police presence at a burglary scene was a fucking joke, and made Gage's job harder. A last look at the paparazzi had him frowning as he snapped on a pair of latex gloves. "Are we attempting to prove we're on top of the case or are we just playing to the cameras?"

Evan smirked. "That's what happens when the queen of social media posts that she's been targeted by a criminal mastermind. I kid you not, that was one of her tweets."

God save him from Twitterheads, Instatrolls, and Facebook freaks. "You'd think she escaped a serial killer. What was taken?"

"Here's where it gets interesting." Evan led the way down the wide marble hallway toward the double-door study at the far end of the house.

Gage noticed the alarm panel blinking incessantly, as if recharging from being set off. "Alarm sound?"

"For ten minutes straight," Evan confirmed. "Miss Bell states she was in the pool with some friends when it went off."

"She had the alarm on with friends in the house?" Gage circled the room, noting the empty pedestal by the door, the open door to the safe, the crooked paintings and mirrors on the walls, as if Nemesis had ransacked the office in his search for the safe. Gage returned to the pedestal. "Either stupid or paranoid. What goes here?"

"According to Miss Bell, a bronze Degas ballerina statue. She also couldn't wait to inform us that it's insured for a cool two and a half million. She's happy to file a claim, of course, as soon as the police report is filed."

"A report she doesn't plan to retract." Gage skimmed his fingers around the pedestal base.

"Oh, she's pressing charges. Wants to testify in court. Whatever we need her to do, media interviews, lineups for suspects."

"Somebody's been watching too much Nancy Grace." Gage squatted, scanned the floor around the pedestal and desk. "Came in through the French doors?" He went to check, saw the faint shoe imprints in the damp dirt surrounding the rosebushes. One set, heading in the wrong direction.

Gage snapped off his gloves, anger and irritation boiling like an overheated pot of soup. "Where is Miss Bell?"

"Now that she's done with her interviews, she's gathering herself out by the pool," Evan told him.

"Hope she's ready for an extreme close-up." Gage jerked his head toward the computer tech with the video camera. "Let's see what the victim has to say, shall we?"

∽

Gage's temper had reduced to a simmer by the time he stepped off the office elevator with a box of donuts in one hand and a carafe of coffee in the other. The SIM card he'd taken from the evidence tech was jammed into his pocket, but the way his blood was percolating, the damned thing would be incinerated in the next five seconds. He found his team in various states of consciousness around the conference table.

"Oh, hey, boss." Bouncer jerked up in her chair, covered a yawn, and glanced at the clock that said two fifteen a.m. "Just waiting for the new case information—"

"It wasn't Nemesis."

Bouncer blinked as Rojas and Peyton sat up and shifted to stare at him.

"Pathetic cry for publicity." Gage tossed the SIM card onto the table. "Found the missing statue in her idiot boyfriend's car. When you want a good laugh, or to get a good mad on, take a look at the Oscar-worthy performance of one Clarice Bell."

"Tell me you outed her to the press," Bouncer pleaded, extending folded hands across the table. "Please?"

"A news story will run in the morning that the investigation has concluded Nemesis was not the perpetrator of the crime."

"How much did that cost her daddy?" Peyton muttered.

"Don't know, don't want to know. Not our concern. What it does show is that our withholding certain information is working. The media hasn't gotten wind of the thank-you cards Nemesis leaves behind."

"Not that they're getting us anywhere." Rojas sniffed the air. "Crullers? From Doh!Knot?"

Gage set the box down, slid it to the center of the table. "Save me a fritter. So the cards were a bust?"

"It's plain white card stock available at any discount store. Solitary gold embossed *N*, run off of any color laser printer. The one he left on your car matches the others, but they've given us zip." Bouncer nibbled on the edge of a maple bar.

"While Miss Bell is discussing her future with the D.A. and the chief of police—"

"They should make her pay for all the overtime. Did

you hear they called in a damned chopper to spotlight search the area?" Rojas looked as if he'd been sucking on a lime.

"The mayor might have been influenced by her father's demands for justice," Gage said. "It'll work itself out." He didn't give a crap about Clarice Bell except to curse her for wasting so many people's time. "In the meantime, I'm sorry I dragged you all in here—"

"No, no. It's good, actually." Bouncer grinned at him. "I've got an idea I want to run past you."

"Go." Gage took a seat.

"So we've been looking into the backgrounds of all of the victims, right? When I did a search, each of these names popped up all within the last two years as being a headline story in the *Lantano Valley Times*."

Gage shrugged. "They've spent most of their lives in the media spotlight. Any publicity is good publicity, as evidenced by tonight's events."

"Yeah, you'd think, but check this out." Bouncer aimed a laser pointer at the first board on the left. "Grant Alvers, Nemesis victim number one. He was accused of calling in a raid on his own sweatshop to avoid paying the illegal workers he'd hired. The fine he was given was less than the wages he'd have to pay. Victim number two, Emily Goodwin—"

"You mean her husband, Herman," Gage interrupted.

"Aha. That's just it. I don't think so." Bouncer shook her head. "Stay with me. Emily Goodwin was accused of refusing to pay the medical bills of two of her maids after she demanded they use unsafe cleaning products on her custom wood floors. One was diagnosed with lung cancer, the other developed severe asthma. What went missing?

Not the Monet painting her husband spent a small fortune on, not the stack of bearer bonds sitting right inside the safe, but Mrs. Goodwin's antique jewelry collection, including the emerald and diamond necklace rumored to belong to the Romanovs of Russia. The collection she'd bragged about in a local TV news interview a few months before. Then there's Adam Swarthmore's negligence at his factory that left half his workforce with pneumonia. All of these stories were headline news in the *Times*."

Gage leaned forward.

"Here's what I did." Bouncer shifted her focus to her computer, hit a few keys, and a projector popped the image of a chart onto the blank wall at the end of the room. "Every Nemesis victim was featured for unsavory actions against their employees, their stockholders, or someone less fortunate than themselves. Then see here, no more than three days later, they're hit by Nemesis and each theft is tied directly to the personal collection of the owner. Nemesis didn't wipe them out. He was selective, meticulous even. He took what he determined would hurt them the most. I mean, look at the stack of cash left in the Cunninghams' safe. That's a freaking fortune and then there's the fact that by stealing one or two items, they're easier to fence, get them out of the country. And then, as we know, the money from selling them comes back to the people Nemesis's targets let suffer. Those two maids were able to pay off their medical bills with what they said was left in their mailboxes."

"Nemesis was the Greek Goddess of retribution and revenge," he murmured. Jackson had been right, and so had Gage's gut. "Every single one of Nemesis' victims stuck his or her foot in their mouth, very publically."

Bouncer added, her face shining with pride. "Every incident connects to a burglary."

"That doesn't explain why they withdrew their charges," Gage reminded them.

"Yeah, well, I've got a theory on that." Rojas leaned into the conversation. "What if Nemesis didn't steal just one thing? What if he took things he knew the victims wouldn't want to report? What if he got his hands on information about these people, information no one would want getting out."

"Blackmail. Interesting idea." Gage nodded. "Got any proof?"

"Not yet." Peyton got up to refill his coffee. "But there is this. What Jackson Tremayne told you checks out. At least four of Nemesis' victims, including the latest, Cunningham, had the same attorney of record." He pointed at the whiteboard and victim number three. "James Van Keltin."

That couldn't be a coincidence, and even if it was, Gage didn't believe in them. "Shift focus to Van Keltin. I want to know everything about him from the time he was born. But this is great work, guys." He could feel the break coming, just out of reach. "Really great work."

"Wouldn't have gotten this far without Bouncer," Rojas said, and Peyton nodded.

Bouncer smiled. "If all this tracks, Nemesis works backward from what we thought. He finds people who need help and then picks his targets. We've been focusing on the 'victims,' when we should be looking at those receiving the money. We just have to keep an eye on the papers and local newscasts for someone fitting the pattern of the victims and tie them to someone Nemesis would deem worthy of helping. The D.A.'s 'threat'"—Bouncer air quoted threat—"did part of the job, but we need to be scouring every paper, every article since the last robbery to see who might be Nemesis' next target. Now that we know how he thinks, what he looks for, we might just be able to catch him in the act."

And then, finally, Gage thought, he could close this case and move on with his life. A life that would hopefully include Morgan.

CHAPTER 12

"Hi, Dad." Morgan hurried into the private dining room at Beaugere's, grateful for the quiet after the crap week she'd had. "Sorry I'm late."

"Don't be." Jackson greeted her with a warm hug before gesturing to one of the chairs at a table equally suited for bank owners or their employees. The soft seafoam green walls and the delicate embroidered silk fabric draping the etched glass windows that overlooked the small serenity garden outside lightened Morgan's heart. How many birthdays, anniversaries, and graduations had they celebrated here?

"I'm just glad you could make it at the last minute," Jackson said. "Nathan's running behind and Sheila is discussing some catering plans with Chef Catalan."

"Sheila's building a solid client list." Morgan pushed her purse under the table so she couldn't access her phone. She'd taken Sheila's comments about her lack of family attentiveness to heart and amended her schedule to fit her father's last-minute request. Weaning herself off her cell phone during dinner was her next goal. She slumped back, tempted to kick off her shoes and give her overworked feet a break. "If I never have another week like this one, I will be eternally grateful. The fact that tomorrow is Friday is the best news ever." All she had to do was get through tomorrow's meeting with the new accountant for the foundation.

Her weeklong quest of visiting every downtown business asking for donations had added up to a cool thirty thousand, which meant she was still a hundred seventy thousand short. Next week she planned on daylong trips to Santa Barbara and then a couple of Los Angeles suburbs. With more than three weeks to go, she was beginning to feel as if she might pull off a financial coup. Add to that she'd found a steal of a deal on a semi-new washing machine on Craigslist, and she was putting this week in the win column.

Her tired smile faded as she caught the faraway look in her father's eyes. "Dad? Is something wrong?"

He blinked as if coming out of a trance. "You reminded me of your mother just then. The combination of exhilaration and dedication." The sadness didn't hover as long as it used to, but Morgan didn't think it would ever fully fade. Her parents had been married for over thirty years and rarely spent more than a few days apart.

And then, one day, Catherine was gone.

"It's her birthday soon," he said. "The first one since the accident."

"Whatever you want to do that day"—Morgan reached for his hand—"I cleared my calendar."

"Appreciate that. But I'll be okay. Besides, you don't

need to add me to your list of responsibilities. Speaking of which, how are things going with the center?"

Morgan bit her tongue. "Kent and I spent the day revamping the construction schedule. The latest inspection revealed a sewer line wasn't properly hooked into the system, so we're looking at maybe a three-week delay." It could be a month, considering they had to schedule another inspection. Morgan was almost numb to the shock of bad news by now. Then again, given the mountain she still had to scale, what was another ten, fifteen, or a hundred thousand dollars? At least that bank account was holding. For now.

"The subcontractor who did the work is going to cover the cost, I assume?"

Morgan nodded and rubbed her temple, wishing away the headache that had been plaguing her for two days. "For the new work and the supplies, sure, but the delay is going to stretch our budget pretty thin." A budget that could still be bolstered by local fundraisers, but honestly, how many bake sales and car washes could Lantano Valley host? "Sometimes I worry I'm letting Mom down. That I'm failing her." When the confession slipped out, a tiny bubble of tension popped in her chest, as if the small admission was enough to let her breathe again.

"You are not failing her." Jackson squeezed her fingers. "No one could have stepped into her shoes like you have. It's been a relief to me knowing how determined you are, how passionate you feel about the foundation and continuing your mother's work. I couldn't have done it, Morgan. Without you, the foundation would have died with your mother."

Guilt and responsibility bore down on her like an

avalanche. She grasped the cameo her mother had given her, wishing it would trigger inspiration or give her some guidance. Maybe she should tell him the truth. Maybe it was time to admit the truth. Maybe she should ask for help—

"If I can find a way to clone Gina Juliano, I will make a freaking fortune." Sheila swept into the room, pale peach fabric skimming the tops of her knees as she teetered on four-inch Pradas. "Do you know she's already found me three new clients and sent out flyers to seventeen grammar and high schools inviting them to participate in her new fundraising test program? And those clients? She talked them into making a donation to the foundation in exchange for certain "perks" that were already included in my standard contract." She fanned herself with her hand as she took a seat across from Morgan. "She hasn't even worked for us for a week and I'm thinking about giving her a raise."

"This would be Gage's sister?" Jackson poured Sheila a glass of white wine as she sat across from Morgan. "Must run in the family."

"She'd take the foundation global, given half the chance," Morgan said.

"Might be something to that. Speaking of Gage." Jackson tilted the bottle in Morgan's direction, but she shook her head. "Will we be seeing him again anytime soon?"

"I'm sure Morgan will be," Sheila teased.

"We've been playing text tag all week." All day. Every day. Into the night. With both their jobs running them twenty-four/seven, Morgan enjoyed the constant communication, the bantering, the opportunity to vent and have someone listen and then joke her out of her frustration or worry. While Morgan missed seeing him, the physical distance kept her sane. Secrets stayed secrets so much easier when you didn't have to look someone in the eye and lie.

And she had to admit, even though Nemesis' latest reported transgression had proven false, she'd needed reminding of the minefield she was traversing with Gage. Not that she could walk away from him now. Not with the success he and his family had been having bringing Drew along. Whatever magic they'd worked on him at J & J Markets, Morgan hadn't seen him frown in three days. She'd even gotten a smile out of him over breakfast this morning.

When it seemed as if her father and sister were waiting for more information on her social life, she sighed, rolled her eyes. "Hard to mesh schedules."

"Mesh, mesh." Sheila waved an encouraging hand. "Please let me live vicariously through you."

"There's nothing stopping you from finding a Gage of your own," Jackson said.

"Dad, please," Morgan said. "Gage and I aren't serious. It's just—"

"He bitch-slapped that CPS woman," Sheila stated. "And saved Drew from the detention center. Even got him a job, which, according to Gina, is going quite well. And then there's that magic wand Gage bought for Kelley. *He bought a magic wand.*" Sheila tapped her finger against her lips as if to hide a knowing grin. "Trust me. He's serious."

As if she needed reminding of what made Gage special. "Sheila, that doesn't mean—"

"Oh, my God. Do not screw this up." Sheila gaped at her. "That man is crazy about you and you know it. Not to mention the fact that he gets your life, the work, the kids, and he's still interested. Doesn't get much better than that."

The idea of thinking long-term with Gage was akin to rolling a grenade into the room with the pin half-pulled. She wouldn't know when, but when the bomb exploded, the fallout would be devastating. Especially now that he was tied to the kids, to Drew.

"Please let's continue talking about my love life because it's the perfect topic to discuss in front of my *father*."

Jackson picked up his drink, considered the ice cubes. "In case either of you needs reminding, you wouldn't be here if your mother and I hadn't had a love life."

"So not a statement you want to hear before dinner." Nathan stopped inside the door, looking as if second thoughts had stolen his ability to walk. "Bourbon, straight, please," he said to the waiter who followed him in. "Actually, make that a double." He shrugged out of his jacket. "What have I missed?"

"Nothing Morgan wishes to discuss further." Sheila grinned. "And what kept you?"

"I ran into Alcina Oliver on my way in. She's trying to convince Malcolm to come back for her birthday celebration you've been planning for her."

"The Malcolm Oliver you dated while I was away at college?" Morgan glanced at Sheila, who couldn't have looked more uncomfortable if she had just sat on a porcupine. "You two were pretty serious, weren't you?"

"That's him." Nathan said, angling a look at Sheila, who was suddenly overly focused on her menu. But before either Morgan or Nathan could pounce, she shifted her attention to their father.

"So what's with the impromptu dinner, Dad?"

Jackson took a moment and looked at each of them, a calm Morgan hadn't seen in some time settling over him. "Well, I'd planned to broach the subject after we ate, but I guess now is as good a time as any." He took a moment. "I'm thinking about selling the house. In fact, I'd like to."

Whatever air was left in Morgan's lungs evaporated. She looked at Sheila, then Nathan, and figured the same sick feeling had to be squirming its way through their stomachs. "Sell Mom's house?"

"You'd like to," Nathan repeated, leaning his arms on the table, ignoring the drink the waiter set in front of him except to say, "Give us a while, will you, please?"

"Yes, sir." The waiter left and closed the door behind him. The trickling of the fountain in the serenity garden echoed in the room.

"Are you sure, Dad?" Sheila inclined her head, as if she couldn't wrap her mind around the concept.

"Why?" Morgan felt cold, as if every molecule of warmth had been snatched from the room. "Why now?"

Jackson placed a hand on each of his daughter's arms. "I've been giving this some thought for some time. It is, it was, your mother's house. We built it together from the ground up, raised you all in it. Every breath taken inside its walls was because of her. Knowing she'll never walk down those stairs again with me in the morning, not seeing her struggle with the coffeepot or try to figure out the microwave—"

"Or the popcorn machine." Nathan laughed.

"Or the time she turned the oven to self-cleaning on

Thanksgiving and cooked toxic turkey?" Sheila wiped a tear from her cheek.

"It was our home, all of ours," Jackson agreed. "Which makes this a family decision."

Morgan couldn't help but feel as if one of her last anchors had slipped its mooring. Family decision or not, she had the feeling her father had already made up his mind. "I still expect her to walk through the door at any minute."

"One reason I haven't been around as much as I could have been," Nathan admitted. "You're right, Dad. It does hurt to be there."

"I can be home more," Sheila offered. "I can make it a point to be—"

"Sheila, the fact that you moved in after the accident was the greatest gift you could have given me, but I refuse to allow my children to live for anyone other than themselves." He aimed a pointed look at Morgan. "A lesson I hope you're learning. The last thing your mother would want is for you to miss out on the chance to be happy."

"We aren't talking about me. We're talking about you and Mom." Morgan's eyes burned, clouded, but she pulled the tears back. Now wasn't the time to give in.

"Do you know that her closet is exactly the way she left it the morning of the accident?" Jackson squeezed her arm. "Her nightgown is still draped over the dresser. The watch she forgot to put on is in the glass dish beside her jewelry box. The dress she needed to press before dinner has the dry cleaner bag half-off. It's like passing by a portal into the past every time I walk into our bedroom. There isn't a moment I would want to forget, Morgan. But something has to change. I have to live for now. Not for what should have been."

~

"These records are a miracle, thank you, Morgan." When he accepted the USB thumb drive, Elliot Dunbar gave Morgan a look of such relief that she might have smiled if her heart hadn't been slamming against her throat. "Ralph's records are a disaster," Elliot continued. "I can't believe he could function under these conditions."

Ralph's records were a mess because the foundation's accountant had been covering for her.

Guilt settled inside her like a hibernating bear, suffocating the regret over having to turn away a doctor who had called her for help with his terminal patient. It was all Morgan could do not to scream at the timing. Even if she'd had the money to give, with the new accountant watching the foundation's funds so closely, there was no way to get to it without arousing suspicion. She was failing. And falling. With no net in sight.

Morgan could only hope the second set of books she'd handed over to Elliot would buy her the time she needed to come up with the last of the money.

"Glad I could help," Morgan told him with a forced smile.

"I know the independent auditor will appreciate your attention to detail."

Morgan's ears roared as if she'd just dived off Niagara Falls. "I'm sorry. Independent auditor?"

Elliot stopped shuffling papers. "I thought you knew. Sorry, shouldn't have assumed. Before I take on any account I like someone from the outside to take a look and make sure we're heading in free and clear. Nothing to worry about." He continued sorting and stacking. "While I can't see where Ralph kept anything on computer, your records are meticulous. Thank goodness you pay such close attention to detail."

"Ralph was old school." Morgan was amazed she could eke out the words. The books she'd just turned over were more fictional than Dan Brown's latest conspiracy thriller. "So, um, when do you expect the audit to begin?"

"A week on the outside. I'd like to get it taken care of before that balloon payment on the first half of construction is due."

"Right, of course." The clock in her head that had been counting down doubled in speed.

"In fact." Elliot frowned. "I think I have an email in here from Talbot and Sons. I went to grad school with their youngest, and since it's for a charity, he offered to do the audit free of charge." Elliot shoved a stack of files aside and unearthed his keyboard. "Yeah. Let's see, they'll be sending someone over on the twenty-fourth. So, next Wednesday. I can have it moved up if you want."

"No." Morgan forced a laugh to cover the fear-induced urgency in her tone. "No, you're right. Getting it all in order before the big payment is due should be our main concern."

"Well, the check from the fundraiser has cleared, so we should be in good shape for that. I'm familiarizing myself with the bylaws now and we should all be on the same page to move forward." Elliot smiled. "Glad to hear you're okay with me as your new go-to guy. We'll make a good team."

"Great. Thanks." Morgan pushed herself to her feet, grateful that her knees didn't fold under her. The walk to the door and into the hall felt like a mile hike, each step agony. Hugging her arms around her chest, she wandered to the window and stared into the blinding sunlight as she chewed on her thumbnail, the pain a welcome reprieve from her racing thoughts.

Five days to deposit money she didn't have.

"Morgan?"

"Huh?" Morgan blinked sunspots from her eyes as Sheila headed toward her. "Oh, hey." She resumed chewing on her finger.

"I asked if you wanted to come see my new office. How did the meeting with Elliot go?"

"Um. Great. Just fine."

Sheila pulled Morgan's thumb from her mouth. "Stop gnawing on your hand like a starving hyena. Did Elliot say something to upset you? Is there something going on with the foundation?"

"What?" Shocked at the suggestion, Morgan gaped. "No, of course not. What would make you say something like that?" What had she done wrong? Had she slipped the other night, said something that made Sheila think she was failing?

"Then what happened?"

For an instant Sheila's face shifted into their mother's —the same coloring, the same concerned green eyes. The same kind tone Morgan had longed to hear for the past year. In that desperate desire to confide in someone, in the mother she missed so much she ached with it, she blurted out, "Did you ever do something very wrong for the right reason?"

Sheila's hand tightened around hers. "Tell me what's going on, Morgan. What did you do?"

Morgan swallowed, considering, debating. She almost crossed over and trusted, but she couldn't take the chance. Anyone she told at this point could be held as responsible as she was, and she wasn't about to put anyone else at risk. "It's nothing. I'll figure it out," Morgan said softly. "I'll, um, I'll call you." She tugged her hand free, headed toward the elevator. Five days. A hundred twenty hours.

"Morgan?" Sheila called before hurrying to catch up with her. "If you can't talk to me about it, there is someone who will listen."

Morgan's heart clenched. She'd been playing with fire getting closer to him, and now look. She was about to be incinerated. Was there any way to extricate herself from this mess without Gage finding out what she'd done? "Gage can't help me."

"At least give him the chance," Sheila pleaded as the elevator doors opened. "Do not turn away because you're scared of what could be. He's good for you. You and I both know how fast people we love can be taken away."

CHAPTER 13

Record heat and an overstressed air conditioner were not the welcome home Morgan hoped for Friday afternoon. While the swamp cooler in her apartment gave a coy rumble of protest before kicking into agreement, the ancient central air system in the main house copped an attitude the second the mercury hit ninety and turned the house into a sauna. By the time Morgan located and wrapped the exposed wire in electrical tape, she'd had enough.

Not even the exuberant squeals and laughter from the backyard as the kids ran through an obstacle course of sprinklers, fired-up mega water guns, and an endless barrage of water balloons were enough to drag her out of her self-imposed hobbit hole of depression.

It was all Morgan could do not to scream and cry and beat her fists against the wall to bend the world to her will. She was starting to suffocate, everything piling up on her, boulder after boulder landing on her chest. The center, the money, Nemesis, Gage, her father selling the house, the endless repairs, Lydia. The doctor and patient she'd had to turn away.

The desire to hear Gage's voice was overwhelming, to be reminded that even though he was unaware of what she'd done, what she was hiding from him, he was there for her. So she'd taken Sheila's advice and called Gage.

She'd hung up before the call connected.

An hour later she'd dialed again, let it ring once before changing her mind again, and turned her phone to vibrate.

She tapped the small stack of insert cards that had been included with Nemesis' "gifts." Where they'd once brought her immense relief and bolstered her belief that all would be okay, now the cards mocked her and screamed failure in their vapid whiteness.

It was too late, they seemed to say.

The incessant vibrating of her silenced cell phone provided background music as she clicked through spreadsheet after spreadsheet, searching out extra dollars, any mistakes that might suddenly fix the foundation's financial woes. Another read-through of the foundation bylaws proved what she already knew: the operating and property fund accounts could not intermingle. There was no wording that led her to believe there was a legal "out" if and when her financial finagling came to light during the audit.

"Lawyers and computers don't make mistakes." Morgan hit the stuttering mouse to get its attention when it stopped moving on the screen. "You do though. Mistake." Click. "Mistake." Click. "Mistake."

The only thing her fruitless search produced was a carpet of scattered files and confirmation that she was out of time.

She'd even gone so far as to check mortgage rates against the house. Surely with her family's sterling reputation she could get one; she might even consider asking her father to co-sign. And that might have been the solution. If she still had a few weeks. But no bank, not even the one her father sat on the board of, was going to get her the amount of money she needed in five— Morgan glanced at the clock. Shit. The banks were closed for the weekend. Three days.

Morgan slammed back in her chair, disgusted that she'd even considered sacrificing the Fiorellis' and the kids' stability because of her rash decisions. The deposit she'd make next week wouldn't be all she needed, but it was something. She lowered her head into her hands, trying to uncover the bright side. Explaining a hundred-and-seventy-thousand-dollar discrepancy was a little easier than two hundred thousand. Wasn't it?

Thank God Nico and Angela were taking the kids to the spring concert in the park tonight. They wouldn't have to witness the massive self-pity party she was throwing for herself.

"Enough." Morgan pushed herself out of the creaky office chair and straightened up, stacked the files, and tapped the cards into a neat pile under her monitor. If only everything in her life could be put in order so easily.

Morgan grasped the cameo around her neck, dragged it along its silver chain. Her mother wouldn't have given up. No, her mother would have kept fighting, kept looking for another way, any way, before surrendering. There had to be something.

She heard the back gate bang open, more excited laughter

pealing through the air as new voices joined the throng, but she didn't take the time to look out the window. Instead, she went into her bedroom and sat on the edge of the mattress. She stared at the photos of her family surrounding the black lacquer jewelry box her grandmother had left her, resisting the overwhelming urge to wrap herself cocoon-like in the down comforter and bury herself in the mattress for the next week.

"Oh, Granny," Morgan whispered as her gaze drifted over the photo of herself, Sheila, and their grandmother, Siobhan O'Donnal Tremayne, under the massive oak tree in the front yard. Between the Irish fire of her father's mother and the strong will of her mother, Morgan had received a double dose of genetic stubbornness when it came to doing what was right. Both women had always done what was necessary to take care of the family.

The stories Granny told of meeting and falling in love with Morgan's grandfather were family legend. Tales of skirting the law during Prohibition, the excitement of defying the rules despite the possible ramifications should they ever be caught, had never grown old—or been forgotten. Morgan embraced the irony that she was carrying on an unusual family tradition. She wished she could learn to live without regrets like Granny had.

Granny had risked going to prison to put food on her family's table and had ended up providing them with everything they'd ever need. Even now that Granny was gone she'd left Morgan this house along with a gorgeous jewelry box filled with her treasures.

Morgan's depression-logged mind cleared as if a fifty-mile-an-hour wind blew the thunderclouds away.

Morgan bit her lip, stood up, and lifted the latch on the

box, exposing the treasure trove of antique jewelry. Oh, but she couldn't. Could she?

That late fall afternoon when Granny had sat both her and Sheila down and let them alternately choose their favorite pieces from her extensive collection was as vivid a memory as a Technicolor film. As was the reading of Siobhan's will four years later when the lawyer presented them with her bequests.

Lifting the box as if it would disintegrate at the slightest touch, Morgan carried her grandmother's jewels to the small table outside the kitchen. One by one, the jeweled brooches, the delicate necklaces, and the too-small bracelets were brought into the light. A rainbow of gemstones and tarnished silver glinted and littered the table.

Morgan looked down at them, sadness creeping over her like ivy around a trellis. Granny was a practical woman. Hell, she'd worked in a speakeasy in the twenties and, rumor had it, had done far more scandalous things than Morgan could ever conceive of. Morgan ran her finger along the edge of the antique diamond engagement ring she'd hoped to wear one day. The thought of parting with it, with any of it, made her belly churn like a whirlpool in the middle of the ocean.

Granny would understand.

Morgan looked up at the ceiling. "Tell me what to do, Mom. Granny. Please, before it's too late."

A water balloon exploded against the front door. Smack!

Morgan jumped. Another smack, this one followed by a peal of laughter that echoed throughout her apartment. Morgan returned the ring to its velvet housing.

The second she pulled open the door, a balloon hit dead center of her chest. Water cascaded down her tank top, soaked her cutoffs, splashed against her bare feet and floor.

"Uh-oh."

The back yard went silent, as if all sound had been sucked into a vacuum.

Morgan swiped a hand over her dripping face and down her neck as she scanned the lineup of suspects. Kelley and Brandon in drenched shorts and tank tops; Drew carrying a loaded water gun over his shoulder like a soldier of fortune and earning appreciative glances from Liza Juliano, who, still in her school uniform, guided Lydia as she waded in the thigh-high kiddie pool.

Lydia was walking. On her own.

Tears clouded her eyes before her gaze landed on Gage, who was frozen in mid-launch with another water balloon in his hand.

"Um. Wanna come out and play?" he asked.

Every minute she'd fought, every second she'd wanted to scream, every tear she'd wanted to shed walloped her like a sledgehammer.

But it was the sight of Gage standing there surrounded by her kids, dripping wet in slacks and a tailored button-down shirt as if he'd come straight from work, that brought the sob up from her toes.

She covered her mouth, but it was too late. Another sob built against the pressure in her chest.

He launched the balloon over his head. "Liza's turn." Morgan heard Gage's sister squeal even as she laughed.

And then he was there, in front of her, his hands cupping her elbows, drawing her against him. Morgan burrowed into his chest, grabbing onto him, absorbing the feel of him, the presence of him, into her as if he were the only thing in her world.

"Bad day?" he asked, pressing his hand against the back of her head. She nodded. "Really bad?" She nodded again. "Is that why you called me?"

She wanted to deny it, didn't want to give in to the weakness of wanting, of needing him. But she took a deep breath, took a chance.

She nodded.

Gage leaned away, stooped down so they were eye to eye. "Thank you." He kissed her hard on the mouth, triggering another sob which made him frown. "Not the reaction I was hoping for. Gotta fix that." The next sob came out as a laugh as he bent down and dumped her over his shoulder, shaking her depression loose.

"Gage." She slapped at his back and kicked her feet as his arm locked around her knees. She choked on the tears, on the laugh. "Put me down! I'm too heavy."

"Make way!" Gage bellowed at the kids. Morgan stretched to one side and, saw Liza pluck Lydia out of the pool and heft her onto her hip. "Take a deep breath," he shouted over her shoulder before he tumbled them both into the water. "Duck and cover."

She came up sputtering just as the kids unleashed their arsenal of water weapons.

∼

The Tumbleweed version of the Battle of Waterloo lasted until Angela called a halt to the war and ushered the kids inside to get changed. Halfhearted protests followed them, but not before Kelley tossed the last water balloon in the air and giggled when it landed on Gage's drenched shoes.

Gage made to catch her, but she shrieked and dashed out of reach.

Morgan lay in a heap on the grass, her shorts and tank soaked, her hair dripping, laughing so hard her sides burned. She knew she must look a fright, but any feminine insecurities threatening to take hold vanished under the heat of Gage's heart-searing gaze.

He turned off the hose before heading over to her. "Now that's the way to start a weekend." He tugged her up, covering her mouth with his so completely that any hesitation, any doubt she had when it came to her heart, vanished.

"You really have a knack with that," she murmured against his lips, the guilt and doubt she had about whatever time she spent with Gage going silent under his touch.

The patio door banged open. "Sorry. Ignore me," Liza called, holding up her hand as if to shield her face and make herself invisible. "I'm not here. Go about whatever it is you're doing. See you tomorrow."

Morgan dropped her forehead onto Gage's chest, wrapped her arms around , and held on. A sliver of her heart was petrified that if she let go, he'd see the truth, uncover the lies, and walk away.

What would she do when he walked away?

Morgan squeezed her eyes shut, locking that part of her heart in the darkness until she was forced to open it. Live for the moment.

Love for the moment.

A soft breeze wafted across them, cool against her damp clothes, the whisper on the wind calling in her mother's calming, strong voice, as if finally giving Morgan the answer she'd been waiting for.

Lead with your heart and you'll never have regrets.

Morgan looked up at Gage, the words frozen behind her parted lips, but she knew.

Angela banged on the kitchen window, held up a towel, waved them inside.

"We're being summoned." She took his hand and led him inside and took the towel Angela offered, not sure what good it was going to do. She handed it off to Gage, who looked just as flummoxed. He left his sopping shoes in the washroom as Angela finished packing up the family picnic basket.

"Where did this come from?" Morgan approached a second smaller basket on the counter, only to have Angela slap her hand away.

"That's a surprise. Leave it."

"Yes, ma'am." Instead, Morgan plucked a Greek yogurt ice pop from the tray Angela pulled out of the freezer and tried not to look at Gage as he joined her by the sink. He trailed his fingers down her arm. She shivered.

"Angela? Morgan? You home?" Nico bellowed.

"He knows we're leaving in a little while. Where else would I be?" Angela shook her head. "Crazy man. In here!" She glanced up from packing a container of fried chicken. "Well?"

Morgan slurped the pop, frowned. "Well what?"

"It's a go." Nico's face could have put the Rockefeller Christmas tree to shame. "We just signed a contract to supply J & J Markets with fresh-baked bread, muffins, and pastries. Three deliveries a week, with an option for more depending on sales." He picked Angela up and spun her around the kitchen. Morgan looked up at Gage as he draped an arm over her shoulders.

"And if all goes well," Nico continued, "in three months Angela says they'll consider expanding the main store downtown into the next building so they can include an in-house bakery. *Our* in-house bakery, exclusive to J & J."

"I knew Mom was up to something the other night," Gage said. "That bread you sent with Morgan for Stephen's birthday did the trick. Mom couldn't stop raving about it."

"Nutmeg, I tell you." Nico came over and shook Gage's hand. "Miracle ingredient. I've always said."

"I'm so happy for you." Morgan wrapped her arms around him as well as she could and gave him a squeeze. "You'll be doing what you love and it won't even seem like work."

"Better yet," Angela said as she finished with the basket. "Now we'll have extra money so you can stop hiding bills from us."

Morgan swallowed wrong and choked. "I don't know what—"

"Did you think we didn't notice when the medication bills started disappearing?" Nico asked in a serious tone. "Or the electricity bill?"

"The water bill? The phone bill?" Angela continued.

"Cable, Internet," Nico said.

"Okay." Morgan held up her hands. "Okay, I get it. I'm not as sneaky as I thought. I just didn't want you to have to worry about—"

"What everyone else has to worry about?" Gage earned

nods of agreement from Nico and Angela. Morgan started to sputter.

"You can't take on everyone else's problems." Nico headed into the washroom and pulled down the stack of picnic blankets. "We went into this fosterage together. We will handle it together. Stop protecting us. We'll make it through. So we will need to sit down and put together a new household budget and payment schedule. Understand?"

"Understood," Morgan said. Was this what it felt like when responsibilities dropped away? As if she'd lost fifty pounds in fifty seconds?

"Excellent. Enjoy your night. We'll be back late. Kids!" Angela called. "Move it. Van's leaving in ten."

Morgan dropped what was left of her ice pop in the sink and followed them to the door. Kelley wore her Princess Ariel mermaid costume that had ripped enough up the back so she could walk. With her magic wand in hand, she waved at Gage as she dashed outside, followed by Brandon. But it was seeing Drew walk behind a determined Lydia that etched permanently in Morgan's mind.

"No wheelchair tonight," Lydia announced as she took the steps one at a time. Twice Morgan saw Drew's hands shoot out when she wobbled, and once they reached the landing, he bent down so she could climb on his back. Morgan saw Drew try not to look at her, but a glimmer of humor shone in his semi-obscured eyes. "Whatever," he mumbled as they passed.

"Drew's going to be okay," Nico told her as they followed. "Good night, you two."

"Oh, wait. The other basket." Morgan moved to retrieve it from the kitchen.

"That's ours." Gage caught her arm. "Good night." He shut the door behind Angela and Nico. At Morgan's confused look, he rolled his eyes. "I called my mother, asked her to send dinner over for us, and Liza delivered." He pulled her closer, dipped his head down, and brushed his lips against hers. "Thank you for calling me."

"I didn't really." But she loved the thank-you.

"One ring was enough." Another kiss, this one deeper, longer. She sighed as his hands moved down her arms, cupped her hips. His mouth moved on hers, erasing the hours of self-pity and doubt, of reminding her that she could have, even for a little while, some happiness. Something just for her.

"Will the basket keep?" she murmured against his lips, wanting more, more than she knew she should take.

"I'm sure that's how she planned it."

Morgan smiled, then turned and dragged him out the back door and picked up the basket on the way to her apartment.

The second she closed the door, she pushed him against it and curved her arms around his neck, stretching herself up to bring his mouth to hers. She broke away long enough to slide her hands underneath his shirt to feel the taut, smooth skin she'd dreamed about. Frustration coiled as she worked the buttons free and shoved the fabric apart to flatten her palms against his chest. She trailed her fingers over shapely abs, skimmed the waistband of his slacks. She heard his sharp inhale as she dipped under. She smiled.

She had imagined this happening. A lot. She'd suspected he had a beautiful physique, but her imagination hadn't come close. The solid form of his body against hers, the heat of him radiating like the sun, warming her water-cooled skin through the layers of fabric separating them.

He was toned, and tanned, and the slight dusting of dark hair made her fingers itch to touch him, to explore, to tease.

She took a deep breath and her head went light at the intoxicating scent of him, as if he'd taken a long walk in the redwoods. "I do have one question to ask."

Gage lowered his head and nibbled the side of her neck. Her brain fogged over as heat suffused her entire body.

"Ask whatever you want," he murmured. He licked the lobe of her ear, took it between his teeth. He nipped gently as she shuddered. "I doubt I'll say no."

Morgan brushed her lips against his, pulled away when he tried to deepen the kiss. "Tell me you came prepared."

Gage kissed her, the smile on his mouth contagious, and they laughed. "I was a Boy Scout. Take a wild guess."

"I've never been so grateful for the Scouts." She slithered against him.

His entire body went rigid as he caught her face in his palms and gazed down at her in the dim light of the entryway. "Are you sure?"

No matter what waited for them down the road, Morgan didn't want to live the rest of her life without having made love to him. "I'm sure. I'm taking your advice and asking for help, Gage." She trailed her lips across his cheek, rubbed her skin against the roughness of his. Who knew stubble could be sexy? Erotic? Arousing.

"Help with what?" His hands were already roaming, slipping under her shirt and over her back.

She shivered and grinned. "There are some things a girl shouldn't have to do on her own."

He kissed her, long and deep, and when he lifted his mouth, he whispered, "I think that's about the sexiest thing I've ever heard." He bent down and scooped her up in his arms, setting her heart to soar. "Bedroom that way?"

"Mmmm." Thank goodness she'd made the bed this morning. She pressed her lips against his throat, kissed him, nipped him. Licked him.

He'd barely set her on the bed when she reached for the zipper on his pants, only to have him catch her hands in his and pull them away.

He brought her hands to his mouth, kissed her fingers as he smiled. "Let's start someplace else," he murmured, and walked over to close the shutters and turn on the bedside lamp.

Morgan's courage faltered with the spotlight. She crossed her arms over her chest and looked anywhere but at him as he returned to her and slid his hands down her arms.

"Morgan, look at me," he ordered, as if he could read her thoughts.

She cringed, lifted her chin, but not her gaze. He bent down in front of her and caught her chin between his thumb and forefinger.

"You are beautiful. Inside and out. I thought so the minute I first saw those sexy legs of yours come out of that Mustang. I've dreamt of nothing else but those legs around me, holding me to you, keeping me inside you." He pressed his lips against hers until she melted against him and her arms went lax.

He moved slower this time, taking the hem of her wet

shirt in his hands and, inch by inch, drawing the fabric up over her ribs, above her breasts. She inhaled him and lifted her arms.

Gage tossed the shirt away and, taking both her wrists in one hand, stretched her out on the bed and settled himself beside her.

He kissed her again and Morgan felt her heart clench at the tenderness of it. He coaxed her lips apart with his tongue, as if asking her permission to delve deeper. She stretched up against him, desperate to feel his naked flesh against hers. She twisted and turned to get to him, only to have him hold her firm as he wedged a fabric-clad leg between hers.

She gasped, tearing her mouth free, and he trailed hot, moist kisses down her throat. He released her hands and skimmed the valley between her breasts before sliding his hands down the sides of her body and then up again to cup her breasts in his palms through the plain white bra. She groaned as her nipples hardened and strained against the cotton. He glided his fingers around her rib cage and released the clasp. Drawing the straps down her arms, he tossed the fabric away and brought her right breast up to his lips.

He kissed her there, drawing the peak into his mouth and laving her with his tongue. She whimpered, tightened her legs around him as the heat built between her still-clad thighs. Morgan dove her hands into his hair and held him against her, not wanting him to stop, wanting nothing more than to feel him hot and heavy inside of her.

Only he could ease the ache that grew deep in her belly. Never in her life had she felt this much, needed this much from another human being. She felt so wanted, so desired, as Gage shifted to treat her other breast to the same erotic care.

She raked her nails up his back and around his shoulders as he lowered himself on top of her. Finally, the weight of him descended and the sensation of crisp, curly hair scraping her bare skin sent her reeling.

"Gage," she gasped, and cupped his face to drag him to her mouth. She kissed him hungrily, drawing his tongue into her mouth as if she couldn't get enough. Because she couldn't. She didn't want this to end. She never wanted to be without him.

He shifted and she raised her leg then hooked it around his hip as she pressed up and against him. He was so hard, so ready for her, that she felt her feminine power ignite. She planted her hands on his shoulders and shoved him onto his back.

Before he could react, she climbed on top of him and straddled his hips. She stared down at him, her long, damp hair draping them like a screen. He stared up at her for a long moment, as if he wanted to say something, needed to, but she kissed him gently, shook her head.

"Not now," she whispered. "I don't want to talk." She rubbed herself against him, feeling the pressure begin to grow once again. He dropped his hands to her hips, his fingers sliding under the band of her shorts, flipping open the button, drawing down the zipper until he slipped his hand around and found her, hot and wet. Morgan groaned. His. She bit her lip as she lifted herself on his hand. She was all his.

She arched against him as his fingers probed her depths, circling and teasing, in and out, as her hips fell into rhythm with his touch.

"Gage," she gasped as she felt herself cresting. "Gage, stop." But she didn't want him to.

"No talking," he ordered, increasing his pace. She cried out as she rode toward the peak. "That's it," he urged. "Let go, Morgan."

Her body rocked as the orgasm ripped through her. She felt herself clench his fingers, holding him inside of her as her body exploded into a million stars.

She collapsed on top of him, unable to catch her breath before he rolled her under him and drew the last of her clothing from her body.

"Gage," she murmured as he kissed her again. She tangled her fingers in his hair, loving the silky softness, how it grazed over her hand like the finest silk.

"Oh, baby," he breathed into her mouth, "we're just getting started."

He withdrew from her grasp and reached into his back pocket before he rid himself of his pants.

She looked at him, standing there in his naked glory, and felt a wave of pride wash over her that this man wanted her. This amazing, wonderful man thought she was worthy of him. The fierce love she felt for Gage washed over her, and she let go and let herself be dragged under.

He returned to the bed, stared down at her as she lay completely exposed and satiated. She smiled up at him as he tore open the foil packet.

"Thanks to those legs of yours, I bought these weeks ago."

She lifted her foot and trailed her toes down his arm. "These?" she teased. "You mean it has friends?"

He let out a growl that had her laughing as he covered himself and settled on top of her once again. His hands gripped her hips as he lowered his head, kissed her belly, her navel, brushed his chin against the mass of curls between her thighs.

Morgan arched off the bed as he dipped his fingers into her heat and tested her, probing gently. Just when she thought she'd go mad from waiting, she felt the strength of him pressing against her, sliding torturously into her. She inhaled sharply, forced herself to relax against the desired invasion.

He withdrew slightly, cupped her hips once again in his hands, and then pushed in again, only to slip himself nearly free. Again, and again, until she couldn't take any more.

Morgan wrapped her legs up and around his hips and pulled him down and into her. She cried out as he filled her, heard him hiss as he struggled to keep control. She clenched her thighs around him, felt him pulse inside of her. She bit her lip to stop the groan. This was heaven. Tears burned her eyes, leaked out of the corners, as she took the few seconds to burn him into her memory.

He felt so right, so perfect, and she wrapped her arms around his neck and exposed her throat to his mouth.

Gage sank his teeth into the sensitive spot on her neck as he moved inside of her. She could feel every inch of him stretching and filling her over and over as the muscles in his back strained. She wanted him faster, harder, and thrust her hips up to meet his, driving him even deeper into her.

They groaned together as his hands searched for hers, his fingers tangling with hers and dragging her arms above her head. She stretched her torso as he increased his thrusts. She felt him expanding inside of her, knew he was on the edge, and she clenched herself around him as she felt herself going over with him.

He fused his mouth to hers as he spilled into her, triggering her second orgasm of the night. Wrapped around him, she rode the slow descent in his arms, listening to his ragged breathing as he rolled over and drew her with him.

This was so perfect. She didn't want to forget this moment, how she felt, how he felt. But already it was slipping away.

"Everything's okay, Morgan." He murmured the words as they drifted into sleep.

She shimmied up his body and pressed her lips to his, keeping her eyes on his as their tongues swept over each other in renewed passion. Then she was under him once more, felt him hardening inside of her again.

She caught his face in her hands and brought him as close as two people could be. Staring into his eyes, feeling his soul brush against hers, any words she might have uttered lodged in her throat. Would she remember what her life had been like before him? Once he learned the truth, once he learned what she'd done and walked away, would she ever be whole without him? "Everything's perfect." She stroked her thumbs across his lips.

For now.

CHAPTER 14

Gage drew lazy circles on Morgan's bare arm. He'd thought the dragging week had been the result of the glacial-moving case. He was wrong.

The anticipation of seeing Morgan had slowed time. Today, this weekend, this moment, couldn't arrive fast enough.

The days and nights of texting were as satisfying as being offered a wheatgrass shot after touring a chocolate factory. When had she become the first thing he thought of in the morning? When was the last time he'd gone more than two hours without checking in at work? Hell, he hadn't even called Bouncer back about the list she'd received from Kolfax's office.

But the list had ceased to matter when Morgan needed him.

All these years he thought that when, or if, he fell for a woman, he'd feel stifled. Trapped. Instead, falling in love with Morgan had set him free. Which was why when she'd called—in the loosest sense of the word—he'd had no qualms about leaving work behind.

Somehow the last two years, the FBI clusterfuck, his recovery, his doubts about his job—none of it mattered except that each event led him to exactly where he needed to be: beside Morgan.

This room, the entire apartment, what he'd seen of it, was so extraordinarily her. The soft yellow walls and winter white plantation shutters. The discount store dresser displayed elegant silver frames with photos of her family: her mother and a little blond-haired boy Gage assumed was Colin. Morgan and Sheila in mid-air jump at Morgan's college graduation. Nathan and Jackson hoisting a beer at a local pub. Kelley and Lydia dressed up for Halloween—although with Kelley, it could have been any day. An unframed picture of Drew and Brandon sat propped against the wall as if awaiting its appropriate housing. Nothing in excess, nothing to distract from her simple, straightforward way of living. Typical, practical Morgan.

"Tell me about your day," he urged.

Her hand stilled from where she'd traced the scar on his chest, as if his words chilled her warm body. He drew the sheet up and around her, kissed the top of her head, brushed his fingers against the cameo medallion around her neck. "What's wrong?"

She snuggled her head into his shoulder, draped a leg between his, and he shifted, wincing as she almost triggered round three. "I—" She tensed, as if the words got stuck, but he stroked his fingers down her spine, felt the tension melt under his touch. "I had to tell a doctor we couldn't help his patient. Five-year-old boy, stage three lymphoma. He's not responding to traditional treatments and insurance won't cover experimental. With the construction delays, the bills that are due—I don't have the money to give them."

She tried to sit up, and he felt her pulling away from him, retreating into the solitary shell he'd been certain he'd never crack. He held on, wrapped his other arm around her and drew her higher against him, refusing to let her turn away from him. Refusing to let her shut him out.

"I had to say no," she whispered as she surrendered, despite the spine of steel he was convinced she possessed. "And that baby boy isn't going to make it." Hot tears dropped onto his chest, the anguish behind them sinking into his skin, into his heart, like molten lava.

"I'm so sorry." He cradled her head against his chest, wished he could take this from her, offer a solution, but all he could offer was himself. "You're only one person, Morgan. It's not your fault."

Her silence echoed louder than any argument she might have made.

Gage scooted up against the iron headboard. "You told Gina the other day that they can't all be saved, that some will die. Why doesn't that same warning apply to you?" He grasped her chin, forced her to look up at him, and the grief in her eyes sliced through him like sharpened obsidian. "You're doing everything you can. No one expects you to do more."

"I expect it." She pounded a closed fist over his heart. "I promised her. I promised them."

"Who? Your mother? Your brother?" He wished he could shake some sense into her. "I'm sorry, but they're gone. It's tragic, and yes, it hurts, but you cannot go through life living up to expectations they never set. There has to come a time when you say *enough*."

A spark of irritation flashed in her eyes like a flint stone in the dark. "If I don't do this, who will? If I don't fight for them, who will?"

Suddenly, everything about Morgan made sense. "Is that what this cause of yours is about? Are you afraid no one will step up to help if you ask?"

"If I don't ask, I can't be disappointed, can I?"

"Oh, baby." He kissed the frown from her lips. "You don't give people enough credit." He tucked her head under his chin and held on. It took a few moments, long moments, before she sank into him again. "You aren't the only person in the world who wants to make people's lives better. Give them—give us—a chance. You're right. If you don't ask, they can't disappoint you. But imagine if they say yes. Imagine what you can do then."

∽

Gage's cell phone buzzed from somewhere in the bedroom, dragging him out of the deepest sleep he'd had in weeks. Sunlight streamed through the skylight in the narrow hallway. He picked up the watch he'd set on the nightstand sometime after midnight.

A slow smile spread across his mouth as he looked over to find Morgan sprawled face-first on the mattress, her hair curling around her shoulders and down her back, tempting him to trail his fingers along the curve of her spine, over those amazing, full hips and those legs. Gage closed his eyes, clenched his fist. They—and she—had lived up to his every expectation.

She'd only been asleep for a few hours, after he'd taken his fill of her—and she of him. But given the day that lay ahead, he needed a boost other than the drug that was Morgan.

Gage extricated himself from the tangle of sheets, then retrieved his still-damp pants and cell phone before draping the sheet over her. She mumbled something and pushed deeper into the mattress in much the same way she'd pressed into him last night. His body stirred, but he went into the surprisingly spacious bathroom, washed up, and then headed into the galley-style kitchen where he programmed a cup of coffee before heading out to his car for the bag he kept in the trunk.

The aroma of fresh-brewed coffee welcomed him back, and steam rose from the extra-large mug he'd found in one of the cabinets. He drank, exhaled, sighed. He sat at her desk, clicked on his phone, and saw the text message from his sister. Running right on schedule, apparently. He needed to keep Morgan distracted until at least eight. Gage grinned. Shouldn't be a problem.

He turned in the chair, knocking over a stack of file folders. He bent to pick them up, placing them beside a small pile of gift cards, before he scanned the scribbled list she'd made of chores to do today. He folded it, popped it into the top drawer, and caught an ancient-looking troll doll with bright pink hair staring at him from the top of her computer screen. He flicked a finger against the featherlight hair.

"Nice to know there's something amusing this early in the morning."

Gage glanced up and found Morgan leaning against the doorway, the cerulean blue bed sheet wrapped around her,

her hair mussed, her face flushed in a way that made his ego spike considerably. "Good morning."

"Mmm." She nodded sleepily. "It sure is." She approached him with a hungry look in her eye and he opened his arms, only to have her pilfer his coffee. She drank deeply, the same look of ecstasy flashing over her face that he'd become acquainted with last night. His ego slipped a notch.

She sighed and, still holding the mug, settled on his lap. "Now you." She kissed him. Definitely something he could get used to.

Gage brought a hand up to the back of her head, held her there until he felt her move, and opened one eye to find her struggling to keep hold of the mug. "I think I'm offended," he murmured against her lips. "I should have enough power to wake you up."

"You have the power to keep me awake," she corrected. "Busy day today. Have lots to do on the house."

Feigning innocence, stroked a finger down her cheek. "I'm sure you have time."

"Never enough time. Where's that list?" She frowned, scanned the desktop. "Could have sworn I left it here somewhere." She stood up, mumbling to herself as she took his coffee into the bedroom. Gage tried not to laugh as she fought against the sheet tangling around her legs. Sexier than the damn dress she'd worn the night they'd met.

Gage programmed another cup of coffee before following her into the bedroom. That list she was looking for wouldn't do her much good anyway since Gina's updated one would supersede it. But right now he had work to do. He sipped his coffee until he heard the shower running. Setting his mug down next to hers, he turned the knob and opened the bathroom door, noticing with some trepidation that steam billowed from the top of the shower. The woman must like to cook herself.

"Yep. Really, really tough job." He stripped off his pants and popped open the door to the stone cubicle.

"Gage." Morgan whipped around, almost slipping as she tried to cover herself. He stepped inside, closed the door, and smiled down at her. "What do you think you're—"

He caught the rest of her question in his mouth, swallowing her words as he enveloped her in his arms. His senses sang. The lavender-scented soap she used caused her to slide against him in the most erotic way. Her arms came up and around, slipping over his arms, her fingers clenching and releasing against his shoulders. Her body went lax, her left ankle coming around to hook behind his calf as she groaned into him.

He left her mouth and trailed his lips down her neck as the last ounce of resistance melted out of her.

"Told you I'm better than coffee," he murmured. Gage turned the hot water down. "We don't want to drain the heater, now, do we?"

"I don't have time—"

He kissed her again, pushed her against the wall, and began the process once more, using his mouth and hands to coax all thoughts of work from her mind. He took his time, tasting her, touching every inch of her, until she trembled in his arms. She gasped, turning her head away for a long moment before coming back to him, pulling him against her with a strength that surprised and invigorated him.

"Want more?" he asked, then took her bottom lip between his teeth, pressed gently, and used his tongue to soothe the sting.

She narrowed her eyes before dragging his mouth down to hers. He knew what she wanted before she hitched her leg up around his waist. He slid his hands down to the backs of her thighs and brought her other leg up and slid inside of her.

She let out a moan that made his heart soar. She arched her back, closed her eyes, and drew in shallow breaths. The water pounded over her and he swelled with male pride.

"Hold on to me," he ordered as he pressed her against the wall and slid his hands up to her waist. Her arms came down and around his neck and her breasts flattened against his chest as he pushed into her, her heat enveloping him. She felt so tight, so perfect, as if she'd been made just for him. God, how he loved her body. How he loved her.

Gage's mind cleared of all thoughts except this moment, of being inside of her, bringing her slowly and torturously to that peak of ecstasy. He withdrew only to plunge deeper, hearing her whimper of pleasure as he repeated the process again and again. His heart pounded, his breathing grew labored, but all he could think was to bring her off first, to send her over the edge. The anticipation of that moment, the promise, had him clenching his jaw, holding off as he felt the telltale spasms begin deep within her. She threw her head back as she came and pulled him with her, draining him to his very soul.

Gage released his hold on her hips and felt her legs slip down his body as the water continued to cascade around them. He kept her in his arms and rotated them under the spray where they stood, kissing and touching, exploring and loving, until the water turned cold.

"Now we have to go get warm," he murmured, rubbing his thumb over her lips. "Back to bed."

"Gage." She protested with a weak laugh as he picked her up, but she pushed open the shower door to give them safe passage.

∼

"We have a problem." Huddled under the sheet, Morgan kissed Gage's naked chest, her lips skimming the edges of the scar left by the bullet that had nearly killed him.

"Only one?" His eyes were closed, an arm tossed over his head, his still-damp hair sticking up in odd angles since she'd all but mashed him into the mattress.

They did indeed have more than one, but only one she was willing to voice at the moment. "I think you forgot to bring something into the shower with you."

"I didn't hear you complaining at the time."

She twirled her fingers in the short hairs on his chest. "What happened to being prepared?"

He stopped breathing for a minute, his arm tightening around her. She tilted her head up and saw his eyes open slowly.

"Well, damn." He lifted his other hand to his forehead, rubbed at the crease of concern that formed.

"That's one way of putting it. Should we have the talk now?"

His smile eased any concern she might have had. "The talk?"

"You know, STDs, HIV. I've always prided myself on being safe."

His eyes narrowed. "Safe with whom?"

Morgan shrugged. She could have so much fun with this. "Oh, you know. Whoever." She couldn't go through with it and laughed. "A boy in college, and that was more out of curiosity than anything. I wanted to see what the big deal was."

"And did you?" he asked with a touch of jealousy in his gaze.

"There was nothing big about it at all." The words were out before she realized what she'd said. "Oh, no." She covered her eyes as he chuckled. "That isn't what I meant. I just meant I didn't think sex was that big of a deal. Almost felt like a waste of time."

"And now?"

She laid her head on his chest and teased his nipple with her tongue. "I think I get it now. I get it really, really well."

This was where she wanted to be. Right there, in bed with him. Where nothing out there could touch them. Where none of her decisions mattered. Where she could pretend she'd never lied to him.

"I'll take that as a compliment, thank you, and just so you know, I got a clean bill of health after I left the department. That good enough?"

"Yeah. It is." She waited another moment. "Actually, there is something else we should discuss." She moved up and over him, her new favorite place to be. "About your mother—"

"Stop," Gage cried, sitting up, and as he did, parts of him shifted into dangerous areas. Morgan shuddered.

"Stop what?" she practically purred.

"Say whatever you want to me in bed, but keep my mother out of it. Do you understand me?"

Morgan leaned in and laid her forehead on his shoulder. "I'm s-sorry," she laughed. "It's just she's so obsessed with you giving her grandchildren. She's going to know what we've been doing the second she sees us together."

"My mother already knows, I promise you that. Why else would she put chocolate cake in that basket of hers?"

"Mmm." Morgan licked his shoulder and found it salty with sweat. "It did make the perfect late-night snack, but it doesn't hold a candle to you."

Gage was still frowning, but his sharp intake of breath told her she was on the right track. She felt his hands slide down to cup her buttocks.

"I don't think we should take any more chances without protection." She nibbled on his neck. "No more, mister." But she couldn't seem to get enough of him. Knowing it could all disappear in an instant didn't worry her as much as it emboldened her.

"Then stop that." His arms moved around her. She'd come to anticipate that motion and pulled away, pushed him flat on his back, and moved down his body ever so slowly.

"I meant no more of the same thing, Gage." She took the hot, hard length of him in her hands. "I didn't say we couldn't try something different."

She smiled and lowered her head as he groaned her name.

CHAPTER 15

"Morning, Morgan."

Morgan missed the last step coming out of her apartment. She looked up to find Gage's brother Jon waving at her from on top of the Fiorelli's roof. Shielding her eyes against the morning sun, she had to blink twice before she recognized Drew crouched beside him. "Um, hi?" What on earth?

"Gage is out front. Said to send you in that direction when you got up." Jon picked up his hammer and gestured to a stack of shingles. "Drew, why don't you start on that section over there and we'll meet in the middle."

"Sure."

Morgan zombie-walked toward the gate, unable to fathom what Jon Juliano was doing on her roof. Or what Drew was doing with him. She scrambled out of the way as her brother carried a stack of siding on his broad shoulders into the backyard.

"Morning, sis." Nathan jerked his head behind him. "About time you got up. Coffee and muffins in the kitchen." When was the last time she saw her brother wearing jeans and a T-shirt? And when did he start looking as if he could try out as a running back for the 49ers? There wasn't enough coffee in the entire state to shake off her eight a.m. confusion.

"Morgan." Kelley popped up from behind a sawhorse, a saturated narrow roller in her hand. She ran at her, navy blue paint splattering her pink overalls.

"Morning, sweetie." She caught Kelley and twirled her away from the side of the house out of fear that she'd pull a Jackson Pollock. "What's going on around here? You having a party and forget to invite me?"

"Not a party. It's family. Lots and lots of family. Gina said so. They all came to help with our house. Come see." She grabbed Morgan's hand and dragged her to the front yard.

Morgan's belly buzzed as if a wasp nest had exploded. She touched a hand to her chest as her soul filled. She forgot how to breathe.

Cars and trucks lined both sides of the street. Gage stood in front of the house, pointing and talking with Nico, and . . . Was that her father? In board shorts and a T-shirt?

Gage's father, Daniel, was whooping it up with her general contractor Kent Lawson and his fellow construction workers as he hefted toolboxes, a table saw, and a stack of industrial extension cords out of the trucks.

Gallons of paint were piled on a tarp on the far end of the lawn, while Brandon bounced between groups like a pinball, stopping to tug on Gage's waistband when he spotted Morgan. Gage bent down to Brandon's level and tightened the little boy's tool belt. He rested a hand on

Brandon's head and said something before giving Morgan a smile that melted her heart.

"Are you mad?" Kelley dropped the roller to her side.

"Mad?" Morgan managed as her throat closed up.

"Gina said you don't like to ask for help. That you might not like people taking your work away."

Oh. Tears burned her eyes as she swallowed. Gage had been right. All she'd had to do was ask. "I'm not mad, sweetie." How could she be? "They put you to work, too, huh?"

"Painting." Kelley squealed with the biggest smile Morgan had ever seen on her tiny face. She waved her roller in the air like a torch of victory. "Me and Daniel and Sheila are going to do the spare bedrooms, and we're going to redo Brandon's."

The cowboy room Morgan hadn't had time to plan let alone start. "Sounds like the perfect way to spend the day. Where's Gina?"

"Inside with Liza and Theresa and Sheila. They're talking about Brandon's party. It's gonna be awesome."

"There's my helper." Gage's dad scooped Kelley into the air, flying paint and all, hefted her against his chest. "I set out some baseboard for you, so get to it, little lady."

" 'Kay." She wiggled to get down, then jetted off like her sneakers were loaded with blasters.

"It's a lot for you accept, having this many people come to help," Daniel told Morgan, a kind smile on his face.

"That's one way of putting it." She couldn't seem to process anything at the moment. Had her obsessive tendency toward self-sufficiency gone too far? Instead of being an example for the kids, had she taught them not to trust anyone? "How did you know—"

"Gina found—what was it Sheila called it? Your clipboard of death." Daniel chuckled. "My daughter doesn't think anyone should have so much to do, and once she gets an idea in her head, well, you've met Gina. Especially when it comes to family."

Family. Morgan clutched at her shirt with the same ferocity that fear clutched her throat, like the claws of an eagle. "But I'm not—"

"Afraid you are if my wife and son have anything to say about it." The tenderness in his eyes, the love that shone when he spoke of his wife or children, twined inside of her and took root.

Daniel continued. "Theresa means well. I hope you know that. I had the misfortune of making her very happy all these years. She wants the same thing for our children."

More people to care about. More people to count on. More people to hurt. God. Did she possess some kind of gravitational force field that pulled people in just as her life was about to explode? Morgan's chest tightened at the potential fallout.

"Morgan?" Daniel touched her arm. "What is it?"

"Nothing." She snatched up the mask of normalcy she'd worn for months, but the facade wasn't as easy to slip on. "Like you said, it's a lot to take in. Gina's even sneakier than I thought."

"Go on inside, check in with her and your sister. Things are under control out here."

"Brandon and Kelley—"

"They'll be fine, Morgan. Stop worrying." Jackson strode over, his greying hair catching the sun as he smiled at her. Daniel slapped Jackson on the shoulder and went in search of Kelley.

"Is that a socket wrench?" Morgan tried to remember the last time she saw her dad pick up a tool, let alone wear khaki shorts and tennis shoes.

"It is indeed. Kent's giving me a crash course in that water heater of yours. I don't think there's anything that contractor friend of yours can't fix. But rumor has it the heater's on its last legs."

Not true. On its last toes perhaps.

"You and I need to sit down and have a serious conversation about what needs upgrading around here, young lady."

"My house, my responsibility," Morgan said automatically.

"My mother's house, once upon a time; *our* responsibility. Get used to it. Now scoot. I have a water heater to fix and you have breakfast to eat." He pushed her toward the front door.

Morgan returned the smiles and greetings of two of Kent's construction workers pulling up the last of the rotted porch planks and replacing them as if they were nothing more than popsicle sticks. "The Twilight Zone has nothing on this place," Morgan muttered, then braced herself as she walked into the kitchen.

She found the female contingent among the baskets brimming with fresh-baked muffins, gallons of orange juice, and overworked coffeepots.

"Morgan, look." Lydia pointed at the giant foam rollers in her bangs. "Liza's making me pretty."

Morgan brushed a gentle hand on Liza's arm in thanks,

stopping to examine Lydia from her perch on the edge of the counter. "You are stunning."

Lydia giggled.

"Gramma Theresa says to get used to them all, cause they're here to stay." Lydia kicked her legs as if she were about to swim across Lake Michigan. "We've got more brothers now and two more sisters. Can you believe it?"

Gramma Theresa? Oh boy. Morgan took a mental snapshot of Lydia's radiant face, filing it away for when she'd need to remember. Liza hoisted Lydia off the counter and they watched her wobble her way into the dining room, where she was going to help strip off the old wallpaper.

Morgan turned on Gina. "So this is all your doing?"

Gina cringed and hugged her tablet computer against her chest like a shield. "I know I probably went too far, and I know I shouldn't have overstepped. Again." The words tumbled out in a rush, as if she was afraid Morgan would stop her once she got going. "But I saw there was just so much for you to do and you can't do it all yourself and, well, Gage agreed with me and offered to keep you busy while we got everything arranged. I'm sorry but I don't care if you're mad—you're laughing," Gina accused, looking as if Morgan had just stomped footprints in her wet cement. "Is this funny?" she asked Sheila and Liza. "Why is she laughing? Why are you laughing?"

Even Sheila rounded the counter with a look of concern on her face, but Morgan held out a hand to stop her, sucking in a breath. "It's just now I understand why Gage distracted me in the show—" Her vocal cords froze as Theresa's head snapped around.

"Distracted you where?"

"In th-the—" Morgan couldn't think. What did she say? Oh, God. "In the sh-show. We went to the movies?" Sheila guffawed.

"At seven on a Saturday?" Liza countered. "They don't start before noon. Ow! Hey." Liza glared at Gina when her sister smacked her hard on the arm. "What was that for?"

Morgan closed her eyes, wishing she could melt into the floorboards like the Wicked Witch of the West. "Please don't tell Gage I told you, Theresa."

"You haven't told me anything." Theresa advanced as Sheila backed away. "Yet. In the show—?" She waved her hand for Morgan to finish the confession.

Morgan looked to Sheila for help, then Gina, Liza, and even Angela, but they all looked anxious to hear the details. "Oh, all right. In the shower. He distracted me in the shower."

Theresa's entire face lit up like a sun gone supernova. "I'm going to be a grandmother."

Morgan groaned.

Sheila laughed.

"The shower?" Gina shuddered. "I don't want to hear this. Come on, Liza."

"No way. Knowledge is power."

"This knowledge is not for you." Theresa shooed them out of the room. "Out. Both of you. We need to talk."

"But, Mom," Liza whined.

Morgan grabbed Gina's arm. "Don't leave me with her."

"You slept with my brother, Morgan." Gina gave a sad, exaggerated shake of her head. "You're on your own."

"We didn't sleep," Morgan called after her, then realized her mistake and spun toward to Theresa. "I'm begging you, don't tease him about this. You have no idea what it does to him."

Gage's mother looked as if she'd hit the jackpot in Vegas. "It'll cost you."

"Cost me what?" Morgan gaped at her. "Blood? Property? My firstborn?"

"Bah. Your firstborn's a given," Theresa said. "I want a wedding."

"You had a wedding," Morgan reminded her, a new panic taking hold. A wedding? Marriage? Nothing like that was going to happen with Gage. Not once he learned the truth, and then nothing, not even the almighty will of Theresa Juliano, was going to change that. "I saw the pictures." She ignored Angela laughing on the other side of the counter.

"I want a huge event wedding for my boy," Theresa explained. "The entire family, all our friends."

"There's not going to be a wedding, Theresa," Morgan insisted, casting a desperate look at her sister, whose eyes had taken on an excited glow not unlike the one shining in Gage's mother's eyes. "Sheila—" she warned, but her sister was already pulling out her phone to make notes, the event planner part of her taking over.

"How many are we talking?" Sheila asked. "A few dozen? A hundred?"

"Three hundred twenty-four," Theresa said. "On our side of course. That doesn't include yours."

Morgan's head spun. She had to stop this. Now. "H-how many? Theresa, you can't possibly know that many people." Was it getting hotter in here?

"We have a lot of relatives." Theresa waved a dismissive hand. "Don't worry about cost. We'll split it with your father. Our wedding gift to you."

"Couldn't you just get me a Crock Pot?" Morgan pleaded.

Angela chuckled and settled a comforting hand on Morgan's shoulder as she walked around the counter. "Looks like this is out of your hands."

But it couldn't be. She couldn't do this, let Theresa and everyone else believe there was anything permanent in the future for her and Gage. No matter how much she might wish differently.

"Theresa, please," Morgan pleaded. "Sheila?" But her sister wasn't listening.

"That's my offer," Theresa said. "I leave Gage alone, I get your wedding." Theresa walked to the doorway and rose up on tiptoe to look out the dining room window. "Gage is on the porch. Should I call him in and ask for the details of last night? Or should we start with this morning's shower adventure?"

"Stop!" Morgan cried, running up behind her and waving him off when he popped his head in the door. "Nothing. Just, nothing. Go do, whatever." Her efforts weren't convincing, as she saw suspicion creep into his eyes. But he withdrew, quicker than she might have liked. Coward. "You are an evil woman, Theresa Juliano. And you're not listening to me. There's not going to be a wedding."

"My son's not good enough for you?" Theresa challenged.

"What?" Morgan balked. "Good Lord, Theresa, of course he is." If anything he was too good for her. "That's not . . . We've only known each other a couple of weeks."

She shifted tactics. "It's too early for anyone, even you, to think about marriage, and besides, things are, um, complicated." And she couldn't very well explain herself at the moment.

"When it's right, it's right." Theresa knocked her fingers gently against Morgan's cheek. "You two will get married. I know it. And when you do, I want what I asked for."

"Take the deal, Morgan," Sheila said, and for the first time Morgan saw a glimmer of concern and understanding in her sister's eyes. She knew this wasn't a joke—at least not for Morgan—any longer. "If there's no proposal, then you have nothing to worry about. And if there is—"

"There will be," Theresa insisted.

"If there is," Sheila continued after a heavy sigh, "then you'll live up to your end of this deal."

"But . . ." Morgan felt the fight drain out of her. "This is ridiculous." But she was withering under the Theresa's piercing gaze. Sometimes surrender was the best option. "Fine, but Theresa, do not say you weren't warned. And I want this on record." She pointed a stern finger at Gage's mother even as her heart screamed at her to walk away. And not dare hope . . . "Not a word about last night or that I uttered the word *shower*. You don't mention marriage or grandchildren or weddings to anyone outside this room. One word, even to your husband, and the deal's off. I have witnesses." She motioned to Angela, who looked as if she wanted nothing to do with this part of the agreement.

"We'll want some say in the event," Sheila interceded before Morgan could change her mind.

"Of course." Theresa nodded once as if they'd created an accord for world peace. "I want location and menu approval, and I get to do the guest list. You can choose the dress, the colors, and the theme."

"We choose attendants and their gowns." Sheila ignored Morgan's repressed squeal of panic.

"Flowers and cake are mine."

"Chocolate?" Morgan looked at her sideways. Damn if the woman didn't already know her weaknesses.

"Of course. It brought you together, didn't it?"

"That's a mention." Morgan pounced on the opportunity. "She mentioned last night, Angela, you heard her."

But Angela shook her head, held up her hands. Sheila shrugged. "Sorry, Morgan, but I'm with her on this."

"You should be married with a brood of your own," Angela added. "Besides, I haven't been to a wedding since my own daughter got married." She grinned over at Theresa. "Need an assistant?"

Morgan leaned her elbows on the counter and hid her face in her hands. What had she gotten herself into?

CHAPTER 16

"Dammit. Hey, Morgan."

At her brother's shout, Morgan looked up from scooping fruit salad onto her paper plate. "What?"

Nathan beat his cell phone against his palm. "Can I use your computer? I'm not getting Internet."

"Go ahead." She took a seat at the picnic table between Sheila and Liza. "Anyone seen Gage? I thought Gina proclaimed work officially finished fifteen minutes ago." Not a moment too soon, as everyone looked as exhausted as Morgan felt. She wouldn't be surprised if people started passing out in their plates.

"He had one more thing to do." Sheila knocked her shoulder into Morgan's as she waved a fried chicken leg in the air. "Said it was a surprise."

"Yeah, haven't had enough of those lately." Thinking of his last surprise brought a smile to her face.

The reward for a full day's work had been a fried chicken feast put together by Angela and Theresa, who chose to work in the kitchen while the rest of the house came together as if Hermione Granger had waved her magic wand.

"I can't believe you and the construction crew came," Morgan said to Kent as he sat across from her. She'd never be able to express her gratitude. After all the work he'd already put in at the center, here he was on his day off, helping her. She'd made it a point to learn each of their names this afternoon.

"Ever try to say no to Gina?" Kent arched a brow. He plowed into the macaroni salad as if he hadn't eaten in a month. "Girl makes Martha Stewart look like a slacker."

Liza's mouth twisted as she plucked apart her buttermilk biscuit.

"You were good with Lydia today," Morgan told her as she stabbed an errant blueberry. "Made her feel special."

Liza shrugged. "I just braided and curled her hair. Put on some blush. No big deal."

"It is for a little girl who likes to feel pretty. Trust me, Liza. You made her very happy."

"Agreed." Sheila popped an olive into her mouth, specks of blue and red paint dotting her face and hair. "Hey, Kent, any chance I can come by the site next week and see the blueprints for the center? I'd like to see what the space allocation is."

"There's some left to play with, including that lot behind the building," Kent said. "I'm there by eight every morning."

"Gad." Sheila shuddered. "Make it noon and we'll talk."

"What are you thinking?" Morgan asked her sister.

"Depends on whether you're open to some new ideas,"

Sheila said. "I know you have things on a schedule and all mapped out on that cell phone of yours—"

Morgan didn't need another reminder of how difficult she'd made things for herself or how frustrating her self-sufficiency must be for her family. "I'm working on being flexible, Sheila, but it won't happen overnight. Out with it."

"Well." Sheila gave a pointed look at Liza. "I'm wondering if we might have the space for a mini-spa for girls. You know, get their nails done, pretty bows and makeup and stuff. Like you said, every little girl likes to feel pretty, especially when they're sick. Maybe a gaming room for the boys? Or a woodworking shop. We could bring in people like Kent to teach some classes."

"Not sure how good I'd be at manicures," Kent joked.

"We did plan on some playrooms, but maybe that's too typical." Morgan tapped a finger against her lips as she smiled at Kent. "What about having a social center, you know, arcade, spa, art studio. Different little stores geared for kids, for teens, since we'll have all different ages. Like a mall for center patients."

"Exactly." Sheila snapped her fingers. "Activities that spark their interests, let them stop thinking about being sick."

"I love it. Liza, what do you think?" Morgan asked.

Another shrug.

"You and Drew could start a club," Morgan muttered. "Think she's up to helping, Sheila?"

"She could be if she stopped feeling sorry for herself."

"I'm not feeling sorry for myself." But the hurt look on Liza's face said otherwise. "It's just—"

"Hard to live up to your sister's overabundance of

confidence and determination?" Sheila nudged Morgan to sit back. "Try it when she's five years younger than you are. Then you'll have something to bitch about."

Morgan's mouth dropped open at Sheila's confession. "Hey."

"When she was six she gave away all of the Barbie dolls, and by all I mean even *mine*. The Dream House, the pink convertible—hell, even Ken didn't survive the purge because this one heard about a fire at a local day care and they'd lost all their toys."

"That was almost twenty years ago." Morgan tried to laugh, but Sheila had hit on something. Liza's frown was easing.

"Or what about the time you went on a hunger strike until Nathan promised to take Ellie Munford to her high school prom?"

"She'd had a crush on Nathan for years," Morgan protested. "And you agreed with me at the time. You even helped her pick out her dress."

Sheila waved a hand in the air. "That's beside the point. Prisoners go on hunger strikes. Not Tremaynes."

"Not like I couldn't afford to miss a few meals." Morgan snorted. It had been one of the few diets she hadn't tried.

"My point is, Liza"—Sheila leaned over Morgan as if she wasn't there—"you have to find your own way in life, and wallowing in the fact you aren't someone else or that you don't do things the way they do isn't going to get you anywhere. Put the talents you do have to use. Like working for us."

"Or working for her," Morgan corrected automatically. Okay. Morgan's brow knitted. Where had that come from?

"Exactly." Sheila nodded. "Wait. What?"

"Your idea. Your project." And the more Morgan thought about it, the more sense it made. Given what might be coming down the road, given that there was every chance she couldn't fix the mistakes she'd made, she had to have a contingency plan for the foundation.

If she was wrong, then it was time Morgan shared the responsibilities of the family's foundation. "I think Liza should be your consultant on this project. She's not that much older than the kids we'll be treating, and you said I needed to ask for help more often. Let's consider this step one." She stood up and picked up her plate, but she bent down and whispered, "Now you get both of them. Oh, and Liza? If at some point you could show me how you get your eyebrows perfectly plucked, I'd love a lesson."

She tossed her plate in the garbage and made a quick round of thank-yous before stopping beside a super sleepy Brandon. "Hey, bud." She bent down next to where he rested his head on his arms. His eyes drooped despite his determination to stay awake. "I think maybe you need to call it a night."

"Want cake," he mumbled, even as he reached for her. Morgan hefted him into her arms, patted his back as she smiled at her father and Gage's dad as they stopped their discussion on the downgrade in property values to say good night to Brandon.

"Cake," Brandon said again.

"We'll save you a piece for breakfast. Come on." She carried him inside, marveling at the finished and polished banister as she inhaled the vanilla-scented paint on the walls on her way upstairs.

Brandon's new room was everything she could have

hoped for and more. The Wild West theme included a sheriff's office made out of a giant moving box. The dresser, desk, and bookcase had all been distressed to match the Old West feel. Cowboy-and-indian fabric draped the windows on either side of the bed. She popped off his shoes and set them on the giant sheriff's badge throw rug. Drawing the bright red sheet up to his chin, she kissed him on the forehead before he rolled onto his side and dropped into exhausted sleep as only an exhausted nine-year-old can.

The room couldn't have been more perfect. Love was indeed in the details: in the desert landscape and ghost town buildings Sheila had painted on the far wall. The year her sister had spent studying art abroad had been worth the months Morgan spent missing her. To be able to create this perfect fantasyland for a little boy was a gift.

Closing the door, she headed downstairs and stepped onto the silent front porch, grateful for a few quiet moments to remember this moment—seeing Gage like this, hot, sweaty, still working to make her home safe for her kids, her family, knowing when he turned around that smile would be on those beautiful lips of his. She squeezed her eyes shut as if taking a mental picture, memorizing this sight, these feelings that wouldn't stop growing, for when she had to say good-bye.

"So what's the surprise?" she asked Gage as she hugged her arms around her waist and walked over to him. He stepped aside to reveal the tire swing knotted to one of the branches. "Oh." Morgan's heart flipped like a dolphin in the summer sea. "Oh, Gage."

"Might be too big for Kelley and Brandon, but they

can grow into it. If you want, I can put up a smaller one on the other—"

Morgan threw her arms around his neck and hung on, squeezing him so hard she heard him laugh as his arms went around her. He lifted her in the air.

"You and tire swings are the oddest combination. But nice to know I know how to get to you."

"It's perfect," she whispered, not wanting this day to end. "This day has been perfect."

"I'm thinking tonight might be, too." He tucked his chin to his chest and grinned. "I snuck off to the drug store at lunch."

Morgan laughed as he lowered her feet to the ground. She turned to look at the loving transformation of the house. Her grandmother, her mother, would have loved it. Morgan loved it. The pale blue siding, the eggshell white shutters and trim. There wasn't a nail to be hammered, a board to be sanded. Even the yard had been replanted with bunches of pansies and daisies and still-to-bloom camellias. It was the picture-perfect-postcard house she'd always known it could be.

"I'll remember this day for the rest of my life, Gage."

Her heart had never been so full.

Or in such danger of breaking.

∼

Morgan's perfect day screeched to a halt when Gage's cell phone vibrated.

"Boy, you two really are made for one another." Sheila glared when Gage pulled out his phone. "Honest to God, one weekend without a cell phone wouldn't kill either of you."

"Given my job, it could," Gage said with a grin, then shot Morgan an apologetic smile. "I've put them off all day. I need to take this."

"Sure, yeah. Of course." Suddenly chilled, Morgan shivered. "I'm going to grab a sweater."

"Wait, Morgan." Sheila ran up the stairs behind her, caught her arm. "I just wanted to say how much I appreciate you letting me help more with the center."

"Just mark it on your calendar as the day you were right." Morgan smiled and tugged her arm free.

"And, um, that I won't let you down."

Where was this coming from? "You can't. I know where you live. Speaking of which." Now that Sheila reminded her. "What do you think about Dad wanting to sell the house?"

"You first." Sheila leaned against the railing. "You seemed to be the one having the most issues with it."

Morgan watched Gage pace while he talked on the phone. After one night she'd never look at her home the same way. Never not see him in her bed, never not remember him sitting at her desk drinking coffee, welcoming her with a warm sleepy smile. She couldn't imagine how her father had managed this long. "I think Dad should do what he needs to do. It's not the same without her."

"You're okay with it, then? Because Nathan is, and it might help ease Dad's mind if we tell him sooner rather than later."

"Agreed. Let me get that sweater and we can do it now."

"Great," Sheila said in a loud voice. "I'm going to get some cake."

Morgan's brow furrowed. "I don't think you needed to announce it to the entire yard, but have at it." As if a single calorie would dare adhere to Sheila's DNA let alone her hips. All Morgan had to do was think about cake and the scale ticked up five pounds. "Oh, Nathan. You're still in here?"

Her brother held up his hand, pointed to his phone as he spun on her desk chair to face her. "Yeah, I'll meet you at the gym at seven tomorrow morning. Sorry." He clicked his phone off and turned off her screen. "Took longer than I thought. Did I hear Sheila say she was having cake?"

"Yes. We thought we'd tell Dad we're okay with him selling the house."

Nathan flinched and looked away as he got to his feet. "Today was a good day. Mom would have loved it."

"Yeah, she would have." For the first time since last summer, the thought of her mother didn't arrive on a wave of pain. When Morgan headed into the dining room, she saw the jewelry box and its contents lying on the table.

"Feeling nostalgic about Granny?" Nathan asked as she scooped up the pieces and dropped them into the box, then closed the lid and headed into the bedroom.

"Something like that. I'll be back out in a second." She heard the door close as she placed the box on her dresser. More and more people depended on her every day. She couldn't let them down. Whatever it cost her in the end would be worth it. She hoped.

"No, Monday is soon enough." Gage's voice drifted up through the open window. Morgan angled the shutter open. "Take a day off, for Christ's sake, Bouncer. The list will wait. No." Morgan frowned at the long pause. "No, we've been watching the papers and the media outlets. None of us has seen anything that looks like a Nemesis trigger. Maybe he's taking the weekend off. You do the same. That's an order. Yeah. You, too."

Morgan was about to close the window when she saw her father approach Gage.

"You look like you could use this." Jackson handed him a beer. "Work won't leave you alone?"

"My overattentiveness to the Nemesis case has rubbed off on my team. Doesn't help we're working against a clock."

"I wasn't aware Evan put you on deadline."

"Not Evan. Suffice it to say I'm trying to stave off any federal involvement. The sooner I can get them out of town, the better. Putting a stop to Nemesis should do exactly that."

"Feds, huh?" Jackson lifted his bottle. "What possible interest could they have in Nemesis?"

"Hell if I can figure it out. But this case is so strange, I can't help but feel I'm not seeing something I should, like all the information is out of focus and I need a new set of eyes to see it clearly."

"Maybe you're focusing too much and need a break. Today should help you see things clearer come Monday."

"Let's hope you're right. I've been meaning to ask you, are you acquainted with a man named Mac Price?"

"Mac?" Jackson's eyebrows shot up. "Yes, actually, I am. He was one of my first investors back when I was starting my business. Once upon a time we lived in the same neighborhood down south." Jackson lowered his chin and shook his head as if in regret, even as his lips curved into a smile. "Easy to forget those days. Mac was always a lot of fun; dangerous, even. Last I heard he was serving time in Soledad prison for a string of white-collar cons. Man could charm the white off rice. Why do you ask?"

Gage shrugged. "No reason, really. How about an FBI agent named Kolfax? He was investigating Price at one time."

"Kolfax?" Her father quirked his head, frowned. "The name's familiar. With the financial world the way it is, I've had more interaction with the Feds lately than I have in the past. It's possible I've spoken with him. Why?"

"Nothing. Just one of those things running in my head. Any idea where Morgan got to?"

Morgan jumped out of sight as both Gage and her father looked up to her window. She dug into a bottom drawer for a lightweight sweater, then tugged it on. Gage wasn't the only one on a deadline.

The question was, which one of them would run out of time first?

∽

"Guess we have to get back to the real world." Gage rolled out of Morgan's bed Monday morning just as the sun made its return appearance.

Morgan burrowed into his pillow, drawing his residual warmth as close as possible, snuggling as if settling in for a long winter.

"Best weekend ever," she all but hummed, but she could feel the gears in her mind clicking into their familiar overworked state even as a satisfied smile curved her lips. After an early morning walk to the park, they'd spent the rest of Sunday finishing up the repair list Gina had pilfered from Morgan's clipboard, before introducing the kids to the tire swing. They, like Morgan, thought it was the best invention ever. Ah, the simple things in life. Watching Gage play catch with Brandon or tossing Kelley into the air had been beautiful, but it was when he sat down for a long conversation with Drew that locked her heart away forever.

She'd almost cried when she heard Drew laugh, then did when he shoved his hair out of his face.

Gage was right. Fantasy couldn't last forever. That didn't mean she wouldn't try to hold on to it as long as she could.

Gage bent down and placed a warm kiss on her neck and lingered long enough for her to reach for him. "Mmmmm. Come back to bed."

His low laugh made her insides tremble like a ten-point aftershock. "Can't. I've already put Bouncer off long enough. I need to get my head around work and not"—he kissed her quick and hard—"be distracted. Why don't you stay right where you are."

As if considering Gage's request a challenge, Morgan's calendar alarm blared its Beethoven-based reminder about her morning appointments and phone calls. Morgan slapped her hand on the nightstand, but Gage had hitched into his pants and picked up her phone first, frowning as he skimmed her schedule.

"Christ, Morgan. Did you leave yourself time to breathe?"

"Gimmie." She waved her fingers as she came more fully awake. Given the week she had in front of her, she didn't want to start the day with a lecture on her overscheduled life.

"Today's bad enough, but you've booked all but five minutes tomorrow starting with a breakfast meeting with Kent, and I'm assuming by breakfast you mean coffee, bank deposit at eleven, final contract meeting with Vanity Cleaners, phone appointments with, what is that, six different doctors? We couldn't wedge a two-second kiss into this schedule with a crowbar."

"You were warned." Morgan pushed herself out of bed and plucked her phone out of his lax fingers as she headed into the bathroom. "And don't try a repeat distraction of Saturday morning. I'm locking the door."

By the time she emerged, the euphoria of the weekend had evaporated with the shower steam, replaced by the reality that in the next two days, the foundation would either thrive or be buried under a public scandal of mismanaged funds.

She buttoned the last two buttons on her lavender shirt, zipped and twisted her knee-length black skirt around, and headed into the kitchen where Gage held out a mug of coffee. "Thanks." She inhaled the steam and felt the caffeine zing through her system as she lifted her heavy damp hair from beneath her collar, then beelined for her computer for her morning email check. As she switched her screen on, her gaze fell to the blank space on her desk.

Her stomach dropped like a deflated basketball after a game-losing shot.

She slammed her mug down and ignored the splatter of

coffee on the back of her hand as she shoved the stack of folders aside, lifted them up, and pushed her cup of pens aside.

"Lose something?"

"Um. There was a stack of white notecards here." She tapped the empty space where the cards from Nemesis had been. The space that suddenly felt like a black hole. She tucked her hair behind her ear, then dropped to her knees to look on the floor and peer under the desk, her breath coming in short, sharp gasps. "Did you take them?"

"No. I'm sure they're here somewhere." He came over, pulled open the bottom desk drawer. "I'll help you look."

"No!" She slammed shut the drawer that held the last of the Nemesis cash and almost caught his fingers. She forced out a laugh, but it sounded more like she was choking on the air she couldn't find. "I'm sorry, I just meant, it's okay." But she knew her eyes had to be spinning like a UFO coming in for a landing. Staving off the dizziness, she pinched the bridge of her nose until she saw stars. Too close. "I'm sure they're here somewhere. I'll find them myself. I don't need help."

The chill that erupted down her spine had little to do with Nemesis' missing cards and everything to do with the icy stare Gage leveled at her. "And even if you did, you wouldn't ask."

Morgan closed her eyes. "That's not what I meant. We both have busy days and neither one of us has time—"

"It's too early for bullshit, Morgan." His words sounded as bitter as the coffee in the mug he set in the sink. "Say you want to do it yourself, remind me you need to do everything on your own, but don't make shit up. Don't ever lie to me, Morgan."

She might have laughed if she didn't think he might have her committed when she couldn't stop. Don't lie? She'd been lying to him from the moment they'd met.

"And don't expect me to change overnight," she snapped back, and earned a cool arch of his eyebrow in response.

She let out a long breath, dug fingers into her hair as she tried to settle her riotous pulse. Where the hell were those cards? The last time she'd seen them was right before she and Gage had—

"You're sure you didn't take them?" Try as she might, she couldn't keep the tremor out of her voice.

"I did not, and since it's obvious you aren't going to tell me what's so all-fired important about those precious cards, I'll leave you to your search."

"Gage, please don't leave angry." She didn't want the weekend to end this way. The coffee threatened to rocket up into her throat like acid.

He stopped, hand on the doorknob, his bag dangling from his hand as he turned his head and looked at her, disappointment shining like dulled coins. "I thought this weekend taught you that you don't have to handle everything on your own."

"It did teach me that. You taught me that. They're just stupid cards. You're overreacting." But she couldn't pry herself from beside the desk, not when Nemesis had her so tied up in knots she couldn't move. "I'm trying, Gage. Please believe that. I am trying."

"Try harder." And then he was gone.

"Shit." Morgan spun on her bare feet, twisting this way and that, looking through every folder. She dug through every drawer, tossed the twenty-five thousand in cash

Gage had nearly found aside, but to no avail. She sat against the desk feeling as if she'd taken a body shot of Novocain.

The cards were gone.

CHAPTER 17

"Good weekend, Gage?" Janice's cheery greeting kicked up the gas on Gage's anger meter. "So not the expression I expected to see on your face this morning, given that you're an hour late."

Rather than incur her wrath by issuing a rude response, Gage lifted his extra-large coffee cup in acknowledgment and proceeded into his office, drawing on every ounce of control to resist slamming the door.

What should have been a quick stop at his house turned into a thirty-minute soak in a lukewarm shower, during which he reminded himself who Morgan was, who she'd always been. She was used to taking everything on herself. She didn't trust anyone to help her. While he'd hoped this weekend had been a turning point, it felt more like a failed intervention.

Stupid cards, whatever they were. She didn't even trust him to tell him that much. Forget banging his head against a brick wall. Morgan was reinforced concrete.

"Did I take your cards? No, I didn't take your

goddamned cards. Almost lost my fingers trying to find them for you, but hey, what's a hand in the grand scheme of things. What?" he bellowed as he paced by his door.

The doorknob turned, and the door opened less than an inch as Bouncer poked her head inside.

This woman had chased down drug runners and carjackers, been thrown out a second-story window, and survived a motorized encounter with a speeding Cutlass, but at this moment she looked pre–training academy pee-her-pants anxious.

"Yeah." Gage let out a long breath, pushed Morgan's irritating self-sufficiency out of his mind, and waved his teammate inside. "Sorry. Shitty morning. What's up?" When she stepped inside, Gage noticed she was sans crutches. "They put you in a walking cast already?"

She gave him a tentative smile. "I went to the emergency room and told them I couldn't stand it anymore, threatened to use a rusty hacksaw if they didn't take it off. Are you sure now is okay?"

"It's fine." Somehow he needed to find a way to separate his personal life from his professional one. This wasn't the last fight he'd have with Morgan. Taking his frustration out on his coworkers would make him the boss everyone loathed to be around. "Sit. Can I get you some coffee?"

"I've already had three cups this morning. That's my limit."

Gage continued to stand, the rustling of papers in Bouncer's hands a telltale sign of nerves. "Okay, let's have it. Does this have something to do with Van Keltin?"

She rubbed fingers across her forehead. "Um, we're still working that angle, actually. This is something else.

But with the mood you're in, I'm not sure how you're going to take it, which is why I thought I should give this to you privately."

Gage felt as if a heavy metal band had taken up residency at the base of his skull. "Let's go with the Band-Aid method and rip this off. Out with it."

"Okay. Well, seeing as we still don't know exactly what case the FBI is working on, I don't know if they're pulling your chain or if there's something to this." She winced and handed him the two stapled pages. "It's a list of search warrants Agent Kolfax has applied for with a federal judge out of Los Angeles. Thirty-seven bank accounts at six branches of Federal Consolidated between here and L.A. He, um, should have the warrants by tomorrow morning at the latest."

Gage skimmed the names, some of them familiar, but nothing that got his pulse going. "I don't—"

"Next page." Bouncer folded her hands in her lap before pressing her lips into a thin line.

He flipped the page, ran his thumb down the list, and felt the world drop away. "What the hell?"

"That's what I said."

"Why is Morgan's name on this list?" Was this what Kolfax had been up to this whole time? "And the Tremayne Foundation?"

"I don't know, which is why I kept calling you this weekend. I wasn't sure what to do, and then you, well, you told me to take the weekend off and I didn't want to ruin your plans so—" She shrugged. "Nothing they could have done on the weekend anyway."

"This is bullshit." And his fault. If he hadn't let himself get distracted, he'd have been here on Friday when the list came in. He could have gotten a jump on this sooner. His head spun like an orbiting astronaut off his tether.

"What are we going to do?"

"Find out what the hell is going on. Janice!" Gage headed to the door. "Sorry." He should just make the apology for his shortness automatic from now on. "Let Evan know I'm on my way up to his office."

"I think he's in meetings all morning," Janice called after him as he stalked to the elevator.

"Tell him I don't care." Elevator wasn't fast enough. He shoved through the door to the stairs and took them two at a time.

"What on earth is going on?" Janice asked Bouncer, who looked to Peyton and Rojas as they came out of the conference room.

"Whatever it is, we need to be ready to help."

∼

"Morgan, how nice to see you." Randolph Morton swept into the pristine white showroom of Curtis & Green Jewelers with a permanent smile etched on his face and a royal blue ascot around his neck. Randolph might look as if he's stepped out of a 1960s Vincent Price horror movie, but when it came to the jewelry business in Lantano Valley, he had no rivals.

The sole owner and hands-on manager of the upscale store considered the West Coast Tiffany's, Randolph prided himself on providing the best, and more importantly confidential, service to his customers. While this storefront was a small one, his reputation for being able to get anything—or sell anything—for anyone was unrivaled.

She set her purse on the Atlas display case and greeted him with a kiss on each cheek, hoping Randolph's decades-long relationship with her mother would work to her advantage. "I appreciate you seeing me this morning. I know how busy you are and I'm sure I should have called for an appointment."

"I am never too busy for one of Catherine's beautiful daughters. I miss you coming in to shop for her with your father." A sad smile touched his lips as he tapped a finger against his heart. "She was a wonderful lady."

"She was very fond of you as well." Morgan waited a beat. "Is there somewhere private we can talk?"

"Yes, of course. Come into my office."

Morgan followed him through the displays of Omega and Tag Heuer watches, Mikimodo pearls, and a selection of Paloma Picasso jewelry that jostled even Morgan's practical sensibilities.

"Please, sit." Randolph indicated the plush purple leather seat across from him as he notified his floor staff he would be in a meeting. "What can I help you with?" He closed the heavy wooden door and joined her.

"I'm wondering if you might be interested in any of these pieces for your estate auctions." She pulled out the velvet bag she'd used to transport her grandmother's jewels in. "I'm afraid I don't know much about jewelry, which I know would horrify Mom, but if you wouldn't mind taking a look?"

"Of course, of course." He pulled out a velvet-lined tray. "This is why I love my job. I never know what beauteous items I might come across on any given day."

Morgan didn't have the heart to tell him he needn't take such care with the drawstring bag that until a few hours ago had contained a hundred dollars worth of chocolate poker chips.

"Oh, my. Morgan, I recognize these. Your grandmother was one of my father's most faithful customers, and of course, these must be what she left you when she passed." Randolph placed the seven bracelets in a single row, using his magnifying monocle to examine the stones Morgan prayed were real.

Morgan tried to stop her mind from ringing like a cash machine. She was so tired of hoping, only to be disappointed, but she couldn't help herself. These jewels were her last chance to save the foundation from ruin or at the very least scandal. She shifted in her chair, clenched her fists, and tried to put the morning's argument aside.

"Judging from these pieces, I'd say you could expect anywhere from five to fifteen thousand each. Maybe more depending on who participates in the auction. I could be sure to tweak the invitation list to ensure they bring in as much as possible. Both Victoria Bolton and Evelyn Cranston recently started antiques collections, and I think the competition could be quite beneficial for you as a seller."

By the time he examined the three necklaces and the half-dozen brooches, Morgan felt her body lift as hope inflated her lungs. To hedge her bets, Morgan withdrew the small black velvet box from her purse and, after a last internal debate, passed her grandmother's engagement ring across the desk.

Randolph accepted it with a mixed look of sympathy and understanding. Soon after he said, "If we add all this up"—Randolph scribbled on his notepad—"you're looking at between one hundred thirty to one hundred fifty for the lot. If." He held up a finger and smiled. "If we get that competitive bidding going."

Morgan sagged in her chair. More than she'd expected, but she'd still need to use the Nemesis cash. She gnawed on her thumbnail. "Your next estate sale is scheduled for when?"

"Oh, not until the fall. We just closed our summer catalog offerings."

Her expectation evaporated. Six months would be too late. She needed the money in two days.

"Not the answer you were hoping for, then?"

"No." So close. She was so close to fixing everything, and yet she didn't want to part with her grandmother's treasures if they wouldn't bring her what she needed when she needed it. "No, I'm afraid it wasn't."

Concern crossed Randolph's waxy botoxed face. "I don't suppose you want to confide the reason for the urgency."

"I'd rather not," Morgan admitted. She was so tired of lying. To everyone. To her family. To Gage. One more lie might just be her undoing. "I appreciate your time, Randolph." She started to reach for the ring box.

"I'll tell you what I can do." Randolph touched her hand. "That center of your mother's is coming along, is it not? And I imagine there's always something new cropping up that needs tending to. Seeing as how she was so dear to me, I do want to help. Let's say I buy these pieces from you now, for the prices I quoted you, and if they bring in less than that at auction, we'll consider the balance a charitable donation to the Center. Does that sound reasonable to you?"

Reasonable? She clasped her cameo in her palm,

giving silent thanks for whatever otherworldly persuasion Catherine had wielded over Randolph. It sounded like the end to all of her problems. Dare she believe?

"That sounds quite reasonable." Which left one issue. "Um." How did she ask without sounding rude? "How soon could I expect a check?"

"Well, I'll need to do some fancy footwork with my accountant, but I think I could have one for you by this time tomorrow morning. Is that soon enough?"

It was all Morgan could do not to sob in relief. The iron band that had locked around her chest months ago clicked free. She wouldn't be able to breathe easy until she put the money back in the account. But for now? Yes, it would most definitely do.

"Thank you so much." Seeing as she had a standing appointment with the bank branch manager at eleven tomorrow, that gave her plenty of time to make it across town.

"Excellent. In the meantime, should you change your mind—"

"I won't." If only she could. They were things, sentimental perhaps, but her grandmother's jewels would do so much more good this way. She ran her finger along Granny's engagement ring one last time, saying good-bye to childhood dreams as she embraced the completion of new ones.

∼

Gage plowed into Evan the second he opened the fourth-floor stairwell door.

"Janice said you were on a tear." Evan caught his balance, rubbed a hand across his chest. "Office. Now."

His boss's cool tone doused the fire that propelled Gage up two flights of stairs, as did the curious gawks and mutterings of Evan's office staff that followed the two of them.

"I've had it with Agent Jerk-Off," Gage blasted as he stepped into Evan's office and found said agent inside, legs crossed, hands folded in his lap, an expression on his face that made him look like a seventies porn reject. "What the hell is this?" Gage threw the list of names into Kolfax's face.

"You saved me a call, Inspector," Evan said, as if he felt the need to remind Gage of his position. Evan closed the door and took a slow seat behind his hideous mass-manufactured desk. "Agent Kolfax was about to read us in on his case."

"How generous of him." Goddamn Feds had to ruin everything they touched. They'd almost cost Gage his career, not to mention his life, but he'd be damned if he'd let them go after Morgan and the foundation.

"I'd make quick work of it, Agent." Evan motioned for Gage to take a seat, which Gage refused. "You've been stalking my inspector long enough."

Kolfax placed Gage's mangled list on Evan's desk, then handed Evan a new file, this one filled with two inches' worth of documents.

Evan went up ten notches in Gage's estimation when the D.A. didn't so much as blink in the file's direction.

"Eighteen months ago I was assigned a new case, a joint undercover investigation with the DEA—"

"You mean this doesn't have anything to do with your

personal vendetta against Mac Price and his previous business relationship with Jackson Tremayne?" Gage demanded.

"No." Kolfax's self-satisfied smirk had Gage seeing murder red. "No, this was an investigation into the Benetiz cartel."

"South Miami." Gage explained at Evan's non-reaction. "They have connections throughout South America. Take them down, the entire syndicate falls apart."

"That was the plan," Kolfax confirmed. "The BC is fast becoming the major supplier of cocaine in the United States. One of our agents managed to get in pretty deep, worked his way up to the number three position just as a huge shipment was due in to port. We wanted to get our hands on those drugs, stop them before they hit the street, so we set up a buy through our agent. Somehow his cover got blown and the bust went to hell."

"Been there," Gage muttered. "What happened to the agent?"

"He didn't make it. We think he was taken out by the number two guy, Carlito Benetiz."

Not a glimmer of emotion crossed Kolfax's face, and Gage's loathing of the agent increased.

"The three million in marked bills we supplied for the buy disappeared in the chaos," Kolfax continued. "The plan had been to buy the drugs then trace the money to its source, take out the entire operation. But with the agent dead, the drugs and cash gone, the case went cold. The remaining cartel members burrowed further underground. Snitches we'd relied on for months disappeared or turned up in the morgue. We thought the case was dead. Most of us moved on, and then six months ago, the money started turning up." Kolfax looked up at Gage. "In Lantano Valley."

"You think the BC shifted its operations here?" Evan asked, the disbelief in his voice echoing Gage's. "I might be new to the job, but I think we'd have noticed if a drug cartel moved to town."

"I didn't say we tracked the cartel here." Kolfax indicated the folder. "We traced cash deposits to Consolidated Federal branches either in Lantano Valley or Los Angeles. The names on that warrant list all made cash deposits on the same dates our money popped in the system. Someone is laundering money for the cartel."

"Wouldn't that be kind of stupid?" Gage asked. "Depositing marked money into the banking system?"

"We weren't able to confirm the cartel was aware the buyer was a plant. Could be they assumed the money was clean, or maybe they figured enough time had passed where they could start using it. Small amounts here and there as a test run. That would explain why the full three mil hasn't been accounted for yet. We think whomever is responsible is testing the system, which is why we didn't give the details on our investigation before now."

"So you don't know much beyond the fact that the money is in circulation," Evan said.

"It's enough to get me my warrants." Kolfax stood to address Gage, his expression daring Gage to argue with him. "Your hostility regarding our presence hasn't gone unnoticed, Inspector, which has led some to suggest you might be involved."

Gage laughed, rubbed his eyes, but when he let his hands drop, he looked Kolfax in the face. "Oh man. I so wish I could say I was surprised you just said that."

"That's ridiculous," Evan said.

Kolfax held up his hand to silence the D.A. "Ever work with Agent Sean Salcedo?"

"Salcedo?" Gage frowned, considered. "Yeah. We did our Quantico training together two years ago. Worked a couple of undercovers."

Kolfax's eyebrow quirked.

"Salcedo was the agent who was killed?" Gage's blood turned frigid, as if he'd body-surfed an iceberg. Oh, shit. "He was just a kid." His head went light and he bent over, tried to catch his breath. "Man. Oh, man. Salcedo's dead." The same as Gage might have been save for two centimeters. His shoulder throbbed. The scar on his back burned as if he'd been branded by the past.

"Sit down." Evan had come around the desk, shoved a chair under him, and pushed him down.

"He was getting married the last time we spoke." Gage couldn't wrap his brain around it. "Talked about having kids and helping his mom buy a new house. He's really dead?"

"When did you last speak?" Kolfax asked.

"You can't be serious," Evan said. "You think Gage had something to do—"

"Of course he's serious, Evan. Me and the Feds are like this." He held his hands a foot apart before burying his face in his palms, tried to focus on the question even as resentment covered him like a suffocating thermal blanket. "It was maybe two years ago? Before either of us went under. We met for a beer to celebrate our grand career achievements." He couldn't have sounded more bitter if he'd tinged his words with vinegar.

"What did you talk about?" Kolfax asked.

"I told you, family issues. Providing for his mother who'd been ill for some time." Gage thought of his own mother, how difficult Gage's injuries had been for her, and Salcedo's mother had had to bury him. He couldn't shake the cold.

"Nothing else? No plans to meet later? Nothing off the books?"

"Nothing like that, and fuck you very much for the implication."

"Your affection for the FBI gives you motive to work against us."

"My affection for the FBI is reciprocal. And apparently you all think I'm idiotic enough to deposit dirty money into the ATM two blocks from my house." Gage clenched his fists. "Let's forget your agency nearly got me killed, and this assumption that I'd throw away fifteen years of hard work for cash I don't need. The idea that Salcedo was a wrong cop—"

"I didn't say *I* thought either of you was dirty. I said it was *a* thought. Personally, I've developed another theory." And didn't he look happy about it. "Jackson Tremayne. He's been known to have, shall we say, less than honorable connections over the years. I don't see it as out of the realm of possibility that he's involved in this money situation somehow. Given his position in the community and what I've witnessed in the last few weeks, the Tremayne Foundation is the perfect front for money laundering. No one would ever suspect them of anything untoward. Although considering your relationship with Morgan Tremayne . . ." Kolfax shrugged as if waiting for Gage to fill in the rest.

"The only reason I went near Morgan was because I

saw—" And then the light dawned. "You son of a bitch. You've had this list for weeks. You were just waiting for the right time to use it. Evan was right. You left their name in the open on purpose that day in your office for him to find because we could get close to what you couldn't." Goddamn it! Heat swept through his body like a sandstorm as his arms quivered. They'd used his personal bias against the FBI against him. Kolfax had played him.

Worse. He'd let them. And thrown Morgan right in his path.

"We knew you'd never look into the Tremaynes for us if we asked, and we wanted someone to keep an eye on her." Kolfax sounded so proud of himself, Gage wanted to pound him into the floor. "But knowing how you feel about the agency, I figured you'd do just about anything to keep us out of your pittance of a robbery case. Gotta admit, didn't take much of a push."

"The Tremayne Foundation is not a front for the cartel. They don't launder money." The thought of what Kolfax was suggesting was so far out of left field it wasn't even in the stadium. "Morgan would never do anything illegal to jeopardize her family's work. And neither would her father."

"If that's true, then monitoring the foundation's accounts for the next month will bear that out."

"This isn't some game, Kolfax," Gage ground out. "This is somebody's life you're playing with. Dozens of lives. The accusation alone could destroy years of work and dedication."

"In my experience, people like the Tremaynes think they're above the law, which means they're more inclined to participate in questionable activity. You look at the evidence in that file. Morgan Tremayne fits. And thank you, by the way, for keeping tabs on her and her family while I finished gathering the information I needed to get my warrant. Besides," Kolfax said with a cocky smile that made Gage's fists clench. "It's not like you didn't get something out of this. Looks like she was good for a ride or two."

Gage vaulted out of his chair only to have Evan block him with a hand on his chest. "Enough." He shoved Gage back, turned his attention to Kolfax. "Just to play this ridiculous scenario of yours out, what's your plan?"

"I've got teams ready to stake out each bank." Kolfax straightened his sallow yellow tie. "Any of those thirty-seven people makes a cash deposit, we verify the numbers on the bills right then. If the serial numbers match, I've got my connection and I get the collar."

"Not to mention your headlines. You're wasting your time. Morgan can't lead you to the cartel money. She doesn't have it."

"And you would know, being such a good judge of character," Kolfax said

"Pegged you as an asshole from the start, didn't I?"

"We both did," Evan added, but he looked over his shoulder at Gage. "You're sure about Morgan? No second thoughts?"

"I know her." *I love her.* "She wouldn't do this. Not to the foundation. Not to her family." *Not to me.* She might have trouble asking for help, might be a little too secretive for his taste, but that didn't mean she was a criminal. Did it? "She didn't do this. I'll prove it. You don't need your teams, Kolfax, if it's Morgan and the foundation you're looking at. She has an appointment at the branch on

Twenty-second Street at eleven tomorrow morning. I'll meet you there."

"To observe. Nothing more," Kolfax said, as if granting Gage a pardon from execution.

"Don't tell me how to do my job, you prick."

"Your job," Kolfax sneered. "You're a glorified private investigator, Juliano. You didn't have the stones for the agency. Your own department couldn't find a place to put you, so you ended up here, running down stalled cases that won't get you anywhere but into an early grave. You're dead weight in a dead-end job and you will not interfere with my case."

"You didn't think him so incompetent he wasn't of use to you," Evan said.

But Kolfax's tirade triggered a calm Gage had been waiting for years to experience.

The underlying roar that had been his companion for as long as he could remember went silent. The tightness in his chest eased. His brain unlocked, releasing the pent-up hostility and frustration that had been mounting since he'd been shot. "You might be right, Kolfax," Gage said. "Maybe I'm not cut out for a job that doesn't take a person's character into consideration before decades of their work is put on the line. Or maybe because of agents like you, I've lost faith in what used to be an honorable system. A system I joined to try to make a difference." Gage scooped up the file Kolfax had brought with him and headed to the door. "You're wrong about Morgan. You'll see that tomorrow morning."

This time he did slam the door.

And relished the sound of breaking glass.

CHAPTER 18

"Is everything okay?" Morgan peered around the edge of the computer screen.

Normally Kate's smile was as bright and welcoming as a model in a toothpaste commercial, but today the assistant branch manager's hands were trembling, her mouth stretched into a thin line as she kept glancing at the clock.

"Slow morning for the computers," Kate said with a lack of conviction. "Needs a few extra minutes I guess. Being temperamental."

Morgan couldn't help but swallow hard as she looked at the last of Nemesis' cash sitting beside the small pile of checks that included the one she'd picked up from Randolph less than thirty minutes before. As terrified as she was to part with the last of the ill-gotten funds—Lord only knew what alarms she might be triggering—her determination to finally set the accounts right overrode her doubts. From here on, everything where the center was concerned was going to be aboveboard, every penny accounted for, every moment notarized. Her life was about to head into fast-forward and she had to do whatever it took to keep things running smoothly. For not being much of a gambler, she was taking the biggest risk of her life, but if it paid off . . .

Temperamental seemed an appropriate description for how Morgan felt today. Aside from a few terse texts from Gage, she hadn't heard from him since their argument yesterday morning.

While the money from selling her grandmother's jewelry had set her free in one way, she had yet to find a way to come clean with Gage without exposing the foundation to a criminal investigation.

She should be on top of the world. Everything she'd worked for was within her grasp, and yet—

No. She'd found a solution to her one problem. She'd figure this one out, too. Of course, first she had to get him to talk to her.

Maybe his lack of communication last night was his passive-aggressive way of showing her she did need him, that she couldn't do everything alone.

She didn't need the extra lesson. In fact, his silence felt like overkill. But she got the message. Loud and clear. "Sorry," Kate said again, her eyes skittering to the office door on the back wall, and she restacked the cash. "I know you're in a rush."

"Actually, it's fine. One of my lighter days." Once she was free and clear of the accounting two-step she'd been dancing the last few months, she was treating herself to a few hours off by picking up Brandon's birthday present before meeting Sheila for lunch—Morgan's idea—at Sheila's favorite café downtown.

Not that she wasn't keeping an attentive ear out for her

phone. Lydia hadn't had a good night and had been running a low-grade fever, which was never a good sign, and Kelley had had one of her rare temper tantrums. Chernobyl had nothing on a Kelley Black meltdown. Morgan's usually precious, precocious pixie had been sent to bed without dessert or a story, which incurred a second round of migraine-inducing screams.

At least the entire house now knew not to touch any of Kelley's princess dresses for fear of ripping a hole—however unintentionally—in the hem.

Morgan tapped her phone awake and tried to dispel the disappointment rippling through her belly when she didn't find a new text from Gage.

She'd try again as soon as those missing Nemesis cards became inconsequential. As soon as the last of the money was repaid, which would be any second now.

"Okay, looks like we're good." Kate's smile wobbled and her gaze skipped over Morgan's as she handed her the deposit receipt.

The second Morgan saw the balance on the account, the stress of the last six months vanished. All the money was accounted for, where it should be. Just in time for the audit.

"Thanks, Kate. Have a great day." She would have boogied out of the bank if she didn't think it might end up on YouTube. The second the sun hit her face, Morgan lifted her eyes and basked in the feeling of rebirth. Finally.

Everything was going to be okay.

∼

From his spot wedged into the corner of the microscopic

security center next to the bank manager's office, Gage concentrated on keeping his face blank as Morgan exited the bank.

He'd spent a sleepless night staring alternately between Barney Miller reruns and the text messages from Morgan that slowed to a trickle as the evening wore on.

He'd replied to the first few before having to stop himself. He had to let this play out, had to let her prove herself innocent. He wouldn't put it past Kolfax to continue this witch hunt by claiming Gage had warned her off. Better to keep any communication between them nonexistent, if only for a few hours.

If only it wasn't killing him.

But it would be worth it once Gage threw Kolfax's failure in his face. Maybe throw in his fist for good measure. "What is taking that assistant manager so long?" Kolfax watched Kate saunter toward the office as if her actions weren't dictated by a federal warrant.

As far as Gage could tell, Kolfax didn't make friends anywhere he went it. Agent Marcus, a middle-aged man with a cowlick and ruddy complexion, along with his partner, a young woman around Morgan's age whose name Gage hadn't caught, looked as if they'd rather be hanged from their toes over a fire-ant hill than be stuck on this operation.

The situation wasn't helped when Kolfax had the bank manager open two hours early because Kolfax hadn't done his research and wasn't aware—or more likely didn't believe—that Morgan stuck to her schedule like a fly to flypaper. Gage sauntering in five minutes before Morgan arrived hadn't improved Kolfax's cranky mood.

Did wonders for Gage's though.

When the assistant manager did knock on the door, Kolfax snatched the cash from her with a curse word Gage was sure even Morgan wouldn't have dared utter.

"You're welcome, Agent Asshole." Kate shot Gage a look as if to ask if he was going to do something to stop this, but he couldn't let himself react.

Instead, Gage nodded his thanks and closed the door behind her. "How long before we—"

"Shut up," Kolfax snapped.

"We just have to type the serial numbers into the program," Marcus said, as if Kolfax didn't exist, his fingers flying faster than Gage could ever hope to type. "Shouldn't take more than ten or fifteen—"

Both the agents' computer screens flashed red lines. The female agent snatched her hands from the keyboard as if she'd been burned. "We have a match."

Gage's body went numb. His head roared as if he'd been dropped into the middle of the ocean. His heart pounded in his ears like a gavel in an empty courtroom. "What? That can't be right. Check it again."

Gage couldn't have felt more ill if he'd eaten a table full of bad sushi. He moved forward, but Kolfax slapped his hand against his chest, a mingled look of glee and triumph on the agent's face. "No need. I was right. Your girlfriend's in this up to her—"

Gage tuned him out, watching, praying as the agents typed in different serial numbers. Same result.

"I'm sorry, Inspector." Marcus glanced over his shoulder. "The money is definitely a match to the funds supplied by the FBI."

Gage couldn't do anything but stare at the screens, at

the blinking red lines that screamed of Morgan's deception. Her lies. Her crimes.

"No." Gage shook his head, unable to dislodge the bass drum pounding in his head. "No, there's got to be some explanation. Her brother died from cancer, for Christ's sake." He'd held her when she'd cried about the little boy she couldn't help, watched her with Kelley and Lydia and Brandon. This wasn't the Morgan he knew. Morgan wasn't a criminal.

"People like her are the cancer, Juliano. Guess you just had to learn the hard way." Kolfax flipped open his phone. "Yeah, Estelle, Judge Walker owes me a favor. Can you tell him I need a federal arrest warrant for Morgan Tremayne ASAP? Yeah." Kolfax glanced down at his watch, frowned for a moment, then shrugged. "Which means we should have the warrant by five?" He looked at Gage. "Perfect. Thanks." He hung up without breaking eye contact. "You say a word to her about this, you warn her or her family in any way, and your career is over. And in case you don't care about that, I'll make sure to bring that frat-boy D.A. of yours down with you."

The second Kolfax went for the door, Gage considered coldcocking him from behind.

"Don't," Marcus said under his breath, catching Gage's arm as he closed the door behind Kolfax.

"Alice, you want to leave, I won't blame you, but he needs to hear—"

"Oh, please, Marcus, like I don't know what's going on? Kolfax has to close this case," Alice said without blinking. "He approved the three million for the drug buy. Without authorization. That operation was supposed to be *the* case that made his career. He doesn't track down the missing money, he doesn't make this lead pay off, he's done in the agency for good."

"Judge Walker's going to issue that warrant," Marcus confirmed. "But he never comes into the office before four on a Tuesday," Marcus confirmed. "If you're right, if there's something else to this, anything else, you've got a little over four hours to prove it."

∽

"I don't know what I'm angrier about." Evan paced the end of the task force's conference room, shirtsleeves rolled up, hair askew. The normally composed D.A. was popping apart like a set of Lego bricks and getting on Gage's last nerve. "That Morgan did it or that Kolfax was right."

"I'm going with Kolfax," Bouncer muttered, hobbling around the room as she sorted through the file on the Miami operation. "I haven't met Morgan, but I trust Gage's judgment. He never would have gotten involved with her if he suspected her of something like this."

"You have heard the expression 'love is blind,' right?" Rojas's question drew Gage back into the conversation.

"Love is blind, but it's not stupid. Even if she did do something, I know she's not linked to any drug cartel." Hell, he'd be surprised if she even knew what one was. But there was something.

"Well, we've got"—Evan glanced at the clock—"three hours and forty minutes at most."

"Any chance we can get some ears in Kolfax's office?" Gage asked him as the brain fog finally began to dissipate. "Someone you've spoken with over there in the last couple of weeks, just so we know what they're doing and when?"

"Yeah, I can do that. Bouncer, where's that file with the FBI numbers Kolfax was so generous with?"

"Here." How Bouncer located it beneath twenty other files, Gage had no idea.

"Use my office," Gage said, but Evan was already headed in that direction. "Okay, now that he's out of the way, somebody start throwing out ideas. We know the money Morgan deposited is part of the buy money from the FBI sting in Miami. How did she get it?" He knew he sounded cold, but detached was the only way he was going to get through this. The only way he'd get Morgan through it.

"According to the file, the first batch of cash she deposited was six months ago," Peyton said. "Let's start a time line. New board?"

Gage flipped the board with the Cunningham burglary details, grabbed a dry erase marker, and drew the line. "Call out the other deposits she made." He made notations for each one, took a step away so they could all stare at the information. "Anyone see anything?" Gage felt Morgan's future slipping away with each second that ticked by.

"Huh." Bouncer tilted her head, leaned her butt against the table.

"Huh good or huh bad?" Rojas asked.

"Huh as in—" She grabbed a red marker, circled the first deposit date, then walked over to James Van Keltin's board and circled the date his home had been burgled.

"I don't get it," Peyton said.

"Not done." She circled the second date on the time line, then Herman Goodwin's theft. Third, Charles Baker. Fourth, Lance Swendon. Fifth, Cunningham.

"About a week apart between the burglaries and the

deposits," Gage said. "You're thinking Morgan's money came from Nemesis." He'd rather she'd have been working for the cartel.

"I'm looking at the information we have," Bouncer said. "But no one in this room believes in coincidences."

Gage didn't. "There's been something foggy in this case, something I know we should have been seeing from the beginning." The only time his pulse pounded this way, as if keeping time to a Rose Parade marching band, was when he was onto something. Morgan and Nemesis? All this time she'd known how important this case was to him, what was riding on it.

He needed to focus on what he could see, not what he was afraid to feel.

"Let's go back to the original statements the victims made after the burglaries. The ones they recanted."

They dived at the files littering the table like Olympians at a swim trial. Once all nine files were in hand, they lined them up in chronological order on the table.

Gage pulled down the photographs of the safes and studies, wherever items had been stolen from, and placed them above each report.

The elevator dinged and Gage frowned at the distraction. "Sorry," Bouncer said. "I ordered lunch before the shit hit the fan. I'll get it. Hey, Rojas, I'm short on cash,"

"Yeah." Rojas took out his wallet, tossed her two twenties. Gage shoved them toward her.

"Cash." Gage's gaze shot to each photo as he pointed at Bouncer. "The other day you said something about cash—"

"Yeah. There was a bunch left at the Swarthmore

estate." She hopped out of the room with the money and called, "Nemesis didn't touch it."

"Nemesis left the cash." Gage circled around to the other side of the time-line board, snapped the Swarthmore crime photo off, and set it with the others. "Cash left behind. And here. Grant Alvers. That's got to be at least a hundred grand sitting right there. What's it still doing there?"

"Crockets, too," Rojas confirmed, circling the money with a permanent marker. "Stack at the front of the safe."

Peyton peered at the other photos on the board. "Is cash listed as stolen on the Fitzgerald case?"

"Ummmm, no." Rojas picked up the picture from the table. "Can't see much on this one."

"You can here." Peyton tapped his finger on the closeup of the safe. "Looks about the right size for a stack of cash, right?"

Both Rojas and Gage peered closer. "Yeah," Rojas said. "Yeah, it does, and here. Lance Swendon."

"Charles Baker and—" Gage put a big red circle on the last picture. "James Van Keltin."

"And none of them listed the stolen cash on their retracted statements," Peyton confirmed.

"Why does everything circle to Van Ketlin?" Gage wondered.

"How does any of this help Morgan?" Rojas asked.

"Getting there," Gage said. "I want both of you on the phones with Swendon, Baker, and Goodwin. Tell them we don't care about false statements or even if they lied before, but ask them the simple yes or no question: Was any cash stolen the night they were robbed. That's all we need right now. If I'm right, that'll be enough to stop Kolfax."

"Gage." Evan stuck his head in the door. "Judge blew his game, came back to the office early. Warrant's been issued."

"Morgan's out of time," Peyton said.

"Shit." Gage's mind spun. The second Kolfax arrested Morgan, there was no getting her back. Kolfax would parade her on the evening news and all over the Internet to showcase his success over a once-blown case. They were so close . . . "Shit." He scrubbed his hands down his face. "Shit. Shit. Shit. We don't have another choice. Bouncer." He pointed at her as she returned with two huge paper bags of food. "You and Peyton with me. Rojas, you make those calls and get the answers we need. Evan, call in every favor you have with a judge."

"What for?" Evan called as Bouncer and Peyton followed him to the elevator.

"An arrest warrant for Morgan Tremayne."

CHAPTER 19

"I DON'T KNOW what's gotten into you, but I like this take-a-day-off Morgan." Sheila helped unload Brandon's soon-to-be-assembled BMX bike from the backseat of Morgan's Mustang. "Where are we putting this?"

"We'll hide it under the stairs to my apartment for now. I knew I should have changed my clothes." She kicked her three-inch black pumps into the grass, wished she could do the same for the tight red skirt and matching blazer, but she had to get this box out of sight before Nico got home with Kelley. The kid could sniff out a present like a bloodhound chasing a fox.

"Well, would you look at that?" Sheila stopped helping, leaving Morgan to struggle to keep the box from hitting the ground.

"Look at what? Oh." Morgan wasn't sure what to think about the image of Drew and Gina walking toward the house together, Drew carrying his wadded-up J & J Markets apron in his hand, Gina in her parochial school uniform.

"Romeo and Juliet: the Next Generation," Sheila joked, and picked up her end of the box again.

"Because that ended so well for everyone. Wait, grab our purses." Morgan grunted and walked backward down the driveway. She pried open the small gate underneath her staircase, waved a bunch of cobwebs out of the way, and she and Sheila shoved the box in. Sweaty, grimy, and exhilarated, Morgan grinned at her sister. "He's going to go nuts."

"Only if you get it assembled in time. Maybe Gage can help?"

"Maybe." It wasn't the first time today Sheila had tried to talk to Morgan about Gage. Hopefully it would be the last time Morgan would have to deflect the inquiry. "I need a drink."

"Works for me. Besides, there's a little boy in there who owes me a Monopoly rematch." Sheila rubbed her hands together, then dropped her purse on the top of the washing machine as they entered the house.

"Lydia doing better today?" Morgan asked Angela as she removed her blazer.

"A little bit." But Angela's smile wasn't as full as usual. "She slept most of the day and her fever's down."

"She's back in the wheelchair, isn't she?" Morgan's throat tightened as Sheila wrapped her arms around herself and set her jaw, looked away. This was the fear battering the back of Morgan's mind—that Lydia was rallying before the end.

"Yeah." Angela blinked, but not fast enough to stop the tears from falling. "I know. I know it's inevitable. Doesn't mean it hurts any less."

"We fight until we can't fight anymore." Morgan

grabbed her hand and squeezed, wanting to cry along with her, but once she started, she might never stop. "It's all we can do." The front door banged shut. "Drew and Gina," she said. "Brave-face time."

"I don't have one," Sheila muttered as she headed into the hall. "Hey, guys. Who's up for some Monopoly with my little guy this afternoon?"

"Could be the best medicine for all of us, right?" Morgan reached for the dish towel as Drew and Gina ambled in. "Well, hello, you two. Drew, weren't you supposed to work until five?"

"Stephen sent me home early." He grimaced at the mention of Gage's manager brother, as if he didn't know what reaction he was going to get.

"Oh, God." Morgan nearly dropped the plate she'd been drying. "What happened?"

He looked at Gina, his sour expression turning dour before the two of them grinned.

"He got a promotion," Gina announced.

"Well, not a promotion, really," Drew said when Angela gasped. "Stephen asked if I'd be interested in working the deli counter for a while."

"Drew, that's great news." She started forward, hesitated. "Can I give you a congratulatory hug?"

He shrugged, which in Drew-speak may as well have been a backflip with fireworks.

She wrapped her arms around him, squeezed hard, and felt his hands on her shoulders. "I am so proud of you," she whispered so only he could hear. "So proud."

"Thanks," he mumbled, ducking his head when she let him loose.

"My turn," Angela cried, and repeated the gesture with far more enthusiasm.

"And what brings you by?" Morgan asked Gina.

"I missed the kids," she said simply. "They're fun to hang out with. Is that okay?"

"More than okay."

"Morgan!" Sheila's scream sliced through the house and Morgan's heart.

She shoved Gina out of the way plunged toward the stairs as her sister bolted down. "Lydia?"

"Brandon." Sheila's face was vampire white. "It's Brandon."

"Call 9-1-1." Morgan ordered Gina. Barefoot, she took the stairs two at a time, plowed around the corner into Brandon's new room. He was lying on the floor, his tiny body convulsing, his neck arched as his hands twitched. Morgan fell to her knees. She couldn't touch him, but he might hurt himself.

She placed her hands on Brandon's shoulders, applied light pressure until his legs stopped moving. Morgan scanned the room, looked for blood. Had he fallen? Hit his head? Tripped? Drew raced in, and in the distance she heard the whirring of Lydia's wheelchair.

"Fix him," Sheila whispered, and Morgan knew her sister would be of no help. She was trembling so hard Morgan was afraid her bones might snap. "Please fix him."

"Keep Lydia in her room," Morgan told her. Nodding, Sheila backed away.

"Drew, come here." Morgan grabbed for his hand and placed his palm on Brandon's forehead. "Try to keep his head still, okay. Don't force it, just gentle pressure. Angela, make sure there's a clear path for the paramedics."

Brandon's skin had lost all color, his chest barely rose. Morgan leaned down, pressed her ear against his chest. Heartbeat. Faint, but there. "Come on, baby boy. Don't you give up on me," she whispered, refusing to let the fear in. "Gina!"

Footsteps pounded up the stairs. "Ambulance is on its way. Three minutes out. What can I do?" She stood over them, tucking her hair behind her ear over and over as she stared down at Brandon, her face a mixture of terror and panic. "What's wrong with him?"

"Don't know." Morgan felt Brandon's body ease under her touch. "Grab the blanket off his bed for me."

Gina whipped it off, handed it to Morgan, who tucked it around Brandon. "I think the seizure's stopped. Brandon?" She felt for the pulse in his neck as a rasping sound echoed from his lungs. Pink foam bubbled from between his blue-tinged lips, blood trickling out the side of his mouth. "No," she moaned, trying to take hold of herself, unable to keep her mind from identifying the symptoms of an embolism. "Oh, God, no," she screamed. "We need that ambulance now!"

∾

"Looks like we're too late." Peyton's voice came over Gage's Bluetooth as he turned onto Tumbleweed Drive.

"God." Gage's entire body tingled as he hit the gas, plowing down the half block, and came to a screeching halt in the middle of the street behind the ambulance. He tapped his ear. "Peyton, keep an eye out for Kolfax. Delay him any way you can, then follow the plan. You got me?"

"Got it."

Gage bolted out of the car and raced up the walkway, into the house. "Morgan!"

As he headed for the stairs he saw a paramedic back onto the landing, guiding a stretcher. Gage couldn't breathe. The thought of that little girl, beautiful Lydia, with her big brown eyes and an even bigger capacity to love, pricked at his heart. Would he ever look at a Tinker Bell T-shirt the same way again? Hear a child's laugh without thinking of her.

"Morgan," he called again, and backed up, watching the stretcher pass and the tiny still form under the blanket.

Gage's entire body went numb. "Brandon. What's happened? What's wrong with him?" He brushed his hand against the tiny cold fingers lying against a too-still chest. The oxygen mask covered most of his face. Gage couldn't tell if he was breathing. This wasn't right. Brandon was okay. Brandon's cancer was gone. It was Lydia they had to worry about. Wasn't it?

"Gage." His sister ran down the stairs, threw herself into his arms as Morgan, Angela, and Drew followed.

Sirens blared a few blocks away, throwing Gage so far into hell he didn't think he'd ever find his way out. Kolfax.

"Morgan, I need you to come with me," he said, trying to console his sister as Morgan walked past him.

"I can't." Morgan's eyes were pinned to Brandon as he was carried out of the house. "I need to be with him. I promised"—her breath hitched and tugged at his heart—"when he had his chemo, I promised him I'd never leave him alone. I can't leave him alone."

Gage cupped her cheek in his hand, tried to get her to look at him, but she was as stiff as steel, eyes glazed so thick he couldn't see his Morgan any longer.

"Have to go." She took a step out the door just as Gage saw Peyton and Bouncer's car pull up to block Kolfax's and the two patrol cars speeding toward the house.

"What's going on?" Angela asked.

Gage moved Gina aside, saw Drew step in, take hold of his sister's hand.

"Morgan, you have to listen to me." Gage bent down, tried to get her to see him. "You need to come with me right now."

Bouncer's voice erupted in his hear. "Warrant's in. Gotta do it now, Gage. We're out of time."

"What's going on?" Sheila flew down the stairs as if the devil was nipping at her stiletto heels. "Gage, what are the cops doing here?"

"Sheila, call your father. Tell him to be ready to meet Morgan at the Twenty-first Precinct when he gets the call. You understand?"

Sheila nodded. "Yes, but—"

"Let go of me," Morgan said, and Gage saw they were loading Brandon into the ambulance.

"I can't." Gage ignored the excruciating twisting in his chest. "Morgan, I can't let you go with him." No matter how much he wished otherwise.

"Get your hands off her!" Drew flew at him, but Gage blocked him, turned Morgan's back to the door and grabbed her arms.

"Sheila, go with Brandon in the ambulance and call your father on the way," Gage ordered.

"I can't," Sheila whispered as she brought a hand to her throat, shook her head as her eyes went wide with terror. "Angela?"

"Nico's due home any minute with Kelley," Angela said.

"I've got the house," Sheila said with a shaky nod and too wide eyes. "That I can do."

"I'm going with you." Drew bolted out the door behind Angela.

"I'll call Mom," Gina said, her normally flushed complexion pasty white. "Where are you taking Morgan?"

"Inspector." Kolfax bellowed as he crossed the lawn. "You're interfering with a federal investigation."

"You're interfering with a local one." Gage pulled out his cuffs.

"Gage," his sister cried, diving forward.

"Don't do this," Sheila said, grabbing Gina's shoulders and pulling her away from her brother. "Gage, whatever it is you think she's done, it's not her fault."

"I don't have a choice. It's my job," he said as he snapped the cuffs on Morgan's wrists.

"Your job sucks," Gina spat. Gage reeled at the loathing in his baby sister's eyes.

Morgan looked down at her hands, then up at him, the glazed detachment turning to shock as Gage said, "Morgan Tremayne, I'm arresting you on suspicion of collusion with Nemesis and as an accessory after the fact."

"To what?" Gina's protest was drowned by the ambulance siren screeching to life as it pulled away.

"It's okay," Morgan whispered, as if Gage's proclamation had cleared her head. For a moment he thought she looked relieved. In that moment, he knew she was guilty, and the truth crashed into him with the force of a bullet.

"It'll be okay, Gina. Just watch Lydia for me? Kelley will be home soon. Don't let her get scared. I'll be okay."

"You won't get away with this, Juliano," Kolfax said as Gage tugged Morgan past him. "Your career is over."

"What career?" Gage sneered.

The walk to his car was the longest of his life. Every step pounded into him like a nail in the coffin of his relationship with Morgan. All that was left now was to bury it.

He stopped to scoop up her shoes that were lying on the grass, tried not to worry about what she must be thinking, what she had to be feeling at the moment. The terror, the worry over Brandon. Not knowing what was wrong with him. He didn't have the luxury to care, not when this was the only way to protect her.

He opened the back door of his car, pushed her inside, and listened to Kolfax bluster and scream at agents Marcus and Alice as they slinked into their unmarked unit.

"Gage, I—"

"Not a word, Morgan." Gage slammed the door and set it in reverse, saw the FBI car do the same in the other direction. "You haven't been Mirandized. Until you are you, keep your mouth shut." He looked into his rearview mirror in time to see her flinch. He tapped his ear. "Peyton? You ready?"

"Whenever you are."

Gage glanced at Morgan, who had pressed her lips into such a thin line they'd disappeared. She stared out the window, looking like a lost little girl without hope. When he pulled in behind Peyton's car at Lancaster Park, he saw Morgan blink, frown. She looked around as if she were coming out of a trance. "What's going on? What are we doing here?"

Gage pulled her out of the car and unlocked the cuffs before walking her over to Peyton's blue Buick. With a confused expression, she got in, gripping the open window with trembling fingers as he closed the door.

"Keep driving around until you hear from me," Gage said, leaning down to talk to Peyton and Bouncer. "Shouldn't be more than an hour or two."

"Gage," Morgan said in a tone that told him she was emerging from the shock. "Gage, I'm sorry."

"For what, exactly?" Gage moved to her window, staring into the face of the woman who meant more to him than he'd ever believed possible. The woman who, despite her own dedication to her work, had shown him there was more to life than a job. The woman he loved. "Forgive you for what? Not trusting me? For putting me in the position of having to arrest you?" Sorrow crossed her face like a shadow at sunset. "Or for lying to me from the moment we met?"

Her silence was all the confirmation he needed. Gage slapped his hand on the hood of the car, signaling for them to go.

∼

"Where the hell is she?" Agent Kolfax stormed into Evan's office with the force of a category 4 storm barreling across the Pacific. His beady brown eyes targeted Gage like an out-of-control machine gun firing blanks. Gage didn't move as he watched maintenance replace the glass window with a splinter-infested panel of plywood.

As if covering the empty pane would make it whole again. As if Morgan's apology made the lies disappear.

"Miss Tremayne is in police custody," Evan said, without looking up from the notes he was making.

"Bullshit. I was just at the precinct—"

"I said police *custody*, not precinct," Evan corrected.

"My federal warrant trumps your local one," Kolfax seethed. "I can have you brought up on charges—"

"Do it." Evan stopped writing long enough to glance up. "Please. Let's put all this on the record so everyone can see exactly what's going on."

"I know what's going on. That woman has information I need."

"We agree." Evan clicked his pen shut. "Trouble is, we don't like your way of trying to get it."

"If you mean I didn't fuck it out of her—"

Gage snapped the pencil he'd been twirling in two.

"I kept him from hurting you once," Evan told Kolfax. "I won't do it again. Things would have been so much easier if you'd been up front with us from the start. Instead, well . . . Don't expect an apology from either of us once this is finished."

Up front from the start. Gage inhaled, counted to twenty, but couldn't quite rid himself of the bitterness circling him like a blood-addicted shark.

Gage's cell buzzed and the shark settled. From Rojas: *Got it. In writing. All four.* Now Gage could breathe easier.

"Ready?" Evan asked, and hit send on the email he'd finished composing before Kolfax's arrival.

"Yep." Gage stood and dialed Peyton, who picked up after the first ring. "Anytime. Interview five. Make the call." Then to Evan, "Let's do this."

"Do what?" Kolfax looked more rabid by the minute.

"Question the suspect," Gage said. "That is what you

wanted to do, isn't it? Just one thing. This time you get to observe.

"I've filed a formal protest with the court along with a motion to transfer custody—"

"It's under review." Evan grabbed his jacket and they headed across the street. For once, Gage had anticipated Kolfax's egotistical behavior and wasn't surprised to find the media beginning to swarm outside the precinct.

"I'll make a statement within the hour," Kolfax snapped at an overzealous, barely-out-of-college reporter who stuck a cell phone in Kolfax's face as they passed.

Gage made it a point to take his time on his way to the interview room. But with Kolfax hovering nearby, the agent's frustration increasing like a missile about to go nuclear, Gage watched for Peyton and Bouncer to escort Morgan in through the door by the break room.

Her clothes were rumpled, her thick blond hair mussed from stress and restless fingers. Her color was better, but not by much. But she held her head high and held his gaze for a moment before she was guided into the interview room. His Morgan was back.

His Morgan could take what he'd have to dole out. His Morgan.

Gage took a deep breath of stale, burnt-coffee-infused air.

His Morgan.

"Observation's this way," he told Kolfax. "Did we thank you for that list of contact numbers you gave us?" Gage pushed open the door to the observation room.

"What are you—?" Kolfax looked as sick as a sailor after a weekend bender.

"Agent Dyson, thanks so much for coming." Evan

greeted the Supervisory Special Agent with a hearty handshake. "Agent Kolfax has been telling us how important this case is to the agency. As we told him from the beginning, we've been anxious to help."

"Looking forward to a swift resolution to this case. You must be Inspector Juliano. Special Agent Nicholas Dyson." If Agent Dyson were to ever quit the FBI, he could always play an agent on TV. Classic Mediterranean features made Dyson look as if he'd been sent by central casting. As opposed to Kolfax, who looked as if he should be selling cars in a late-night commercial. "I hear you worked with Sean Salcedo. Terrible loss to the agency. I recruited him myself right out of the Boston Police Academy. I'm not at all pleased about the rumors someone's been circulating about him and you."

"Sean was a good guy," Gage agreed, wanting nothing more than to check to see if Kolfax was hyperventilating yet. "And thank you. You've been brought up to speed on the case?"

"On both cases, yes." The sour look Dyson aimed at Kolfax was the best thing Gage had seen all day. "I'm thinking this woman has some interesting information to impart."

Because Gage knew Kolfax would love nothing more than to discredit Gage by revealing Gage's relationship with Morgan, Gage said, "So you're aware, Agent Dyson—"

"Nick, please." Dyson took a long drink of what passed as coffee at the precinct. "Oh, good God. That was a mistake."

"Depends if you'd planned to blink again this week."

Gage said. "I think you should be aware I've had a personal relationship with Morgan Tremayne."

"Recently?"

"Currently," Gage admitted, and finally allowed himself to look through the two-way mirror at Morgan as she paced. She looked so lost. Alone. Part of him, the part that loved her, wanted nothing more than to fold her into his arms and hide her from the world. The other part, the cop, wanted to close the Nemesis case once and for all and forget any of this ever happened. "I realize there's a serious conflict of interest—"

"You think?" Kolfax sneered.

"But you believe she'll be more forthcoming with you than someone else," Dyson said, giving barely a passing glance to his subordinate.

"I think we should use whatever we have to our advantage. If that includes an FBI presence during her questioning, I'm fine with that. And by presence, I mean you and not him."

Dyson held up a hand to stifle Kolfax's sputtering protests. "I agree. Keeps things aboveboard. But I will step in if I don't like the way things are headed."

"Understood."

Gage left Evan and Kolfax and found his team huddled outside Morgan's interview room. Rojas handed him the finalized information. Gage looked it over, made sure it was in the order he needed, and, angling his body away from Dyson, scribbled a note in pencil on the top right corner of one of the pages.

"This is either a Hail Mary pass or an end to your social life," Bouncer said, looking over his arm.

No shit. "You guys did amazing work with this. It's stellar. Couldn't have asked for a better team."

"You going somewhere, boss?" Peyton frowned. "We heard about what Kolfax said to you in Evan's office—"

"Feel free to watch in observation," Gage told them as he saw Jackson Tremayne entering the lobby of the precinct.

All the pieces were in place.

Gage closed his eyes, tried to forget how it felt to have Morgan in his arms, laughing up at him, kissing him. Surrounding him. Because it couldn't matter. Not if this was going to work.

Her time was up.

Gage opened the door and stepped inside.

CHAPTER 20

"I CALLED THE HOSPITAL. They're still running tests on Brandon."

Morgan spun to face Gage as the door opened to the interview room, her blood pumping so fast her head spun.

Because Bouncer had lent Morgan her cell phone, she already knew about Brandon's condition. She and Angela had assured each other all would be fine.

Neither one of them believed it.

Brandon. Her heart ached to the point where she couldn't feel her fingers and toes. She needed to do whatever she could to get to him. She'd promised.

"Thank you," Morgan said. Peyton told her before they got out of the car behind the station not to volunteer any information. She was to let Gage take the lead. If there was ever a time to follow instructions, for her to surrender the control she prided herself on, it was now.

She'd always assumed the recent renovation to the police station had extended to the interior, but the yellowed linoleum and water-stained walls made Morgan feel as if she were trapped in a 1950s asylum. The gag-inducing stench of scorched coffee with undertones of sour guilt threatened her gag reflexes. Sweat dotted her face and dripped down the back of her neck, as the ten-by-ten room had little space for occupants let alone circulating air.

She blinked against the harsh fluorescent lights, unable to stand still without feeling as if she were being burned alive by a spotlight.

As far as arrests went, she'd expected worse.

The fact that Gage had yet to step inside the room, as if he couldn't bear to be near her, lodged deeper in her heart than even she expected.

She took a step toward him, but even with his eyes glued to the file in his hands, he winced.

Morgan fought the urge to curl her arms around herself and retreat into the corner like a cowering hedgehog.

"Gage, I—" Morgan saw her father appear in the hall. "Dad?" Morgan's heart dropped as if she were the sole rider on the Tower of Terror.

"Quiet, Morgan." Her father, dressed in his impeccable navy blue Hugo Boss suit, looked every inch the powerful executive she knew him to be. He leaned in far enough to hold up his hand and silence her with the same look he'd scolded her with when she was a child.

Morgan pressed her lips shut, heard him speak in hushed undertones with a tall, thin man who could have been passed over multiple times by the Grim Reaper. This didn't make sense. "How—"

Gage shifted his gaze to the mirror across from her. Had she not known him as well as she did, she would have missed the imperceptible shake of his head. Then she remembered, at the house, Gage's instructions to Sheila and now his indication that they were being watched.

Hope trickled into her heart.

Morgan swallowed the tears burning her throat as her father entered and grazed Gage's shoulder with his hand.

She searched her father's face for a hint of what he was thinking, but all she saw was a heavy concern, as if her arrest deposited the weight of a small moon on his already overburdened shoulders.

"I'm so sorry, Dad."

"You have nothing to be sorry for," Jackson said with a silent warning similar to what Gage shot her moments ago. "This is your attorney, Aaron Shackleford. You don't say a word without his approval, you hear me? I'd like to stay," Jackson told Gage as Shackleford pulled Morgan's chair out for her.

"If it's all right with your daughter and her attorney." Gage closed the door. "Sit down, Morgan."

With her father's hand on her shoulder, Morgan sat. When Gage looked across the table at her, she had to stop from twisting her hands together. She folded them and placed them on the table, wishing, searching for the Gage she loved. The man who had tried to help her. The one person who was able to convince her there was more to life than blind devotion to a cause.

But all she saw was the cop.

Her chest constricted as if she'd taken a punch to her heart.

"For the record, this interview is being recorded. Also present is Supervisory Special Agent Nicholas Dyson of the FBI." Gage indicated the tall, sturdy looking man who had taken a position in the far corner of the room before gesturing to the rectangular camera wedged in the upper corner of the room above the door. "You've been advised of your rights, Miss Tremayne?"

Morgan tried not to take his cool, detached tone personally. "Yes." FBI? Fear plumbed new depths in her belly. What was going on?

"And you understand those rights, correct? Which is why your attorney is present?"

"Yes."

Gage flipped open the file without breaking eye contact. Morgan considered it a personal challenge not to look away. How many times had he asked her to confide in him? To let him help? How would things have been different if she'd listened?

"Have you been to Miami in the last five years?" Gage asked.

"Miami?" She glanced at Mr. Shackleford, who was writing down every word spoken. He gave a short nod. "No. I've never been to Miami."

"We'll be verifying that."

She shrugged. "Okay."

"Have you to your knowledge had any involvement with the Benetiz Cartel?"

"Th—the what? I don't understand, I thought this was about N—" Mr. Shackleford touched her hand while Jackson tightened his grip on her shoulder. "No," she said, feeling as if she'd been thrown into the deep end of the pool without swimming lessons or a life vest. "What's a Benetiz Cartel?"

"Have you had any contact with any agent from the FBI before today?"

She glanced up at the man in the corner. "No."

"To confirm, you're stating you have no knowledge of the Benetiz Cartel, have never traveled to Miami, Florida, nor have you had any previous contact with any agent from the FBI."

"Correct."

The ice in Gage's eyes thawed. His jaw unclenched and she heard him let out a soft breath. Whatever answer he'd hoped to hear, she must have given it.

Gage placed a piece of paper in front of her. "Did you make this deposit into the Tremayne Foundation's bank account yesterday at nine minutes after eleven?"

Morgan looked at a copy of the receipt she had yet to take out of her purse. The lawyer tapped the back of her hand. "Yes."

"And that deposit included twenty-five thousand dollars in cash."

Another tap. "Yes." Her heart picked up speed again, like a race car taking a left turn. Here it comes.

"Where did that cash come from, Miss Tremayne?"

The way he said "Miss Tremayne" made her feel as if they'd never met before, let alone shared a bed. "It was a donation."

"Made by whom?"

"I can't say." Her lawyer's hand jerked away, and in her peripheral vision she saw him look up at her father. "The donor wished to remain anonymous."

"That answer won't work well for you. Let me run this down so you'll understand." She heard the edge of frustration in Gage's voice, saw his jaw re-clench as cool fire burned in his blue eyes. "The serial numbers on the bills your anonymous friend gave you are identical to the numbers on money used in an FBI sting against the

Benetiz Cartel in Miami eighteen months ago. A sting that left an FBI agent dead and ended a joint investigation with the DEA. So tell me, Miss Tremayne, how did that money end up in your possession?"

"I—"

"Just what is it you're hoping she'll say, Inspector?" Shackleford asked.

"The truth." Gage glanced up at Jackson, to Morgan, and he tapped his fingers hard on the table. "The truth is the only thing that will clear your name where the Benetiz Cartel is concerned. The truth will clear you in the death of a federal agent. The truth is the only thing that will convince the agents watching us in there"—Gage jerked his thumb to the window behind him—"that you haven't been using the Tremayne Foundation to launder money for the biggest drug cartel to come out of South America in the last twenty years. Now look again." He tapped the top right corner of the list of deposits he'd placed in front of her moments ago.

Morgan peered closer. Her breath caught in her chest. *Trust me.*

"Where. Did. You. Get. The. Money?"

Morgan sat back in her chair, crossed her arms over her chest, and wished anyone other than Gage Juliano was asking the question. All the time he'd spent trying to find Nemesis, to stop him, to close the case in honor of his friend's memory. All the time she knew she shouldn't get involved with him. Was she ever going to be able to live without regrets?

"Morgan, he's right. Tell him," Jackson urged. "It'll be okay, I promise."

Except it wouldn't. Now her father would know what

she'd done, the mistakes she'd made. The mess she'd created out of the decades of work her mother had devoted her life to.

"My advice is to answer the Inspector," Shackleford murmured.

"Please, Morgan," Gage whispered, so softly she wouldn't have heard if she hadn't seen his lips move.

The plea in his eyes, the memory of their argument the other morning, his accusation that even when backed against a wall she wouldn't ask for help, swept any reservations she might have had aside.

"Nemesis." She looked down at the chipped Formica table. "The money came from Nemesis." The last bubble of deception burst inside her. For a moment she felt as if she'd taken a hit of pure oxygen and forgot the confession destroyed whatever trust Gage had in her. For that instant, she felt free.

"And you know it was from Nemesis because?"

Morgan took a shallow breath, felt tears prick her eyes. A solitary tear escaped her control. "Because he included gift cards with the cash." She swiped the tear away with a hard brush of her fingers.

Judging from the flash of understanding that crossed Gage's face, she'd given him the final piece of the puzzle. "What kind of cards?"

"Small," she said. "Rectangular. Plain white with a gold embossed N on one side."

"You have these cards in your possession?"

"No. Not any more." If only she did. If only she had proof.

"Do any of these look like the cards you received?" Gage placed four sheets of paper on the table, each showing a selection of gift cards of different sizes, colors, fonts.

Morgan touched her fingers to one page. He'd put it together before he'd walked in the room, knew the evidence that would have proven her story was gone. But he was giving her the opportunity to produce it in another way. "This one." She tapped the center image on the third page. "Each of the four I received looked like this one."

Gage nodded, gathered the papers up. "The District Attorney's office announced we'd be pressing charges against anyone suspected of accepting funds from Nemesis, for whatever reason. You were aware of this?"

"You don't have to answer that," Shackleford said, but when Morgan looked at her father, she interpreted a different suggestion. The same one she saw reflected on Gage's face.

"I was, yes."

"But you took the money anyway. Why is that?"

"Because I needed to replace money I wasn't supposed to use."

"Money you used for what?" Gage's voice was as tight as a rubber band about to snap.

She was already in over her head. No reason to stop now. "Nine months ago I took a hundred thousand dollars from the property payment account to pay for a child's experimental cancer treatment in Texas. He wasn't going to make it and he wasn't going to live long enough to be admitted to our facility. Only one other hospital in the country offers it, so I gave his family the money to see he got it."

"Morgan," her father whispered. "Why didn't you tell me?"

"I couldn't." And she couldn't look at him now. "Legally I shouldn't have done it, I know that. With the way the foundation's bylaws are set up, it was a clear violation of our financial practices, but I couldn't let that little boy die. And then more patients needed help. I couldn't say no, but I couldn't keep up with paying it back and the final payment on the property is due soon. I thought I had another few weeks and I was getting there, but then Ralph Emerson died and the new accountant called for an audit of the books. I didn't have a choice. I had to use whatever money I had, and that included what was left of what Nemesis had given me."

"So you're admitting to mismanaging the charity funds, to violating the bylaws of your foundation, and to accepting donations from a source you knew left you open to criminal prosecution."

Oh, God. Just when she thought she'd gotten out of the hole she'd dug for herself, she'd just fallen into a deeper one. "Yes."

"No." Jackson's voice snapped through the air like a whip. "She can't confess to mismanaging charity funds or violating the charity bylaws."

"Dad." Morgan rubbed a hand against the creases in her forehead. "Please stop. I can confess. I have to. I did it."

"No, you didn't." Jackson insisted. "This entire situation is my fault. Just after my wife's death my attorneys and I amended the bylaws of the foundation. I only just discovered I'd neglected to file the updated paperwork with the state. Aaron?"

Shackleford opened his ancient leather briefcase and withdrew a stack of stapled papers. "As you can see, the updated bylaws were notarized on July twenty-second, last year. A copy for your files."

Morgan stared at the copy of the bylaws, dumbfounded at the clearly defined stamp that proved what her father claimed. Proof of her innocence. She swung around on her chair. "Dad?"

"I can never apologize enough for allowing Morgan to believe she'd broken the law by using funds not at her disposal. Whatever cost this part of the investigation might have incurred, I'm more than willing to reimburse."

"That won't be necessary." Gage slid the amended bylaws onto the bottom of his stack of papers.

"And the pending charges for accepting the money from Nemesis?" Shackleford inquired.

"Our discussion today will be taken into account. We'll verify this information and be in touch. To use a cliché, don't leave town, Miss Tremayne, but for now, you're free to go."

Morgan couldn't seem to move. Couldn't seem to think. "I can go?" she whispered, not quite comprehending that the nightmare she anticipated would take over the rest of her life had come to an end.

"Come on, honey." Jackson took her arm. "Let me drive you to the hospital."

"One question." Agent Dyson spoke for the first time since the interview began, and Morgan jumped at the sound of his voice. She'd forgotten he was there. "Miss Tremayne?"

"Yes?" She tried to meet Gage's gaze, wanted to, but couldn't bear to see the betrayal in them, not if this was going to be the last time she saw him. Instead she focused on Agent Dyson.

"What was his name? The boy in Texas?"

Fresh tears erupted, and for the first time in months she didn't try to stop them. They splashed onto her cheeks, unheeded, unchecked.

"Colin," she whispered and felt her father stiffen beside her. "His name is Colin."

∼

Had Gage been in a celebratory mood, he might have suggested popping the champagne cork with his team. Instead they reassembled in Evan's office along with Agents Dyson and Kolfax.

"You don't honestly believe that bullshit about the amended bylaws," Kolfax blustered at Evan, who looked as if he'd just won the World Series.

"No reason not to." Evan grabbed bottles of beer out of his mini-fridge and passed them around. "Jackson Tremayne isn't someone I want to call a liar. He says it was done, it was done. I won't argue."

"Yes, I can see where you wouldn't want to challenge one of your main campaign contributors," Kolfax chided. "He's not the saint everyone paints him to be. And neither is the rest of his family."

Dyson twisted the cap off his beer and sat on the edge of the window ledge, acting as if he hadn't heard a word Kolfax said. "Nice that you were able to clear your girlfriend of any wrongdoing, for the most part," he added as he toasted Gage. "That still doesn't tell us where the money came from, aside from Nemesis, that is."

"No." Rojas glanced at the text message that just came through. "But Bouncer might be able to."

"What's a Bouncer?" Dyson asked.

"Officer Thorne," Gage clarified. "She, well, she has this odd penchant for bouncing off cars."

"She's also requesting our presence in the conference room downstairs. All of us." Peyton sneered at Kolfax. "Even you."

Had Bouncer not already earned her nickname, Gage might have given it to her seeing as she was hopping around the conference room like a rabbit with ADD. "Thanks, Janice." She snatched a file from the older woman's hand and shifted the chairs around as they filed in.

"You called?" Gage asked, handing her a beer. She took it, looked at the clock. "Something tells me you earned it."

"Oh, I earned it." The smile that split her face was contagious. "I got him," she whispered.

"Him who? Nemesis?"

Her smile dimmed. "No. Sorry, no, not Nemesis, but I know where the marked money came from."

"Officer Bouncer, I presume." Dyson stepped forward. "We weren't introduced at the precinct. Nick Dyson."

"Hi." Bouncer shook his hand before spinning around to Gage. "It was right there the whole time. The statements Rojas got this afternoon were the last bits we needed."

Once everyone was seated around the table, Bouncer handed them each a file folder. "Pages one through four. Copies of the initial reports filed by four of Nemesis' victims: Swendon, Baker, Goodwin, and Cunningham. In each of those statements there's no mention of any missing cash. But after we examined the crime scene photos more closely, we figured that had to be wrong.

Which begs the question, why wouldn't they have reported it?"

"Because someone told them not to," Peyton said.

"Right." Bouncer hobbled toward the other end of the table. "And there was money. Pages five through nine. Statements Rojas got this morning from each victim claiming that yes, a significant amount of cash was stolen, but they were instructed by their attorney, James Van Keltin, not to include it in the list of stolen items. Which means we can assume—"

"Because assumptions always lead to convictions," Kolfax said.

"Maybe not convictions, but they can lead to evidence. Evidence you had at your disposal if you'd gone back far enough. Or bothered to look beyond your prejudices," Bouncer snapped before ignoring him again. "Time-line wise, James Van Ketlin was the third victim, but he was the most recent victim when it comes to when the missing sting money started showing up. Nemesis steals the money from him, gets it out to people he thinks needs it."

"Including Morgan," Gage said.

"Right. Which is when it pops in the system and sends up flares for this guy." She jerked a finger at Kolfax. "Except Lantano Valley should have already been on your list even without the money."

"How so?" Dyson asked as Kolfax's face turned bright pink.

"Well, I got to thinking about some of the questions Gage asked Morgan. Had she been to Miami in the last five years? Had she ever heard of the Benetiz Cartel."

"Which she hasn't," Evan reminded her.

"But Van Keltin has. Page seven. He bought a house in

Miami twenty years ago. The purchase was made under his wife's name, but he co-signed the mortgage."

"No way," Peyton breathed.

"While I couldn't get a hold of his travel records yet," Bouncer continued, "I did check his license to practice law, which he holds in California, New York, and, wait for it..."

"Florida," Rojas whooped.

"You've got more, don't you?" Dyson said as he flipped to the next page.

"Uh-huh. At the time Van Keltin bought his house and got his license, he was an up-and-coming defense attorney who took on high-profile cases pro bono. So I typed his name into the judicial records in Florida and downloaded a list of all the cases he defended. I highlighted the name I thought might interest the FBI." She clasped her hands behind her back, swayed on one leg until she almost tipped over.

"Son of a bitch," Dyson said. "Claudio Benetiz."

"Who was at the time moving up in the cartel before becoming the number two guy your investigation targeted last year. Van Keltin defended him three times in four years, each time on drug charges. Charges dismissed on two, another was dropped when the evidence disappeared out of the evidence locker."

"And then Van Keltin moved to Lantano Valley," Gage noted.

"To take over his father's practice on the west coast," Bouncer confirmed. "If the FBI had gone back another ten years, they'd have found the connection between Van Keltin and Benetiz."

"That still doesn't tie Van Keltin to the money," Kolfax

noted, but even Gage had to admit the guy looked impressed. Or maybe sick.

"Well, I don't have the proof yet, but I did have a nice phone conversation with one of his maids a few minutes ago, after which I texted Rojas. I think if you look into Van Keltin's travel itinerary for the last two years, you'll find he's traveled to Miami at least three times. One of which the maid is sure was the week of February seventeenth because it was her daughter's birthday and she was still expected to work. I'd bet he brought the money back with him to keep it as far from Benetiz as possible until they knew they were clear to use it."

"She got him." Dyson stared at the file, to Bouncer, over to Evan and Gage. "She fucking got him."

Gage grinned. He knew he hadn't been wrong about letting Bouncer spread her wings on the task force. Given the evidence Bouncer uncovered, turning Van Keltin against his client was the one thing that would save the lawyer from a lifetime jail sentence.

"It's not concrete yet—" Bouncer insisted.

"It doesn't have to be for a warrant." Dyson waved the file in the air. "I'm keeping this and submitting it as part of my report. If that's okay with you?" he asked Gage and Evan.

"You give credit where it's due, fine with me," Gage told him.

"Kolfax, I hear you're the one who riled the press into a frenzy outside, let it leak that Morgan Tremayne had been brought in for questioning for her connection to a drug cartel?" Kolfax's mouth twisted, but he remained silent.

"Then I guess you won't mind if I take that over for

you," Dyson continued. "Evan, if you would please join me? Gage, you and your team as well, especially Bouncer—"

"Hallie," she corrected as her cheeks tinted pink.

"Hallie," he acknowledged as he led them out of the conference room to the elevator. "You ever think of working for the FBI, Hallie?"

The group went silent, save for Kolfax, who sounded as if he might be suffering an asthma attack. Gage wouldn't be surprised if Dyson had him in front of a review board the second they returned to the home office. Kolfax may have finally gone too far.

A mix of excitement and pride shot across Bouncer's face before she smiled and shook her head. "Appreciate the thought, sir, but I'm happy right where I am. If they let me stay."

"I'd say the odds are pretty good," Evan said as the elevator doors opened.

"I'll catch up," Gage told them as they crowded in, and instead of joining them, Gage headed into his office. "Thanks for all your help the last few weeks," he told Janice, who was gathering up her belongings to head out. "I know we didn't make it easy on you."

"You did good work, Gage." But the sad smile on her face told the story of his day. "I hope somehow you can make it work with Morgan."

"Yeah." He nodded, unable to respond. "Good night, Janice."

He closed his office door, took a seat behind his desk, and listened to the media circus roar across the street.

CHAPTER 21

Morgan bent at the waist, her lips pressed so tightly together she couldn't feel them. Air moved in and out of her constricted lungs. Her eyes burned. Her ears thundered. She rocked, stemming the flood of agony that accompanied Brandon's diagnosis. It was what Morgan had feared: an embolism.

The silent, unpredictable side effect of intensive chemotherapy had struck without warning or remorse.

How was it that, standing amidst the family she'd created, surrounded by her father and Angela, Nico, Drew, and Gina, Morgan felt utterly and completely alone?

Part of her was missing. No, not missing. Carved out, hollowed. Gone.

"How long?" Angela's voice broke. "How long do we have with him?"

"That's up to you," the doctor said in that I'm-so–sorry-but-I-really-have-no-hope-for-you tone Morgan hated beyond reason. "Brandon's as comfortable as we can make him, so now the decision is in your hands."

Decision. The decision.

"Thank you, Doctor." Nico wrapped an arm around Angela's shoulders and drew her over to the waiting area that consisted of two laughingly conceived of sofas and a coffee table that looked as if it had been time-warped in from the not-so-fashionable seventies.

"We'll, um, we'll sit with him for a while," Gina said, blinking back tears. She clutched Morgan's arm, but Morgan couldn't stop staring at the floor. If she moved, she'd shatter. If she breathed, she'd shatter. If she did nothing—

Jackson drew her to him, wrapped his arms around her until she couldn't help but clutch at him. "I never knew," she whispered as he shushed and hushed her sobs that grew painful as she tried to contain them. "I never knew how much losing Colin hurt you."

"I'd give anything if you didn't." He tucked her against him the same way he used to when she was little. Before she knew the world could be a painful and horribly unfair place. *Brandon. Her Brandon.*

"How?" She pounded a fist against her chest as if she could restart her broken heart. "How did you?"

"We had you and Sheila and Nathan, and I had your mother."

"Mom," Morgan choked. "God. This explains so much."

"You will get through this," Jackson told her. "I promise we'll help you get through this, and then one day, while the pain will still be there, it won't cut as deep. One day, instead of remembering the loss, you'll remember his life."

"I'm so sorry, Dad. For everything. I never meant—"

He pushed her away from him, clasped her face in his hands, and forced her tear-stained face up so she had no choice but to look at him. "I've never been so proud of you as I was today in that interview room. Admitting your mistakes, knowing what it might cost you—"

"I embarrassed the family. Put the foundation, the center at risk."

"You did what your mother always taught you to do, Morgan Elizabeth Tremayne. You followed your heart." His own eyes filled with tears as he smiled at her. "You saved Colin. Maybe not our Colin, but one is alive who might not be otherwise, and for that I thank you."

"Gage will never forgive me." She tried to stop the tears, to regain control, but there was no fighting it anymore. "I've lost him."

"I know it feels that way." Jackson pulled her into his chest again, rocked her, stroked her hair. "But Gage is a good man. I think he just needs time."

Morgan wanted that to be true. She also wanted Brandon healthy, laughing, spinning in circles in the backyard as he threw water balloons at her head. She wanted another broken washing machine. She wanted to fix the garbage disposal again or have to rewire the toaster or anything. She'd never complain about it again. For as long as she lived. But time wouldn't heal the wounds she'd inflicted on Gage.

She'd betrayed him. Lied to him. Deceived him.

How could she expect him to forgive her when she couldn't forgive herself?

"I can't believe you arrested that beautiful girl."

Gage let out a long breath and dropped his head against the lawn chair in his parent's backyard. On the one hand he'd come for some peace and quiet. On the other, if he'd wanted peace and quiet he should have gone home. To his empty house. His empty, quiet house.

He'd grown accustomed to the noise children made, to their laughter and arguing, to their constant running and crying and bantering. To the chaos of water fights, and in the center of it all, Morgan.

Morgan.

"Have another beer." His father handed him a bottle, took the chair beside him as the sun settled into the night.

"I'm driving." Gage set it on the grass, rubbed his fingers into his eyes. "Christ, what a day."

"You've had better," Daniel agreed, cringing when he heard Theresa banging dishes in the kitchen. "Took your life in your hands coming here tonight."

"Maybe I thought she'd end my misery."

"My future daughter-in-law." Theresa's voice blasted through the open patio door. "What on earth goes through that boy's head?"

"I was doing my job," Gage yelled and then, "Wait, your future what?"

"Your job sucks." Theresa's proclamation echoed that of her daughter from hours before. Hours. Had it only been hours since he'd had to arrest Morgan? Since he'd questioned Morgan? Treated her like a common criminal? Good God, what had he done?

"At least the D.A. won't be pressing charges," Daniel said. "Saw the news conference a while ago. That Agent Dyson was very complimentary of you and your team."

"Damage control," Gage muttered. "But yeah. My team did great." His team. "Dyson was kind to credit Morgan, the foundation, and even Nemesis with providing evidence to bring down the Benetiz Cartel. Nothing like thanking a criminal for committing a crime that exposed an even bigger one." The fact that an arrest warrant had been issued for James Van Keltin upon his return to the States took the sting out of the day's events.

"Nemesis has been your target for a long time." Daniel took a long drink. "Your focus."

Nemesis. Gage never wanted to hear the name again. He'd destroyed too much. Cost Gage too much. At one time that might have made him even more determined to find him.

Instead, he wanted to forget that the case, and the criminal, existed. Before Gage ended up in the grave next to Brady Malloy.

"You have considered that if it wasn't for Nemesis, you never would have met Morgan." Theresa stormed up behind them.

"Actually, no." Gage frowned. "No, I figured that was—"

"I raised an idiot." Theresa waved her wooden spoon in the air as if it would help her take off.

"*We* raised him, dear. I have to agree with your mother," Daniel told him. "Not to mention the fact that what Morgan did, she did for a good reason."

"There's never a good reason for breaking the law." Except, knowing what she'd done, why she'd done it—was he wrong? Maybe he was wrong about a lot of things.

"Told you." Theresa shouted. "Idiot." The front door slammed, indicating Gina's arrival since Liza was staying the night at the Fiorelli's to help Sheila with the kids. But instead of the normal greeting yelled out by either twin, silence followed. "Gina?" Theresa asked. "Baby, what is it?"

The sound of his sister's sobs forced Gage's eyes closed as grief landed on his chest like a pouncing bear. His father's chair creaked as he got up, leaving Gage alone in the yard. Gage's ears echoed with the broken words his sister could get out. "Matter of time. Gone. Machines. Dying."

Dying.

He got up, walked slowly at first, and then picked up speed as he headed for the back gate.

"Gage. Where are you going?" his father called, but he didn't stop. He couldn't. Because the second he did, he might just break.

∽

"I'm looking for Brandon Monroe's room." Gage flashed his Inspector's badge at the nurse's station.

"I'm sorry, Inspector, but if you aren't family—"

"Gage?" Judging from the look on Angela's face, she must be thinking he'd come to take Morgan into custody again. "It's okay, Thelma. He's a friend of the family. Morgan's downstairs getting coffee. I'm sure she'll be back in a few minutes if you want—"

"Can I see him?" It was all he could manage.

"Of course." Angela guided him inside. "Nico took Drew home. He's bringing all the kids by tomorrow so we can—" She didn't finish.

As much as he tried to prepare himself, the sight of the

frail little boy lying so still in the center of a too-big bed, the respirator pumping air into his lungs, would have driven Gage to his knees if he hadn't been holding on to the wall.

It hurt to breathe. The tears that tightened his throat made his head go light. "Does he . . . ? Is he . . . ?"

"No way to know for sure." Angela gripped his arm, rubbed his back. "Would you mind staying with him while I check in at home? Morgan promised him he'd never be alone."

He remembered. He'd always remember and be haunted by Morgan's protest at the house when he'd prevented her from getting in the ambulance.

And then Angela was gone.

What did he say? What did he do? How was he supposed to act when a child lay dying in front of him?

Was this how Morgan felt every day of her life? How did she bear it?

The thought of no new paintings on the wall, no more water fights, no more broken sinks or experimental disfigurement of DVDs . . . How had this happened? One day he'd been happy, healthy, and exploding with energy, and now—

In a few short weeks this child had awakened a part of Gage he didn't know existed. Not just this child. All the children. Not just the children.

Morgan awakened him.

Gage walked over to the bed, took a hold of Brandon's cool hand, and bent down. He held the tiny fingers against his cheek as the sound of the respirator echoed in his ears.

Watching this life fade was more torturous than the bullet that had passed through his body, more excruciating than dealing with the death of a fellow officer. Yet Morgan did it, time after time, beginning with her brother. And instead of turning away as most people would, she embraced the sickness, the struggle. The child.

All those years, all those children. Making sure every sick child she came across was given every chance at life.

A chance at love.

She was the strongest person he'd ever met.

Gage smoothed Brandon's thin blond hair from his face. What he wouldn't give to see those big blue eyes of his again, to see that smile.

Gage placed Brandon's hand back on the bed and kissed his forehead. "Thank you, little man." Gage squeezed his eyes around the tears, unable to stop them from splashing onto Brandon's cheek.

Gage pulled his ID out of his pocket, the badge Evan had given him the day Gage had accepted the inspector job. When he'd accepted it, he'd hoped it would put his life right again—that he'd find his purpose.

He slid the hook of the badge over the top edge of Brandon's gown. He pressed his hand over it for a moment, then, when Angela returned, he left without saying another word.

∽

At noon the next day, Morgan sat at Brandon's bedside, her hand holding his as the machine beeped his heart rate. Slow. Slow. Slow.

She let the tears fall unchecked, looking down at the frail body that continued to house a beautiful, strong soul.

"Morgan?"

Morgan wiped the tears away as she saw Kelley in the doorway, with Angela and Nico, who carried Lydia, behind her. "Oh, hi." She sniffed, let go of Brandon's hand, and opened her arms to the little girl.

Kelley ran to her, threw her arms around her neck, and began to cry, her body shaking in Morgan's grasp.

"It's okay," Morgan whispered brokenly, cupping the back of Kelley's head and rocking her gently. "He doesn't hurt anymore."

Angela pressed a hand to her throat, the question in her eyes.

Morgan could only shake her head before her eyes blurred again. She didn't know if she'd ever stop crying. The pain felt endless.

"Time to say good-bye." Nico set Lydia beside Brandon on the bed so she could tuck one of her stuffed bears under Brandon's arm.

"You always liked Mr. Bundle. Take him to heaven, okay? Maybe you can give him to my mom."

Morgan shifted Kelley in her lap as Nico picked up Lydia again. She linked her arms around his neck and buried her face in his shoulder.

"Can he hear us?" Lydia asked.

"I hope so," Morgan said.

Angela and Nico took turns, coming over to Brandon, bending down and whispered their good-byes.

The monitor beeped. Slower. Slower.

"I don't want him to go," Kelley cried. "I want him here, with me."

"I know, baby. So do I." Morgan didn't think she could withstand the pain. Hers was bad enough, but the kids' . . . "He can't stay. His body's just too sick."

"You can make him better. You made me better. You make everyone else better."

"Kelley."

Drew stood in the doorway, his own face wet with tears that came from defiant eyes. "Brandon's body can't fight anymore. It's time to let him go. We need to tell him it's okay to let go."

Morgan sobbed, then covered her mouth as Drew came into the room. She held out her hand.

"I told him I'd stay," Drew told her as he took it. "The other night he asked if I'd made up my mind and he told me to say yes only if I could promise. I don't break my promises."

Morgan gave him a sad smile. "I'm glad you're staying." *Beep. Beep. Beep.*

Morgan took a deep breath, let it out slowly. "It's okay to let go, Brandon. We'll be all right now."

Nico, still holding Lydia, sat on one side of the bed, Angela the other. Drew stood sentry still behind Morgan as they waited for Brandon to leave them.

Kelley continued to cry as his heartbeat slowed until, finally, he went still.

CHAPTER 22

THE FORECAST SAID RAIN, but the clouds disagreed and blew through Lantano Valley as if the sun's rays chased them away. The brilliant blue sky was accented with fluffy marshmallow clouds—as if Brandon had painted the day himself.

Morgan stood graveside, her hand wrapped around Kelley's tiny one, her gaze drifting over those whose lives had been touched by one little boy. Friends from school, their parents, and students from the martial arts class he'd just started. His teachers, intermingled with the Julianos—Liza and Gina, who stood to the side with Drew, Theresa and Daniel and their sons. The Fiorellis' grown children had come as well. The construction workers who had helped with the house had come, along with Kent and his partner, Craig; even Oscar, their UPS delivery man, and Evan.

Everyone was there.

Except Gage.

She didn't think her heart could hurt so much, but hour

by hour, minute by minute, she was surviving. Just as her father had said she would. Maybe not living, but surviving.

Morgan glanced over to where her father, brother, and sister stood, knowing they must be feeling what she did—that the past and present had intermingled in a perverse and horrific way.

Sheila worried her. Finding Brandon that day, not being able to help, had changed something in her and created a distance Morgan wasn't sure how to breach. She was afraid this time Sheila was broken and that she might never fully mend.

Save for being questioned by the man she loved, Morgan's fears about revealing her connection to Nemesis had been for naught. Somehow, in the midst of her betrayal, Gage had protected her. Her family had stood by her, defended and sheltered her just as she should have known they would.

And yet, surrounded by those who cared about her, all those who wanted to help—it wasn't enough.

Her mind attributed the feeling to Brandon's loss, but her heart screamed Gage's name in response.

Flowers cascaded over Brandon's casket. Her little man had loved being outside, his hands in the dirt, his face smudged as his mouth split into a wide, crooked grin.

Once again the tears flowed free. She was done fighting herself—she had other fights that needed winning. Other children who needed saving. The center would do that. She'd make sure of it. It would be enough. It would have to be.

She stared down at the coffin, her heart twisting as she drew in a shuddering breath.

Coffins shouldn't come so small.

The minister spoke of the fragility of life, the promise of innocence and eternal life, and while Morgan had told him about Brandon, there was no way to capture what he'd been to everyone who loved him. To try made it all the harder to accept he was gone.

She felt a hand on her shoulder and realized Sheila was letting her know the ceremony had ended.

People moved away. Kelley shivered beside her, and Morgan bent down to button her new coat, tugging the purple velvet hat down over her ears as she wiped away the little girl's tears.

"He's an angel now." Kelley looked up to the sky. "You said he'd be able to see us every day. Do you think he likes my new party dress?"

"Yes." Morgan smoothed her hands down Kelley's arms. They'd had a girls' day yesterday—just her and Kelley and Lydia, but Morgan knew Brandon had tagged along in spirit.

"Come on, Kell." Drew stooped down and picked her up. He met Morgan's gaze and Morgan saw the man he was becoming. He had a long way to go. He'd still be difficult, but at least he was here. Part of the family now.

"Give me a few minutes?" Morgan asked her family as cars pulled out of their spaces and headed to the Fiorelli's to celebrate Brandon's life. As a tribute, they'd gone ahead with the birthday party he would have enjoyed today, including the giant bouncy house.

Now the healing could begin.

Morgan stood beside the casket, breathing in the fresh air despite the tightness in her lungs. She placed her palm against the soft, polished wood.

She held the batch of daisies she and Kelley had picked

from the Fiorelli's garden this morning. She placed the wilting flowers on top of the mound of red and white roses.

Tears splashed onto her hand. "Be a good boy up there." She kissed her fingers then touched them to the casket. "We'll miss you."

When she turned around, she found Gage standing under a nearby tree.

She started, stunned, thrilled, terrified. He'd stayed out of sight, as if he didn't want to be seen. Or didn't want to see her. But if that was the case, why was he still here after everyone else had gone?

He didn't move, simply watched her. She pressed a hand to her mouth to stop her lips from trembling. Dare she hope? Dare she believe?

When he walked forward, her heart skipped a beat. He looked so handsome in his black suit, shirt, and tie. He'd combed his hair straight back, wore dark sunglasses that sat stark against the olive complexion of his skin.

She'd wanted him here so much it had been a palpable ache, yet she couldn't help but worry that he'd brought his anger, resentment. But in that moment, she didn't care. All that mattered was that he was here.

He took off his glasses as he reached her. "Beautiful service."

"I'm glad you came."

He stood not two feet away from her, yet it felt as if miles separated them. "How are you?"

She met his gaze and was startled to find his eyes void of hostility and instead filled with every kind of love she'd ever dreamed of. "I've missed you."

He let out a harsh laugh, looked up at the sky. When he

looked at her again, there was a smile on his lips. A smile. That was enough. "I missed you, too."

He opened his arms, and Morgan did what she'd dreamed of doing since their fight the other morning. She walked into them.

The second he wrapped her in his arms, she knew she was safe. That she was forgiven. That she was loved.

"I'm sorry," she said. "I never wanted to hurt you. I wanted to trust you, to tell you the truth, but I couldn't see a way out. I didn't think you'd understand—"

"I might not have," he said. "Before. But I do now."

"I never wanted you to have to choose between your job and—" Morgan reached into her pocket and pulled out the inspector's badge he'd left with Brandon in the hospital. "I was hoping I'd have a chance to give this back to you."

Gage closed his hand around hers and the badge. "I won't be needing it."

"What?" Dread pooled thick and deep in her chest. "But you love being a cop. An inspector," she corrected. "Did they fire you? Because of me? Oh, Gage, no—"

"They didn't fire me." The words were spoken without bitterness or sadness, but rather with a strength and confidence that surprised her. "No, I liked being a cop when I started, but I haven't for a long time. I stayed because I didn't know what else to do. Didn't think I could do anything else. I didn't want to take any chances." His gaze shifted to Brandon's coffin. "But he showed me otherwise."

"But what about the case? What about Nemesis and the task force?"

"They'll get him," Gage said as Morgan searched for

doubt in his eyes and found none. Instead, she saw peace. Acceptance. "Nemesis will slip up, but it won't be me who brings him in. Dealing with Kolfax opened my eyes. He's been on the job too long. He's bitter, angry, obsessive, and obsessing over the Nemesis case is what drove Brady to an early grave. I won't go down that road. I can't. Not when I see a much better way to spend my life."

Morgan's breath hitched in her chest. "But you've worked so hard—"

"Stop trying to talk me out of not being a cop, Morgan." He captured her face in his hands, lowered his forehead to hers. "It's not who I am anymore. I want to be happy, and I'm happy when I'm with you."

"What will you do?"

"I might go back to school. Get my contractor's license. I've already talked to Kent to get some ideas. What do you think? I loved working on the house that Saturday. Bringing it back to life. I can do that with other homes. It wouldn't be as rewarding as what you do, but—"

Morgan kissed him, quick, hard, and with every ounce of love in her heart. "I love you." Then she laughed, her heart lighter than it had been in years. "I was so afraid I'd never get the chance to say that to you."

"I love you, too, Morgan," he whispered against her lips.

Gage wrapped his arms around her so tightly she feared she'd never breathe again, and she'd be okay with that. "Just promise me no more secrets. No more lies. Not ever again."

"You understand why I couldn't tell you, right?" She pulled back, gripped his arms in her hands until her knuckles went white. She needed to know because she couldn't let it come between them again.

"Because you had to." He stroked her cheek. "Because if you hadn't risked everything to save those kids, you wouldn't be the woman I love. The woman I want to spend the rest of my life with." Was that nervousness she saw jumping into his eyes? Doubt? Gage glanced around, grimaced a bit. "Not the setting I'd hoped for, but since I met you, nothing's gone according to expectations."

"What—"

"I stopped by your father's this morning for some financial advice. You know, to cover all my bases." He pulled out her grandmother's engagement ring. "He thought I might know what to do with this. A wise man, your father, suggesting I turn today into a happy memory. I suppose I could wait and do this later. Somewhere less maudlin and, you know, where we'd be surrounded by our families—"

Morgan wasn't quick enough to stop the sob/laugh from escaping her throat. Nor could she stop staring at the ring she never thought she'd see again. The ring she'd sold to Randolph earlier in the week.

Tears blurred her eyes as she thought of her father finding out about her final transgression. And how fitting it seemed to be reminded of hope and beauty and love in the middle of a cemetery, where so many of her loved ones had been laid to rest. It might not be ideal for most people. But for Morgan, this moment couldn't have felt more right. Besides, who better to witness this moment than the spirit of the little boy who had helped bring them together? "Where did Dad—? How did he—?" She couldn't seem to find the right question to ask.

"A very nice man named Randolph called him a few days ago to say you were in trouble. That's how you paid back what you'd taken from the account, isn't it? You sold your grandmother's jewelry?"

She nodded, blinded by the sun sparkling against the stone, touched that Randolph had called her father and that her father had entrusted the ring to Gage.

"Only one way you get it back," Gage teased. "Don't make me look like an idiot, Morgan. Yes or no?"

"Yes or no what?" she asked. Then she grinned.

"Of all the times for you to get traditional on me." Gage sighed, set her back, and dropped to one knee. "Morgan Elizabeth Tremayne, will you marry me?"

"Yes." She pulled him up and in, stopped before she hugged him. Then she froze. "Oh, God. Oh, no." She covered her mouth as laughter bubbled over tears, watching confusion then fear mar his handsome face. "Yes, of course yes I'll marry you. But about those secrets you didn't want me to keep?" She bit her lip, struggling to find the right words. "I think I need to tell you about the deal I made with your mother."

EPILOGUE

The Fiorelli house was filled with family and friends celebrating Brandon's life and mourning his loss, an odd combination of reluctant happiness and gut-churning grief amidst music, laughter, and tears.

It was a fraction of the sorrow that had encapsulated Sheila from the second she'd found Brandon lying unconscious in his room.

Feeling invisible, she'd climbed the stairs and stopped in the doorway of Brandon's room, the unbroken part of her expecting the little boy to race into her arms and challenge her to a ferocious game of Monopoly. Instead, her arms felt empty, as if the life had been drained from her. Taken from her.

The anguish she'd sworn she would never experience again suffocated her.

The cowboy bedspread and matching pillows had been straightened, the sheriff's badge throw rug that had cushioned Brandon from the wood floor set back in place. The toys, the coloring books, the conglomeration of crayons and markers lay scattered about as if waiting for their master to return and put them to use.

But Brandon wasn't coming back. Just like her mother wasn't coming back. Just like her brother.

Had it really been less than a week since she'd brought the Old West to life on the far wall of Brandon's room? How she'd loved sketching out the sheriff's office, adding weathered detail to the rickety swinging saloon doors, filling in the lines with thick, glossy bright colors so as to transport its cowboy-obsessed resident into the world of his dreams. She'd filled every brushstroke with love, wanting Brandon to know how much he meant to her, wanting to give him everything he'd always wanted.

The heaviness in her chest had yet to lessen. Why was it that whenever she surrendered to the gift she'd been given, whenever she let the happiness take over, someone she loved died?

The question turned her legs weak and she stumbled to the bed, staring at her last creation without seeing. The room spun and she closed her eyes, reached out to grip the soft pillow hard enough for her nails to dig through the fabric and into her palms. At that moment, Sheila both hated and admired her sister. That Morgan could put her heart in jeopardy with every child she took in, every child she tried to save.

How did she see past the possibility of losing them? How did she survive it time after time? Sheila couldn't do it. Not again. Never again.

"Sheila?"

Somehow, thankfully, her father's sympathetic voice cauterized the wound in her heart.

She swiped a hand under her eyes, felt the tears that

had escaped her control and shifted into her composed, presentable self. "Hi, Dad." She hated the crack in her voice. Tremaynes were strong. Tremaynes didn't crumble under pressure. They didn't surrender to emotions.

Tremaynes did what it took to get the job done. She blinked and another tear slipped free. How did she have any tears left?

"You did a beautiful job on this." Jackson wandered closer to her painting. For an instant, she let herself bask in her father's pride, but not long enough to dampen the urge to grab a paint roller and paint the entire wall black. "You have your mother's touch."

And another knife to her heart. "I was never as good as she was."

"She believed you were better." Jackson shoved his hands into the pockets of his tailored pants as he glanced at the floor, a sad but amused smile on his face. "It's why she wanted you to study in Europe. She saw your potential. Hoped one day you would embrace it."

Bitterness tickled the back of her throat. "I've always been more comfortable copying others' work. It made forging the notarization on the so-called amended bylaws easier." She grabbed hold of the opportunity to change the subject. "Thankfully Nathan found those note cards from Nemesis when he accessed Morgan's computer to find out what she'd done. She saved all our butts even if she doesn't know it. Speaking of Morgan, is she here yet?"

"She arrived a few minutes ago with Gage." The smile on her father's face widened and the cloud of melancholy lifted. "No official announcement yet, but if Gage's mother's attentiveness is any indication, we can expect one soon. Morgan's wearing your grandmother's engagement ring."

The joy flooding Sheila's system was tempered by irritation. She huffed. "Thank God Randolph called you." The idea of her grandmother's collection being sold to strangers, or worse, to their fellow Lantano Valley residents, stoked the fire in Sheila's belly. She'd make sure Randolph was rewarded somehow.

"Would have been suitable payback, wouldn't you say?" Jackson said. "If it wasn't for Nemesis' arrogance and miscalculations, Morgan never would have been put in the position of having to do so."

"Contrary to what the police believe and what you might think, Nemesis was a team effort," Sheila reminded him. "You needed, we all needed something to focus on after Mom —" She cleared her throat. "After last summer. Nemesis was an inspired creation, Dad. Lantano Valley needs him, and we've done a lot of good. Besides, it wasn't as if we knew Van Keltin was stupid enough to hide drug money in his clients' homes." Knowing the mob-lawyer would have to choose between solitary confinement in prison or the witness protection program kicked fragments of her pain aside.

"Losing myself in Nemesis didn't rid me of the grief over losing your mother, Sheila. It delayed it. But you're right. Knowing what we know, given the information we're privy to, I think we were onto something. It doesn't change the fact that Nemesis almost cost your sister her freedom, not to mention the man she loves."

"Yeah, well, imagine the position she'd have been in if you'd let her in on the family secret." Feeling steadier now, Sheila kicked her legs out, crossed her ankles, and leaned back on the bed. She could do this, block out the pain, turn it off. She'd done it before.

"You've always had an exceptional talent for saying 'I told you so' without uttering the words." Jackson bent to pick up a drawing off the floor, then appeared to think better of it and left it where it was. "You were right. Neither your sister nor your mother would have understood what we've done. Catherine believed, and Morgan still believes, in the inherent good in people. That people, when faced with a choice, will do the right thing. You, me, and Nathan, we know most people need a push in the right direction."

"More like a kick in the—"

"There you two are." Nathan leaned around the doorframe, slapped his hand on the wall. His smile faded as he looked at Sheila and then his father. He stepped inside, closed the door and lowered his voice. "I know those looks. I thought we agreed not to discuss Nemesis outside the house. You've got cops not to mention the D.A. downstairs. Any one of whom—"

"Relax, Nathan." Sheila sighed. "No one's paying any attention to Nemesis at the moment."

"Lucky for us," Nathan muttered. "I was thinking we need to ditch the last of that cash we got from Van Keltin and his clients. We don't want anyone else getting tagged by the Feds. Especially that Kolfax guy. He got a little too close, if you ask me."

"He did indeed. But we're still here. Mail the cash to Evan," Jackson said, and smiled as he chuckled. "Better yet, since you've perfected your method of breaking into secure facilities, deliver it personally. Be sure to include a thank-you note letting him know Nemesis is going on an extended vacation."

"And what is Nemesis going to do on this vacation?" Sheila asked, desperate for a new task. A new target. Something, anything to take her mind off her grief.

"My darling daughter." Jackson reached his hand out for her. "It's time for Nemesis to reinvent himself."

AUTHOR'S NOTE

A note from the author:

Thank you so much for spending your time with Gage, Morgan, and the rest of the Tremayne family. I hope you'll forgive the few dated references in this story that was originally published in 2014.

Every author has a book of their heart and Nemesis in the Night is mine. This was the first book I ever finished and the first I ever submitted to publishers. That it's back in my hands feels like a full circle moment. *For those interested in continuing, book 2, Nemesis on the Prowl features Sheila Tremayne and her ex, Malcolm Oliver. Trust me when I say these two will take you on a roller coaster ride of emotions. Nathan will end the trilogy with Nemesis in Disguise and if you thought his sisters were a handful, you ain't seen nothing yet. Laurel Scott is definitely going to keep Nathan on his toes.*

As far as more Nemesis books are concerned, I'm not ruling anything out. I do have a spin-off series planned (and if you read Nathan's book, you'll be able to guess

AUTHOR'S NOTE

who it would feature). Given the time and effort it takes to write a new series, I'd need to know readers are interested. So please! <u>Email me</u> *anytime and tell me what characters you'd love to see* get *their HEA!*

In the meantime, if you enjoyed Nemesis in the Night (or even if you didn't), please consider leaving a review. I can say without hesitation that authors appreciate each and every review *we receive.*

Until next book, readers.

~Anna J

ACKNOWLEDGMENTS

Huge shout out to Abigail Owen at Authors on a Dime for her fabulous new covers and to Nicole for working her formatting magic. You made my author heart happy.

To Romance Writers of America© and especially the Sacramento Valley Rose Chapter of RWA for making me a better writer with each and every conference and meeting. Thanks to Jon Dennis Schmitz and Harry Gunsallus for their advice and putting up with my tedious and frustrating questions.

To the world's greatest critique/support system: Judy Ashley, proof reader extraordinaire and one of the best people I know. To my personal Yoda and mentor, Melinda Curtis, for pushing me when I wanted to quit, and to Cari Lynn Webb who lets me cry on her shoulder with each and every book.

Thank you to Loucinda McGary and Jennifer Snow for

their feedback and advice as I dive into this crazy world of self-publishing.

To Brenda Novak, author, boss, friend, and cheerleader. You never let me forget this was the goal. I hope to live up to the stellar example you've set. Thank you, Margaret Bail of Fuse Literary, my former agent. You helped make Nemesis possible.

Lastly, and most importantly, to all the families, friends and loved ones dealing with cancer and other illnesses on a daily basis: your steadfastness and strength are humbling as you fight on the front lines of these diseases. And to the cancer treatment centers around the globe who inspired this story and that strive every hour of every day to find a cure, thank you.

Fight on.

ABOUT THE AUTHOR

Anna J Stewart is the USA Today and National Bestselling author of The Nemesis Files (light romantic suspense), The Butterfly Harbor stories for Harlequin Heartwarming, and the Honor Bound series for Harlequin Romantic Suspense. She's also a "founding member" of the Christmas Town, Maine, sweet romance collection which launched with Anna's very first official publication, *Christmas, Actually*. Most recently, she's returned to her first love, paranormal romance with the Time Warden novella series. For a complete list of her published and soon to be published books as well as buy links, please visit www.AuthorAnnaStewart.com where you can also find links to her Facebook, Twitter, and additional social media pages.

ALSO BY ANNA J. STEWART

THE NEMESIS FILES

by Anna J Stewart

Nemesis in the Night

Nemesis on the Prowl

Nemesis in Disguise

Printed in Great Britain
by Amazon